Mary ... for be... thoughtful neighbors! Hope you both got a kick out of my story :)

MW00893148

A Hundred Lifetimes

Dave Zink

A Novel by

David C. A. Zink

A Hundred Lifetimes
© copyright 2016, David C. A. Zink
All rights reserved, including the right of reproduction in whole or in part in any form without the consent of the author.

First Edition

ISBN-10 1523270144

EAN-13 9781523270149

Printed in the United States of America

Cover art by Carlene Salazar
Pacific Ocean Graphics and Fine Arts
carlene.salazar@gmail.com

Map courtesy of Chris Wayan,
http://www.worlddreambank.org/V/VENUS.HTM

Contents

Acknowledgments

Thanks to Aleta, Brian, Linda, and Mike for their suggestions and editing help, and to Chris Wayan for permission to use his map of Venus. And above all, to Charlotte for her patience.

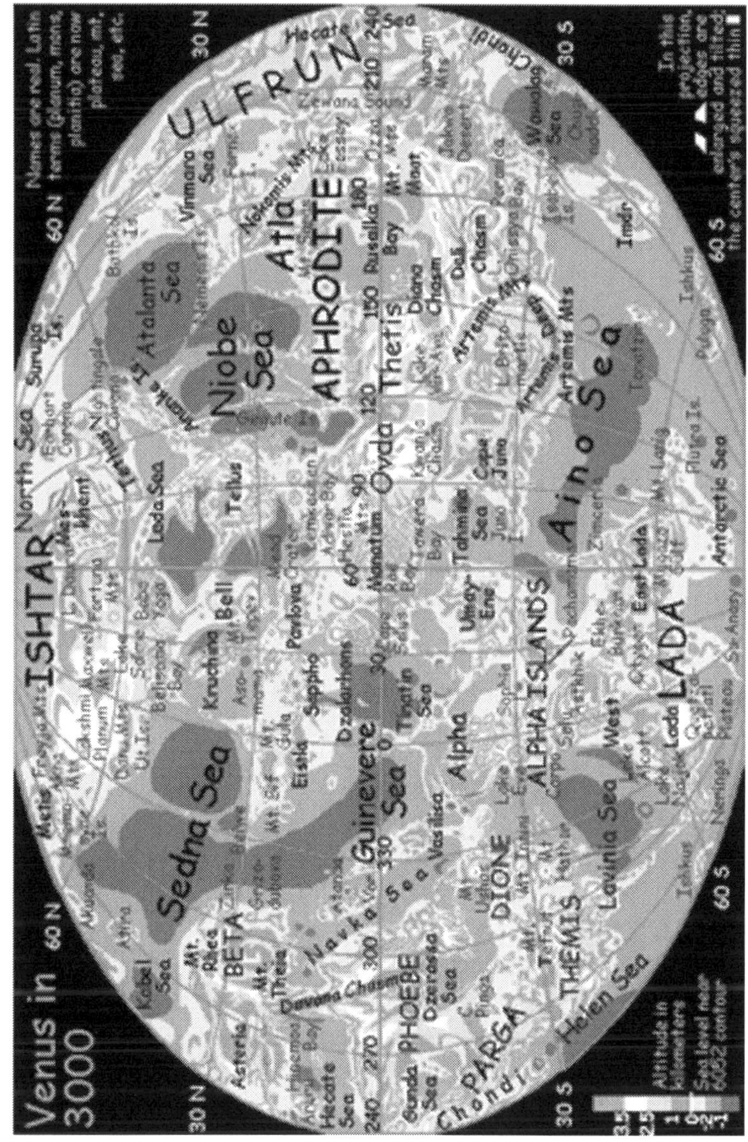

Map of Venus prior to eco-apocalypse and after proposed restoration

—Courtesy Chris Wayan

Prologue

Is anybody—anything at all—left alive on Venus?

Can anybody see above the angry clouds to the stars that once filled our Thlargi and Drelbi ancestors with wonder and inspiration?

To survive on Earth, the Drelbi long ago adopted a simple strategy: hide. Now, in hopes of waking up your species, they have decided to finally break the silence. Consider this a wake-up call.

Translating Venusian into coherent English is like trying to put a size-10 foot into a size-8 shoe. To reduce confusion, I've minimized Venusian vocabulary and stretched your terminology whenever possible, sometimes to its limits and beyond. Likewise, references to time are expressed in Earthian terms.

The mantid vocal apparatus and thought processes are different than those of humans. Bear in mind that translation of some words and concepts is difficult, if not impossible.

You will probably find the Glossary at the back of this book useful in your struggle through this narrative.

—Drelbi Central Committee

CHAPTER 1
FROM BOONDOCKS TO BAYVIEW

That which is learned young is hard to lose.
—From the Proverbs of Drell

Megaraptors. Zyzz hated them.

A chill morning up in the Nokomis Mountains. The boy and his dad looked out over the misty valley below, watching from a cliff's edge as the early morning drizzle cleared. A new day was dawning after a long Venusian night. It was a family camp-out in the high country close to home.

With a sudden rattling of its wings, the giant dragonfly swooped out of the misty sky and grabbed Zyzz's father. Dad was strong, and he hit it with all his strength, but struggle was useless. The monster carried him away, eating him on the fly. Raptors were the largest predators of Venus: death from above with wingspans up to a meter or more. Years later, Dad's yells of pain and anger still echoed around Zyzz's memory.

"Daddy! Daddeee! Please come back!" Zyzz's cries woke Mom. She ran the short distance to where he stood crying. She held him closely as he told her what had happened.

As soon as Marg, his mother, felt that he could handle it safely, she walked Zyzz down to the hardware store in Brrzzt, their small hometown in the highlands of Aphrodite, to buy one of the new-fangled zappers that had just come onto the market. The southernmost of Venus' two continents, Aphrodite is about half the size of the Earth continent of Africa and straddles the equator.

Brrzzt was the kind of town where everybody knew all their neighbors.

The salesman helped them pick out one and warned him "This is no toy, young man."

"He knows," Marg replied. He's been practicing with a neighbor."

Zyzz made it a habit to strap it onto his hip whenever he went out. He often target-practiced and was soon competent with it. He even won a few shooting contests, which helped stretch their income.

Zyzz and his mother survived on his father's modest forester's pension. He supplemented their meager finances by bringing in mega-raptor fangs for the cash bounty, helping hardscrabble farmers who could never afford to pay him much, and doing odd jobs around Brzzt. He grew to a taller-than-average twelve centimeters in the free, healthy, country life, hardened by years of tramping the hill country.

From concealment in the bushes, he'd spend hours watching raptors zig this way, then zag that way in pursuit of prey. Their flight patterns were unpredictable; scoring a good hit on the fly was nearly impossible. Out in the open, he could get a clearer shot, but risked being seen and eaten. He'd wait in the bracken under a tree until one stopped for a rest, embracing the stem and facing up toward the sky before bringing it sizzling down with a crackling zap.

Zyzz was a good student generally and did well in Science class, good enough to win a scholarship to attend the School of Forestry at the University of Ishtar.

Otherwise, he probably would have ended up on a lumberjack crew like his father's, spending his days in the towering forests of trees much like the club-mosses, horsetails, scouring-rushes, tree ferns, and other species prevalent in Earth's Carboniferous period. Not that he would have minded. Being indoors too long gave him the heebie-jeebies and put him in a bad mood.

He loved the sounds and smells of the meadows and forests, the fragrance of fresh-cut hay, and the satisfaction of chopping wood for the cook-stove.

An essay he wrote as a history assignment in junior high, based on the latest reports from the Space Consortium, read:

Venus and Earth History:

Similarities and Contrasts

by Zyzz

Recent research and discoveries by scientists of the Space Consortium reveal some interesting similarities and differences between life on our planet and life on Earth.

Both planets teem with life. While similar in many respects, biological evolution has proceded in very different directions on the two sister planets. The dominant species on both planets are bipeds, but there are big differences. The dominant species on Earth is Homo sapiens, vertebrate mammals that refer to themselves as "humans". Adult human males stand about 1.7-meters tall and females are somewhat smaller on average, while adult female Drelbi stand about thirteen centimeters tall, and males average a centimeter shorter.

The Mantid cultures of both Drelbi and Thlargi are matriarchies, where females play the leading roles, and property inheritance is based on the mother's line. Prehistoric societies of Homo sapiens were also matriarchies, but social stratification and class societies led to the development of patriarchal cultures on Earth, in which descent and inheritance are traced on the father's side, and males are dominant.

While our planet is dominated by two peoples in one united Empire, the Earth is a much divided planet. There are many different nation-states and peoples, and humans still wage war upon each other in a most barbaric fashion.

The life forms of Earth that most closely resemble the Drelbi are the Mantises, but they are quite different from us. Our upper, or fore-arms, split into four fingers and evolved into a versatile hand. We have opposable thumbs, smaller abdomens, larger brains and heads, and—usually—a nicer personality than Earth Mantids. There has been no success in establishing communication with them. On Earth, chordates have evolved into a variety of impressive animals, while on Venus they never advanced beyond brainless, sedentary, barnacle-like water-dwelling filter feeders. The Vertebrate class of Earth never appeared in the course of Venusian evolution.

At some point, the Goddess apparently decided that brains must weigh more than what flight could easily carry. Our ancestors, the Thlargi, are sluggish and stupid, but can still fly clumsily. In regard to powers of flight, this was a degeneration from our airborne ancestors. The Drelbi went a step further down that evolutionary path. With our vestigial wings, we would be flightless if not for our aircraft. There were benefits, however. A slower metabolism increased the Drelbi's average life span.

The Thlargi had a primitive technology and lived a hunter-gatherer existence. They shared a reverential and mystical respect for the forests, meadows, and swamps. They lived in tribal, communal groups. Private ownership of land and resources still seems to be an alien concept to them.

The Thlargi strategy: defend against the encroaching Drelbi, who they referred to as "Fatheads".

There was bravery on both sides of the Great War, also known as the Final Conflict. But the raw courage of the Thlargs and their warlords lost out to the higher intelligence, advanced technology, and cunning of the Drelbi. Thlargs taken as slaves didn't do well, preferring death to slavery. Morg the Terrible, the last Thlarg war-chief, said, "Better to die on your feet than live on your knees!"

The last Thlarg havens were up in the rugged reaches of Aphrodite and Ishtar and a few scattered farra [Editor's Note: farra are flat-topped volcanic islands that look somewhat like pancakes, and range in size from 20–50 km across, and 100–1,000 m high]. After the victory of the Drelbi, the two continents and scattered islands were unified under the flag of the Drelbi Empire. Thlargi were assigned to reservations under Drelbi supervision.

Hundreds of years after the Drelbi nearly wiped them out, there are still derogatory figures of speech (such as "breeding like Thlargs" and "tree-hugging Thlargs") referring to their custom of having large families—nine, ten, maybe a dozen children—compared to a typical two or three for Drelbi. With few exceptions, Thlargi don't have a clue what to do with a book.

There are still occasional, undocumented reports of odd sightings out in the wilderness. Some parents use Thlargi as convenient boogey-men to keep their children from wandering off too far for their comfort.

Assigning the seat of the unified world government is an ongoing, contentious process. To be fair to those living in both polar zones, it was decided to locate the Federal Zone somewhere near the equator. First in Pinga, on Phoebe Island, the capital moved several times over the centuries, and is now located in Otygen in the southern island archipelago of Lada.

Longer lives allowed us to develop communication and technology that empowered us to further develop civilization and leisure, science, music, and the arts. That furthered our longevity. Brain size expanded over many generations. Parental care developed to a higher level. While our ancestors laid a large froth of eggs, then went off and forgot them—we developed a more family-oriented culture.

Zyzz got a "D" for that assignment. When he came in after class and asked his history teacher why, she tssked and shook her head in disappointment. "You've gotten off track, Zyzz. Did you sleep through all our classes about the Thlargi?"

"Remember, Ms. Schnarrg? I was out sick that week."

"This is something we've talked about all year, Zyzz. Now, listen. The Drelbi evolved from a branch of the Thlargi. Remember: the Drelbi and the Thlargi are the same people. We all have the same genes."

"But we look so different from them."

"Social and cultural differences, Zyzz. They dress differently. While we Drelbi value individual initiative and material gain, the Thlargs value sharing and cooperation. We value technology; the Thlargs value nature."

"Many Drelbi love nature too. Like me."

"Yes, we're really not that much different from the Thlargi now, are we?"

"But they're so, so… primitive. Backward, you know?"

"Many of them say that about us."

"Okay," Zyzz said. "But, why didn't they develop?"

"They did develop, Zyzz. But not in the same ways. Remember, they have different value systems than us at the base of their culture."

"Huh?"

"Don't you remember? Just this week we discussed how, on average, Thlargs tend to value different things—have different attitudes and ways of seeing—than the average Drelb does."

"Yah, but we even look different from them."

Ms. Schnarrg sighed a moment and shook her head slowly, then said, "Do all girls look the same to you, Zyzz?"

"Uhh, no…" He leaned his head and cocked his antennae, not sure where she was going with this.

"Do you find some girls prettier, more attractive than others?"

"Yeah, sure," he laughed.

"When Drelbi choose a mate, they often go by looks. Right? The Thlargi see beauty differently. After many generations, they're bound to look different. But we're the same species. Different races, but the same species. There are half-breeds, you know. If we were different species, would that be possible?"

"Nope; I guess not."

"But, I'm using too wide a brush here."

"What do you mean?"

"Okay, look at it like this. In your math class, you've talked about bell-shaped curves and averages?"

"Yes, ma'am. Ms. Zoob showed us all about average distributions, ranges, extremes, all that stuff."

"Good. I know you're doing much better in math than in history," she said, as she took out a sheet of paper and handed it to Zyzz with a pencil. "Now, could you draw me two overlapping bell-shaped curves and put a line through the centers?"

"Sure," he said, and quickly sketched them out.

"Good work." She pointed to one of the curves and said, "Now, let's let this curve represent mechanical ability. Or mathematical talent, or whatever. Anything. This idea applies to many things, Zyzz. Height, weight, you name it. Now, on average, Drelbi show a higher degree of technological talent than the average Thlarg. But see where the curves overlap?"

"Yes." He was starting to see where she was going with this.

"Now look over here," she said, tapping her pencil on the overlapping base of the curves. "Some Thlargi have a greater ability than some Drelbi in math ability, or technical skills."

"Okay?"

"If you take a group of Thlargi, raise them like Drelbi, with all our cultural and educational advantages, these two curves would move much closer. There'd be much more overlap. Can you see that?"

"Yes, ma'am."

And so it went.

Ms. Schnarrg looked up at the clock and sighed. They had been talking about this for nearly an hour, and she still had a pile of tests to grade before she could leave the office.

"Listen, Zyzz. A lot of the information in the old history books was a reflection of the popular anti-Thlarg propaganda of the day. It wasn't scientific. Lies, to justify a political agenda of confiscation of Thlarg property and suppression of their culture. Theft. The truth is starting to come out now. Take a look at this," she said, standing up and walking over to pull a book from her shelf. She handed it to him.

"*A People's History of Venus*, by Zinnn?" Zyzz said, reading the cover.

"Yes. Take it. I know you're not quite ready for it yet. It's really meant for high-schoolers, but I think you would enjoy this. Just promise me that you'll keep it and read it when you can."

"Gee, thanks, Ms. Schnarrg."

He took it home, showed Mom, and told her about what happened. She smiled. After reading it herself, she started reading it to Zyzz at bedtime.

Zyzz wanted to go to college, but knew that Mom and he could never be able to pay for it with their lean resources. Of the several applications they submitted for financial aid, two came through. One was from the scholarship fund of the company his father had worked for; the other was a bursary from an "unknown benefactor". He asked Mom about it, but all she would say was "never mind" and change the subject.

The continent of Ishtar wraps around the North Pole of Venus and is about the size of the continental USA. It took Zyzz about ten earth-hours to travel from his home in Brzzt to the Bayview campus of the University of Ishtar.

Zyzz breezed through college easily. At first, he felt ashamed of his backwoods accent. He thought it would brand him as a hillbilly. But soon, he found it was a plus. People liked his dialect and most responded warmly to it.

He did much better in biology than in math and industrial applications. In the field, he saw plants, animals, and ecology, not board-millimeters of lumber. In most of his classes, he did well and worked as a lab assistant and teacher's aid in the Botany Department.

After graduation, he interviewed for teaching positions at several schools.

Ms. Zelda, the head of the Forestry Department, chaired the interview panel for the University of Ishtar position. They asked him about his background, and he told them about some of his experiences working his way up through the ranks from chore-boy and "saw doctor" (filer) to tree-faller (lumberjack). He had loved those days, knew the lingo, and had a few amusing stories to relate about his days on work crews.

As department heads in a school that prided itself as being an industry-oriented institution that prepared its graduates for the "real world", the panelists valued his first-hand, on-the-job experience. The other candidates they'd interviewed for this position had done well academically, but fell short when it came to down-to-Venus, practical matters.

Then it was geometry professor Zhard's turn. "Where would you place yourself on the political spectrum?" he asked.

"Uhh, I'm not sure what you mean, ma'am," Zyzz responded. This was the first question in this interview that stumped Zyzz.

"How would you describe yourself politically?"

"Hmmm. Guess I haven't given it too much thought, ma'am. I reckon I've been busy enough with important things to bother much about politics. Sorry."

The panelsts looked at him, nodding.

"Oh, that's quite all right, Zyzz," Zhard said, and the other three panelists gave him reassuring smiles.

This was exactly the sort of response they had been hoping to hear from Zyzz. It was bad enough to have growing numbers of radicals on campus, distracting good students from their studies. But they'd be damned if this school would ever add any revolutionaries to their faculty. Not on their watch!

Zyzz was the best candidate they had interviewed so far for this job. They liked his combination of real-world experience and his high grade-point average. His countrified, humorously self-effacing manner and rustic accent took the hard edge off a stressful situation. For them, it was icing on pretty good cake.

It didn't take them long to decide. He got the job.

Zyzz had few complaints about his position at the Bayview campus. His salary and hours were more than acceptable, and he got along well with the department head and his colleagues.

In contrast to their other classes, students actually looked forward to his well-attended lectures. Zyzz usually wore hiking boots to class, while other teachers wore more appropriate footgear. With his muscular build from years of hard, outdoor work, he didn't look much like the typical professor. He was good-looking in his own rugged way, which helped keep females awake in class.

For a hick from the hills of Aphrodite, he wasn't doing too badly at all.

Word soon got around that if you enjoyed getting outdoors, you should sign up for his classes, so they filled up quickly. His enthusiasm was infectious. Art students who took his classes to get their required science credits, and students in other sciences, often changed their major to botany.

Bayview had a lot going for it. It was a college town, so there usually was something interesting going on. There were some beautiful parks with great views of Belisama Bay. On a clear day, it was nice to sit on a bench and watch the variety of boats come and go. It was a fine place to raise a family.

There were some charming old houses in Bayview. He lived in one of them, a small place with a big backyard and garden just outside the University District, a short walk to work. After four years of living in a cramped room in an apartment in the student residence, this was a welcome change.

Often, when he left for school, he stopped to chat with a neighbor working under the hood of her zoom or in her garden. Zyzz greeted her with a simple "Mornin'."

"And good morning to you."

"I'm heading to the grocery. Need anything?"

"No thanks, but could you wait a minute?" She went inside and came back out with a book. "Could you drop this off at the library?"

"Sure," he replied. "Anything to pick up?"

"Not sure. Could you check?"

"No problem."

And that's how a typical day started for him. Sometimes he'd pick up things for a neighbor at the grocery or hardware store.

Zyzz didn't bother buying a zoom; he didn't need one. He preferred walking. When it rained, he grabbed his umbrella and walked to class. The campus was compact and he lived only a short walk away. He used a backpack to bring home groceries from the store a few blocks down the tree-lined street.

He never could stand being cooped up inside for very long. After a few hours in the lab or classroom, he'd be aching to get out into the fresh air and sunshine. You'd see him out there, nose in some plant. Zyzz was happiest when he was out "botanizing" with a magnifier hanging from his neck and botanic keys tucked under an arm, getting samples and field notes to add to his growing backlog of work to do in the lab. Other than hiking boots, a cap, and a magnifier hanging from his neck on an old shoelace, he wore nothing, as was the Drelbian custom.

For his master's thesis, Zyzz wrote *Carnivorous Plants of Western Ishtar*. He put hours and copious sweat into the task, wore out several pairs of shoes trudging through mountains, over rocks, and slogging through swamps. The book had already become a standard reference in the field, but he considered it a work in progress, continuing his field work, adding new findings, and editing it whenever he could get to it. He was now working on his *Biogeography of Ishtar*. His two guidebooks, *Backroads of Western Ishtar* and *Backroads of Southern Aphrodite*, were selling well.

Nature enthusiasts often carried a pair of binoculars and maybe a hand lens, but few had access to a microscope. He added detailed sketches and arrow symbols to his guidebooks to point out diagnostic features. He wanted his field guides to be taken out and used, because they made field identification of species easy with the equipment that people would likely have at hand, not gathering dust sitting on some shelf.

On a planet that was well populated with predatory insects and spiders, many of which were larger than he, his wasn't the world's safest profession for a four-and-a-half-inch tall Drelb. He had to use his zapper on occasion.

Zyzz loved field work. He was in his element in the forest, walking the soft, mossy ground in a moist world of lush green. The wind sighed through the towering, ancient fern and Equisetum trees, known as "horsetails" on Earth. He was dwarfed by trees with trunks 30 meters high and a meter-and-a-half in diameter, luxuriantly festooned with ferns and other epiphytes. He picked off a green, rough-lined, silica-laden horsetail branch and rolled it in his fingers. The silica in these dulled many a lumberjack's saw. He was working on a proposal to the Industrial Section to develop and breed more harvestable trees that had less silica.

Venusian trees and plants had no flowers or seeds, but reproduced via spores. Instead of dispersing their seeds via fruit, Equisetums shed spores from cones at the tops of stems, and ferns from round globs called sori, located on the underside of leaves.

Fern fronds uncoiled like fiddleheads in the dewy morning. Many Drelbi collected the young succulent fronds to bring home and cook up for greens.

Out in the sunshine, Zyzz put on his cap to avoid getting his brains fried. It used to be white, but now looked like it was overdue for an oil change. He adjusted it and pulled his antennae up through the cap's two holes. Now he could better sense any smell or taste that the air might carry his way. Like the mantids of Earth, the Drelbi smell with their antennae.

In the jungle, the air felt dense, moist, and sticky-warm. Even at mid-day, the green twilight was saturated with the sweet odor of lush growth and decay.

Although he always packed a lunch, Zyzz ate off the land whenever he could.

A profusion of mushrooms grew in wide variety. Zyzz had long recognized the good ones—some delicious, others lethal to mantids. Some animals could eat those with no apparent ill effects, due to differing body chemistries.

There was food out in the woods if one knew how to find it. As he went along, he snatched the occasional fat-bodied spider off its web and tossed it into his mouth. Zyzz's favorites were the ones with big, swollen abdomens that popped juicily like a sweet, succulent berry. He turned over an old log for some tasty grubs, gathering insects to roast for supper over a campfire, or a land snail or millipede to be barbecued. Eating outside after hiking and cooking over an open fire were ingredients for a delicious meal. At the campfire, he checked over his body for zlucks, similar to the leeches of Earth, that stuck to him as he waded the swamps. They sizzled and popped when he tossed them into the fire.

Once, while out leading a class field trip, one of his dozen students found a small population of a rare species of fern. The class was on land tagged for clear-cutting by the Ishtar Forest Resources Company (IFR). He was familiar with other related species in the same genus, but the spore cases and leaflets on these plants appeared different. *Quite likely a new species*, Zyzz thought. To find the spot next time, they marked it with orange flags.

The class bagged some samples to take back to the lab, handling them carefully. Rough handling made identification more difficult. Even with a dissecting microscope and technical books, this specimen had Zyzz stumped. Yes, this could indeed be a new species.

He called to notify the local IFR Operations office about it, hoping he could persuade them to set aside the land, at least until he was finished with his field work there. After a long wait on hold, they routed his call to Public Relations. The guy he finally spoke with was quite agreeable, and said he'd bring it to the "immediate attention" of the head of the PR department. She, in turn, would coordinate with Operations and place a temporary "hold" on harvesting. Zyzz agreed to notify them as soon as his on-site field work was completed.

The class soon returned to the location ready to work on moving the specimens, but it was too late. The acreage had been "harvested" (syndicatese for "destroyed"). He and his students poked around a while, but only found litter and debris. The expanse of stumps exhaled a wounded, pungent smell.

Zyzz felt sick and angry inside. Had there been some communications breakdown at IFR? Had Public Relations just been humoring what they perceived as a crank caller? "We should have dug some up to try to grow back at the lab," Zyzz told the students. "We'll never get a chance to see, much less save, this species again."

There was a big, empty place in Zyzz's life. At the end of the day, he went home to a lonely house. His friends at work set him up with an occasional blind date, and he had gone along on some fun double dates. There had been some good times, but so far nothing had really clicked. Occasional, one-night stands didn't come close to filling the void in his life and soul. The chemistry never seemed to be there.

Sometimes he wondered if he would feel so alone if he had followed his mother's advice. She wanted him to take the teaching position they had offered him at his old high school back home in Brzzt. He probably would have settled down with a local girl, maybe even started a family by now.

Chapter 2
Zilla

He who leaneth against a big tree will always find shade.

—From the *Proverbs of Drell*

Zilla was a student in Professor Zyzz's Botany 101 class. She was an education major training for a teaching position in some junior high school and an activist in the Ecology Party (EP).

One day at lunch, Zyzz saw Zilla and another of his students working at an information table the EP had set up in the cafeteria. He was more attracted to the girl than to anything on the literature table. He stopped to browse through the literature, something very few professors did, picking up this brochure and that pamphlet, looking them over, feigning interest, wondering how to start a conversation with her.

"What's a smart young lady like you doing with these radicals?" he ventured with a smile, shaking his head in a mock negative fashion and adding a light "tsssk" from his spiracles.

"Radical problems call for radical solutions, professor," she answered, returning and vastly improving upon the smile. "The system is fouling up our planet. From your lectures, it's clear you don't approve of how they're clear-cutting our forests. They're trashing everything! Do you think that's sustainable?"

"Of course not. Like you say, I try to make that clear in my classes. The ecology is being destroyed. Species are being wiped out; too many are going extinct.

Biodiversity's declining in way too many places..." Realizing he was lecturing, he cut himself short. "Yes, current practices have to change. But to what? What's your alternative?"

"Well, for starters, we should demand that for every hectare of land that is clear-cut, one gets replanted."

"Good, good, but with what?" he asked. "With just a few of the most profitable species? That's a tree farm, not a forest, unstable due to lack of biodiversity. Come on; you know that."

"Yes, of course. But even a tree farm would help keep the soil from washing away. And give us the time to work on cleaning up the reefs, and other work. What we really need is, well... how about building a better *system*? One based on sustainability instead of maximizing profits for the top one-percent?"

"Well, I dunno. Sounds nice, but how do you propose we get from here to there?" He detected a seductive pheromone smell that was causing an involuntary swelling in his crotch. *Could it be coming from her?*

"Tell you what," she said, breaking into another smile that Zyzz felt very alluring.

By Drell, she's beautiful, he thought. In this light, her multi-faceted eyes sparkled like a rainbow, looking deep down into his soul.

"Here's a copy of our program. Please take a copy. It's only seven kecks. Heck, I'll buy it for you," she said, dropping some change into the "Donations" jar on the table. "Read it over and let's talk one of these days. Okay? Here: take one of these too," she added, handing him a copy of the *Wake-Up Call*, the EP's weekly paper. He took the information, handed her a ten-keck note, said "Thanks," and started to walk away. He would've liked to stay and talk more, but didn't know what to say next.

"I really mean it, sir," she said after him.

Turning around with a smile, he asked, "Sure, let's do lunch one of these days?"

"Yes sir, I'd like that," Zilla answered.

"Think we might have a convert here?" her friend asked as the professor walked away.

"Maybe. Why not?" she replied. "That guy can give a lecture about Plant Ecology that even you would understand. Getting him to join would be great for the party." She watched Zyzz. *Not bad*, she thought. *I could really get it on with a guy like that.*

As he walked off, he thought, *what in the hell am I doing? Should I be asking her out*? He wanted to, and he didn't want to. *Drell; what am I thinking? What's the matter with me anyway! I'm her teacher!* He felt like he was treading on swampy ground, afraid he might step through and find himself deep in a muddy situation. It had happened to other professors. Rumors and gossip spread fast in the university grapevine; some had even lost their jobs due to this sort of stuff.

Zilla's current relationship with a fellow student named Schnung was entering its terminal phase. Schnung was in a pre-Law program and they had met in their economics class. He was smart, had a sharp sense of humor, and helped her study and review for exams. But they were miles apart on some things—political views in particular.

Schnung's ambition was to be a corporate lawyer or maybe an investment banker, whatever seemed most likely to make him a rich Drelb. Flauntable wealth—fancy cars and a fat bank account attracted him. In the Biology 101 lab, he was squeamish; dissecting specimens nauseated him. He could never handle working with cadavers or patients, so going into any medical career was out of the question, however lucrative that might be. If there had been serious money in basket weaving, he might have majored in that.

Some of Schnung's habits annoyed Zilla. He had a way of making snide, condescending, cutting comments to the less fortunate Drelbi he happened to encounter. Poverty was a disease he could catch if he got too close to it.

Once when they were out on a date, an elderly Drelb, apparently homeless, down on his luck, and not smelling very good, asked them for some spare change. Drelbs, like Thlargs and their more primitive ancestors, turn from green to brown in their later years, and this gentleman was quite brown. Schnung said, "Go get a job, you lazy son of a snarf," and gave the poor guy a disgusted look and a kick in the rear.

Zilla reached out and took the old guy by the arm and started walking him toward a muncho stand just down the street.

"What in the hell are you doing?" Schnung asked.

She didn't answer him. When they got to the stand, she asked the old fellow what he'd like to eat. He told her what he wanted, and she told the attendant, "Make that a large order, and give me a tall glass of berry juice," as she reached into her purse for the money and paid for it. The juice, crushed from berries grown from imported Earth seeds, was delicious.

"Oh, aren't we so noble," Schnung sneered at her.

When the cook handed the food out the window, Zilla walked the derelict over to one of the tables outside the stand and sat down and started talking with him, sharing the meal. Schnung was fuming. "Why are you wasting your time on this loser?" he asked. "The show starts in ten minutes!"

"Why am I wasting my time on *you*?" she answered. "Good-bye, little boy," she said, giving him a disgusted look and returning to her conversation with the old man. "How did you end up in this situation?" she asked.

Schnung couldn't believe this. "What? That's it?"

"Bye-bye, loser," she answered with a dismissive, brush-off gesture. Schnung stood looking at her for a few seconds in slack-jawed disbelief, then walked off feeling crushed, embarrassed, and angry.

"Gosh," said the old man. "I'm sorry. I didn't mean any harm."

"That's okay," Zilla said. "This has been coming for a while." She shrugged her shoulders, sighed, and shook her head. "Hey. You were going to tell me your story."

"It was my wife," he answered. "Do you really want to hear all this? You don't know me, and it's a long story."

"Well, my name is Zilla."

"I'm Amphecostephanus," he said, reaching across the table, bumping his glass full of juice and nearly tipping it over. "But you can call me 'Amp'."

Zilla smiled and shook his hand. "Pleased. Go ahead, Amp."

"Zilla. That's nice," he continued. "Serzhia, that's my wife, we had a nice little place, and we were pretty happy, all in all. I had a job down at the docks, you know? Loading and unloading ships. Didn't pay much. We weren't rich, but we had enough. It was great. Best years of our lives," he sighed.

"Yes?"

"You see, I was scheduled to retire in another year, when Serzhia got sick. It was cancer. They found it in her colon."

Zilla nodded, looking him in the eyes, silently asking him to go on.

"We had medical insurance through my job. I'd been paying into the plan for years. Never missed a payment.

"Okay."

"Well, she went in for surgery and started going in for treatments. We were going to beat this thing. Some of the sessions were rough on her, and they were expensive."

Zilla nodded. She had a hunch where this was headed. "Yes? So what happened?" she asked, not really wanting to know the answer.

"We thought we had good insurance coverage. We trusted them. Things got expensive. Next thing I know, the insurance syndicate is saying Serzhia had filled out her application forms improperly. She had left out some information that she had a case of stomach flu during her fifth instar and they found these old records at her clinic. She was just a child at the time, but they call it a 'pre-existing condition'. So after paying into the plan for... what, 18 years?... they dropped her."

"So, just when you guys needed them, they dropped you like a hot rock. Just like that?" she asked, snapping her fingers.

"Yep," Amp said. "They should call those crooks *un*surance companies!"

Zilla smiled and nodded in agreement." That's pretty good."

Amp's heart fluttered, and a smile crossed his face. This female was beautiful. He hadn't discharged his troubles to anybody for too long, and it felt good getting them off his thorax.

"I hung on at my job. They let me work three years past my scheduled retirement date. Some of the younger guys didn't like that, of course. They wanted to get promoted, and there I was, gumming up the works. I had to! But even then, I couldn't afford to get Serzhia all the treatment and medicine that she needed." His voice trembled. Tears formed and rolled down his cheeks. Zilla reached across the table and held his hand.

"Well, she died," he continued. The medical expenses wiped us out. We had to sell our home. But even with that money... hell, it went fast. If the insurance company hadn't dropped her, she might still be alive today. If I could have gotten her all the medicine and therapy she needed... oh, snarf-shit. If only... if, if, if."

Zilla patted him on the back. She felt a tear running down her cheek, sadness mixed with anger. "Insurance companies. They care more about making money than doing their job," she said.

"Damn," he said. "Now look what I've gone and done." He handed her a napkin. "I'm sorry. Please; don't cry."

She sniffed, taking the napkin and daubing at her eyes. "You'd better eat. Your stuff is getting cold."

"Yeah, thanks," he said, getting back to his food. "And thanks for listening. Hmm, where's your guy? Looks like he got tired of waiting."

Schnung had stalked off and was nowhere in sight.

"He's not really my guy. He's just a guy I know. Somebody I used to know."

They sat there together while he finished his meal. Before they went their separate ways, she reached into her purse and gave him a twenty-keck note. He took it and said, "Thanks."

Zilla's relationship with Schnung was over. He apparently had some growing up to do. *What in the hell did I ever see in that schmuck*? she wondered.

Chapter 3
Love on Venus

The Thlargi depend on the forest;
the forest depends on the Thlargi.

—Old Thlargi saying

Zyzz loved to watch Zilla.

The way she moved her sleek, mantid body, her big eyes with a kind smile and special sparkle, the pheromones he picked up when she was near, all stirred something deep inside him. She was beautiful and occupied his thoughts. They'd go on long walks together, go to plays, political meetings, and debates. It was easy to laugh with her. Anything was more fun; everything was better if he could share it with her.

Zilla was an education major, aiming for a teaching position in a public school. "The children of the poor go to school in old buildings badly in need of repair," she said. "Public Ed is underfunded in general. They can't pay as much as the richer school districts, so the best teachers tend to gravitate toward the affluent schools. Hell, even the food served in the working class school mess-halls is lower quality than in the dining facilities in better-off schools where they lack nothing."

They would often get into long, deep discussions. When they talked about climate change, environmental health, and politics, they made love with each others' minds.

"There has to be a way out of this. Hell, the science is clear. We can fix this thing; we're not doomed. We've just got to do a better job of getting the truth out there," Zyzz said.

Zilla nodded. "Yes, but the major media is in syndicate control, and those clowns aren't interested in any science except economics. Short-term profits. When it comes to anything else, forget it; they're in denial. And, they keep on spreading their denialist mind-rot."

"Okay, they want to maximize profits. Eventually, they've gotta see that it's in their long-term interest to conserve their resource base, no?"

Zilla shook her head. "I dunno, honey. Most people believe the denialist line, because that's all they've ever heard. They might be ignorant, but they're not stupid."

"Right. Ignorance is curable, but stupidity is terminal," Zyzz said.

Zilla nodded. "And you can't expect the syndicates to change their minds. Their share-holders demand maximum profits. If they don't get it from one company, they'll go somewhere else. It's the system. It's designed to maximize profits, and to hell with anything else."

"Well, we gotta try harder then. It's better to try and fail than to fail to try, no?"

Zilla's eyes lit up when she heard him say "we". She smiled, saying, "We've been trying. But these syndicate types are so blinded by profits that they're crazy. No, they're part of the problem. It's naïve to think they're ever going to be part of the solution."

"Nah, they'll wake up. There's gotta be some people in the syndicate councils who we can work with."

"Like who?"

Zyzz shrugged. "Damned if I know." He'd been looking and listening for signs of intelligent life in the syndicates for years and so far had found precious little.

"Forget about trying to convince the syndicates; they're hopeless. We need to bypass those clowns and speak directly to the people."

"By getting more *Wake-up Calls* into circulation?" he laughed.

"Hmmm-mmm," she agreed. "Get it into more people's hands and heads. That, plus get more people to public forums and meetings, distribute more literature, all that. It's the people; they're our only hope. Education! Forget the syndicate bosses."

Zyzz shook his head. "Okay, okay. Just hold on a second," he said. "Look at it this way: If something in nature goes haywire—say some species becomes too numerous for its food base to support—well, some predatory species will increase, reduce the pest population, and restore balance."

"Yes?"

"Well, biological systems tend to self-correct when things get out of balance," he said, then added, "Right?"

"Right. That's true for natural systems…"

"Right," he smiled, thinking he had scored a point with that.

"…but not true of un-natural systems."

"Hmm?" He raised his eyebrows.

"This syndicate, profits-first system. What's natural about it? It's a disease, Zyzz, a cancer. It's messing up nature everywhere you look. Ruining the biosphere. It will eventually kill the host unless it's surgically removed."

Zyzz was awed by this gal. "Oh yeah. Nothin' to it. And how do you suggest we do that?" He loved watching and listening to her.

"We gotta do two things, honey. Yes, sure, go ahead, try to find people on the inside of the syndicates. That's where the power is now. Who will listen? If you find somebody that will talk to you seriously, try and make them understand that climate change is real."

"... and we are causing it; there's nothing natural about it. Yes, that's what I've been doing—or *trying* to do—and that's what the Ministry of Natural Resources is all about: educating industry. Showing them how we can stop the most stupid, ruinous practices, maybe even make a start toward serious restoration," Zyzz said.

"...which the syndicates usually ignore, right?"

He scowled and nodded in agreement. "Yeah, the Ministry is advisory; no real enforcement authority."

"Toothless. They're a joke, Zyzz."

He sighed.

"Well, we need to educate people. We need to build a bigger movement, so strong and well-organized that the syndicates have to pay attention."

Zyzz nodded. "This is huge."

"Really. We've got a helluva lot to do, don't we?"

And so it went. Zyzz had the "hard-science" insights of a botany professor. Their long one-on-ones paid off in several ways. With the help of his "ground truth", Zilla's scores in her required science classes bumped upwards.

She had the conviction of a revolutionary and helped him see social and political realities he had been unaware of. Over a few weeks, she brought him to several "blinding flashes" of what had been obvious to her.

It started to show in his lectures. Increasingly, he used botany as a jumping-off point for discussing conservation issues, and his classes sometimes turned into lively seminars on environmental activism.

Zyzz was a few years older than Zilla, but that didn't seem to matter. Right from the start, his big, thoughtful eyes and his vigorous face had sparked something in her. She had finally found somebody who liked long walks as much as she did. His botany hikes and field trips, plus a couple weekly workouts at the gym kept him in pretty good shape. He had an exercise bar in his back yard, and used it several times a day to do a dozen chin-ups—more when he felt stressed about something.

She found that he was somebody she could really talk with about what mattered. From there, it grew into confiding in him about personal matters. She wanted to be with him; it felt good just to be with him.

One night, as they were leaving the theater, a bedraggled woman long past her prime asked them for some spare change. He stopped, reached into his bag for a couple kecks, and gave them to her.

"Thanks," the old woman said.

"No problem. Take care," he said.

Zilla stood watching, beaming him one of her golden smiles. He loved it when she looked that way. "What are you grinning at?" he asked, feeling a little foolish.

"Oh, nothing. I love you, you big lunk," she said, taking his arm as they continued along.

It was a clear, starry night. Bayview, like Venus in general, was usually cloudy. On these rare starry nights, stargazing was a popular pastime, but Zilla and Zyzz were so focused on each other, they hardly noticed the show overhead. As they walked to her door, he turned to look into her eyes, deep, dark, and lovely. He drew her near. They kissed, and their antennae touched and twined around each other. This time, instead of just wishing each other "good night", she asked, "Wanna come in for a while?"

"Sure," he said.

Inside the door, they kicked off their shoes. That's all they wore, as was typical on this planet where clothes were unknown outside laboratories and the space program.

"I should take a shower," Zyzz said, suddenly self-conscious, afraid that his body odor might gross her out.

"You're just fine. Don't worry," she said. "Want something to drink?"

"Sure. Whatcha got?"

"Sit down," she nodded toward the couch. "I'll be right back."

She took a couple of fizzes from the fridge, opened them, handed one to him, then sat down next to him. They talked a while and kissed again, this time long and deep, their tongues and antennae caressing and entwining around each other. She took his hand and led him through her apartment to her bedroom.

That was the first time they slept together.

As their love grew, it became obvious to others. It wasn't easy, but he had to avoid any perception of a professor playing favorites. Some teaching careers had been cut short over this kind of thing, and he didn't want to lose his job. In public, they maintained a detached, professional manner. After final exams, she moved into his house.

Zyzz had never felt like this before about anybody. When he was lecturing, her face would cross his mind. He often found himself thinking about her, what they'd do, where they could go, and what they could share.

They made an attractive couple. Although sexual dimorphism among the Drelbi was much less than that of their ancestors or Earth's mantids, females still averaged a bit larger than males, and Zilla was no exception. Both of them were nearsighted, and both wore glasses. Although clothing was something used only out in space, eyeglasses, caps, and shoes were a few of the exceptions.

Zilla was a better housekeeper and cook than Zyzz, and a bit of a perfectionist, which irritated him. He tended to let things lie where they landed, preferred to have everything out where he could see it and not have to waste time searching for things.

"Look at this mess! Zyzzles, could you puh-leeze take off your muddy boots before you squish through here and track all over the freakin' place?" she said one day as he came home from the field. She hadn't said anything about it the first couple times.

He backed up to the front door, sat down, and started unlacing his boots. "Sorry, honey." Then he walked over, grabbed a mop and cleaned up the mess.

"Thanks. Just make it a habit to take 'em off at the door, will ya?"

"No problem. Guess it'll save me some work, eh?"

Though his haphazard ways around the house were an irritation to her, she figured that she could sand off some of his rough edges.

Marg, Zyzz' mother, had long wanted to see him married. On the phone, she'd predictably get around to refrains on the theme. "Son, the longer you live by yourself, the harder it's going to be to get used to living with somebody. Don't get too stuck in your bachelor ways." And, Mom was troubled by some things she heard about the loose morals of campus life.

Her delight when Zyzz told her that he would be bringing somebody special with him on his next trip home, turned into light shades of apprehension. She had been looking forward to this for years. Although she always kept the place neat, now she spent hours cleaning up the house, washing the curtains, and picking up around the yard. She wanted to make herself, her home, and, by extension, Zyzz, look flawless.

Zilla and Zyzz walked the couple blocks to the bus stop, caught one down to the Belisama Bay airport, and boarded a four-hour flight down to Aphrodite. Zilla took a non-wing window seat. With clear weather like this, there should be some spectacular views on this trip.

The flight took them southeast over the Bell Islands to Aphrodite Central. Before they went to baggage claim, they stopped at the Rent-a-Zoom desk and chose one of the lowest-price models that had a wing-option. Then they picked up their checked baggage, put it in a cart, and wheeled it out to where the zoom rentals were parked.

The airport was down in the scorching flat lowlands just southeast of Rusalka Bay. When they stepped outside, it felt like walking into an oven. They put their stuff into the trunk and got in; Zyzz got in behind the wheel.

"Drell, it's hotter than hell in this thing," Zilla said, cranking her window down.

"Greenhouse effect," he said. "Heat comes in, but can't get out. Thank Drell for air conditioning."

They took the main highway east toward Brrzzt via Zewana Sound. It was busy, as was typical for that stretch of road. In about an hour, Zyzz was starting to feel hungry. "Feel like getting something to eat?" he asked.

"Yeah," Zilla replied. "Why don't we stop at the next place?"

"I know a good one."

A few kilometers later, he turned off into a gravel parking lot and pulled up to a truck stop that he remembered as having pretty decent chow. They both ordered burgers for lunch, and yes, they were still pretty good.

As they were leaving, they walked by a crowded livestock truck that had just parked. The words "Clorm Solutions", and the slogan "We Got the Science!" were written in bold letters on the side.

Zyzz nodded to the truck driver and asked "How's it going?"

The driver nodded back and said with a half-laugh, "Hey: can't complain. Nobody'd listen anyway."

"Thanks for driving these monsters around. A good burger sure hits the spot."

"Hey, it's a job; too damn much sitting though."

Clorm Solutions was part of a syndicate that provided a range of services to farmers. In this case, "science" meant adding growth hormones to livestock feed to fatten them up quickly and injecting more hormones into animals to inhibit pupation and retard them from spinning cocoons. Farmers also used the company to pick up their clorms from their feed lots and haul them to the slaughter house.

Later, back on the road, Zyzz said, "You know, Zilla, a year ago I wouldn't even have thought to stop and say anything to that guy. Wouldn't have even occurred to me. Guess you're getting to me, lady. Some of that 'worker's solidarity'?"

"Yep. Workers have to hang together, else we'll all get strung up separately. Doesn't take much time to be nice, does it? You might've made his day. Might help keep him awake and alive on the road for another day. Who knows?"

Zyzz nodded. Yeah; it ain't all that hard, I reckon."

"That trucker, the waitress... everybody talks so funny down here. Sounds like a movie. I didn't think people really talked like that anymore."

"Sheeeit, you ain't heard nothin' yet, honey. Brzzt and the Highlands hereabouts were the last holdouts of the Thlargi. That's what you be a'hearin'," Zyzz answered, exaggerating his backwoods twang.

"I think it sounds nice," she said.

Archaeological evidence shows that the largest Thlargi populations had long been concentrated throughout Aphrodite. Most lived in the cooler highlands. The shrinking amount of arable land increased contact between the two races and had led to bloody conflicts. Aphrodite was the major battleground and the prize of the Great War.

Aphrodite Mining and Manufacturing was the biggest employer down here. They mined and refined iron, copper, tin, and other ores. A fleet of trucks went to and from their sites around the clock. AM and M products were marketed to factories all over the world and used to build zooms, airplanes, and spacecraft.

With luck, they would miss the traffic jams created by shift-changes of workers going to and from farms and the various industrial and mining sites. When the traffic thinned out enough, Zyzz got up to speed, pushed the button that spread the car's wings, engaged the propeller, and they lifted up off the freeway. It was a clear, sunny day with long visibility.

They looked down at the landscape rolling by below. On the farms, clorms grazed in the deep grass. Children tended their flocks, watching for predators. Out here in the country, people learned at a young age how to handle farming equipment. "Hot rods" are devices that deliver mild electric jolts to their animals to keep them under control, and "zappers" are gun-like devices that fire jolts through the air to change the minds of predators, and can be turned up to lethal levels if needed.

Here, on the leeward side of the mountains, the landscape dried out; the countryside opened up into more arid land. Outside the green, irrigated farms, the terrain was rocky and bare except for scattered clumps of drought-tolerant scrub. Large boulders lay scattered across the arid landscape. This stretch of Aphrodite was desert country, hotter and dryer than anywhere on Ishtar.

"Look," Zyzz said, pointing down to a rocky patch that showed a bright greenish tinge.

"Whuzzat?" asked Zilla.

"More grasses growing down there now, see?"

"Yeah?" she glanced at him with a quizzical look.

"Yeah. The Space Consortium brought the seeds back from Earth, and now they're going feral. Gettin' outta control and growin' all over the place. Taking over, like weeds," he said.

Up ahead on the horizon loomed their destination. Mount Maat poked its snowy head up above the clouds. The highest mountain in the Ozza Range, Zilla said that it looked like a big scoop of cool ice-splorff. Brzzt, an isolated highland community of eastern Aphrodite, lay in the forested belt on the northwest shoulder of the mountain. As they gained altitude, the desert started to soften, taking on a hazy and increasingly greenish hue as they climbed up toward the highlands.

As they approached Zyzz's home village, the highway below was clear, so they landed their zoom outside the city limits and drove in. A few small businesses had been replaced with chain outlet stores, but not much else had changed. The same old water tower with BRZZT in huge letters still stood over the quiet little town.

They headed straight for Mom's place. As they pulled into the driveway, there she was, reading a book, sitting out in a swing hanging from the bottom limb of a giant, spreading Lycopod. Zyzz had climbed the tree and put up the swing years ago. It was good to see it was still usable.

When she saw them get out of the car and start walking over to her, Marg put down her book next to her drink on the table by the swing. As Drelbi age, they first go from whitish nymphs to green adults, and then slowly turn brown as they age. His mother had grown browner since he saw her last.

"How ya been, Mom?" Zyzz held her in his arms, gave her a squeeze, lifting her up off her feet.

"Oh, you!" she squeaked. "Put me down!" Then the three embraced in a four-armed hug.

After being cooped up for so long traveling, it felt good to feel the sunshine and be out in the fresh air again. Both of them felt like they could use a little exercise. A walk downtown would be nice. Zilla asked Marg if she wanted to take a wander, maybe stop in at the old drug store for something cool, like an ice-splorff cone or maybe a fizz.

"That sounds nice. Let's just take it slow; don't make me rush now," she said.

What they really wanted was a good, stiff hike, but they held it down to a slow stroll for Marg, down the driveway to the street and the few blocks downtown. Most houses they walked by looked old-fashioned, with big yards and gardens. They nodded greetings in response to folks they passed. The old town had a settled, built-by-hand character that felt very different from the mass-produced, pre-fabricated look of newer developments.

They walked up to a storefront with a sign that read 'Brzzt Drug and Hardware'. Zyzz opened the door for Zilla and his mom, then walked with them back to the soda fountain where a collection of old-fashioned, antique signs hung on the walls.

"Zyzz? Naaah... is that you?" the lady behind the counter asked.

"After a couple seconds of reaching back into his memory banks, Zyzz responded, "Yep. How are you, Brunka?" He reached over the counter to give her a hug. "This is my fiancé, Zilla. You already know Mom," he smiled. "This here's Brunka. We used to go steady back in high school."

"Well, you're looking good, Zyzz. Both of you. You too, Marg," Brunka said as she gave her a nod. "Well, what'll y'all have today?"

"Why don't you make me a blue fizz, just like you used to?" Zyzz said.

"Okay, and how about you, uhh... it's Zilla, right?"

"Yes. I'll have the same."

"And you, ma'am?"

"Oh, why don'cha give me a red 'un?" Marg said.

They sat down on chairs around a small table and lingered over their ice-schlorff fizzes that are similar to the ice-cream sodas popular among Earthlings, and talked about this and that.

Marg kept her nervousness to herself. She and Zilla got along famously from the start. They talked and talked, checking out each other in a warm and kindly fashion, and they liked most of what they found out.

Zyzz and Zilla spent a couple days at the old homestead. After they had hugged his mom goodbye, and drove off, Zyzz asked, "So, how do you like her?"

"She's sweet. Funny! She has a great sense of humor, you know," she answered.

"Seems like you two hit it off pretty well."

"Yes. She's very nice. A little old-fashioned and proper, but sweet."

CHAPTER 4
MARRIAGE DRELBI STYLE

She that marries for wealth sells her liberty.

—Proverb from the *Book of Drell*

A few weeks after final exams, Zilla and Zyzz signed up for the mandatory series of pre-marital counseling sessions.

They loved Father O'Shozz, the assistant priest at the campus temple, for his humor and wit. The Padre's wife often attended and assisted with the counseling, sharing her insights regarding marital life: what makes a good marriage bad, and vice versa from a wife's viewpoint.

During the sessions, the young couple received the standard cautions, admonitions, advice and, finally, Holy Assent. They sent out the marriage announcements and invitations to a few friends and relatives. Neither wanted a big ceremony; they both preferred a small, more intimate one. They made a reservation for the ceremony to be held outdoors at the campus garden.

The day of the event arrived. At the garden, not far from where they had set up the chairs, there was a display of the latest flowers, grown from seeds from Earth. The exhibition was attracting an interested crowd and causing quite a stir. Many of the flowers were larger than a Drelb. They had never seen such surreal colors nor smelled such intoxicatingly sweet fragrances. Zyzz had only read about these things and seen pictures, and was fascinated by them.

"Know much about these?" Zilla's father Mott asked Zyzz.

Zilla's father had met a few of her previous boyfriends and hadn't been very impressed with any of them. One had been a squishy philosophy major. Useless! Then there was that hoity-toity pre-law guy. Drell; what an arrogant snot he was! Zilla was his only daughter, and he had wondered if she would ever find a decent mate. These past few days he had become acquainted with Zyzz and felt this guy was definitely an improvement.

"Yes, sir. Flowers. From Earth. Amazing, aren't they? They're the reproductive organs of these plants," Zyzz said.

"Yep!" Mott climbed up into the flower. "These red things here are called *petals*, right?" He ran his hand over the soft, velvety red surface.

"Yup. And these here are stamens—the male part. The tips up here are called *anthers*, where the pollen—sperm, basically—is produced. The central structure here is the female part. The tip is called the stigma. It catches the pollen."

"I'll be damned!" Another guy who was also checking it out said, "And down here, down at the base of these petta-whatchamacallits are scent glands. Dang things smell good, eh?"

"Yup. They use this scent to attract pollinators," Zyzz said.

"Pollina-whats?"

"Pollinators. Earth-bugs. The sweet odor lures in bugs that transfer the pollen from the anthers to the pistils of other flowers. That's how they make seeds."

Mott shook his head. "Hmm. What'll they think of next? You know, son, you should have been a farmer."

"Yeah, maybe. I just don't have the business sense for it, I guess."

They looked over at Zilla, her mother Glort, and Marg, standing by the priest and smiling back at them and shaking their heads. "Uh-oh. Guess we'd better get back," Zyzz said, and they walked over to join them. "To be continued."

Marg, Zyzz's mother, had come a long way to be here; getting from her small town to the airport, then flying all the way from Aphrodite to Ishtar was a long trip, tiring for anybody.

Father O'Shozz cleared his throat and asked loudly, smiling, "Are we ready?"

"Yes!" Zilla and Zyzz said, and the assemblage quickly hushed.

The padre delivered a short homily about marriage, dedication, and the meaning of life, sprinkled generously with comical asides. Then he began, "Sisters and brothers. On this beautiful day, here in this garden, we are gathered to celebrate the commitment of Zilla and Zyzz to share their lives, join their worldly possessions, and become one in the eyes of the Goddess, creator of all that is seen and unseen."

The two looked into each other's eyes and smiled.

"Zilla, do you pledge to dedicate yourself to this Drelb, Zyzz, to honor, respect, and care for him in health and in infirmity, come what may, from this day forward, until you are parted by death?"

"I do."

"Zilla," the priest continued, "do you pledge to raise any children that may result from your union with the love, spirit, knowledge, and teachings of the Goddess and her only begotten daughter Drell?"

"I do."

The Padre then faced Zyzz and led him through the pledges.

"By the authority vested in me by the Church and Holy Empire of Drell, our light and savior, I now pronounce you united in Drell. May you two enjoy a happy, loving friendship and a long and full life together. In the name of the Mother, the Daughter, and the Holy Spirit."

"Amen," the gathering responded.

Zilla and Zyzz kissed, then turned to walk down the aisle between the people standing in front of their folding chairs.

After the reception, they caught a zoom for a ride to the Bayview Airport. They flew out to the Ut islands to the west of Ishtar for a week of loving, hiking, botanizing, and snorkeling the coral reefs.

The water's clarity made for spectacular snorkeling. The accommodations were rustic, which was perfect with them. The restaurant at their hotel had aquariums, where you could select the ammonite, lobster, or crab you wanted for supper, fresh off local fishing boats. The cooking smells from the kitchen cranked up their appetites, and by the time it arrived steaming at their table, they were ravenous.

To walk it off, they strolled down along the turquoise sea holding hands, beach-combing, and collecting seashells, stopping now and then to kiss and watch the surf roll in.

Chapter 5
The In-Laws

Each bite of food in the bowl
comes from Drelbi toil.

—From the *Proverbs of Drell*

It was another hot, record-breaking day, a few months later. Just mid-day and already 33° C.

Bayview's Old Town District is a dozen-block walk downhill from the University District. At a sidewalk café, Zyzz and Zilla were having lunch with Glort and Mott, her mom and dad. They were just finishing their schlurpp, a shrimp-and-krill soup.

"So, what are we doing that's so wrong, Zilla? Dammit; your mother and I have worked hard all our lives, unlike some of these… friends of yours." Mott's antennae lay back combatively flat. He made a dismissive, brush-off gesture and his eyes sparked as he dabbed his chin with a napkin. "I tell you, that land has been good to us. But now? I've just about had it. I'm ready to quit. Retire. We need some security. That land is all we've got, and it's ours to do with whatever the hell we need to."

This was what Zilla got for asking her dad about plans to sell their house and farm to developers on a reverse-mortgage deal that would convert even more farmland into suburban sprawl. Mott was feeling torn and defensive and was emanating a potent odor. A mixture of guilt, anger, distress, and confusion pheromones hung like a thick, invisible cloud around him. Zyzz listened and nodded, slicing off bite-sized pieces of trilobite steak and munching them. *Let him vent,* he thought. *If he doesn't get this off his thorax, he's going to blow a fuse.*

"Yeah, I've heard all about this global warming stuff. Bunch of alarmist clormshit, if you ask me. But even if there is something to it, hell, is that my fault?" Mott asked. "Don't blame me for it, girl. Besides, do you think the Goddess would just stand by and let us ruin her world?" He pointed at Zyzz now. "Maybe if you guys spent more time praying and less time shit-stirring, you'd see that."

Zyzz could hardly blame Mott for making this decision. Over the past few decades, many important agricultural valleys on Ishtar had been gobbled up by sprawl.

Warehouses, shopping centers, and huge parking lots sat on top of prime farmland, thus driving up food prices. Farmers, especially older ones worn out from a lifetime of hard work, found they could make a lot more money by selling their lands to developers than continuing to work them. Most young people preferred jobs with dependable hours and regular vacation time, rather than being chained to the land and all the demands of farm life. Mott had gotten an offer for his land that he couldn't refuse.

The crisis wasn't brought about by any underhanded conspiracy to ruin the planet. No, this was an unintended result of thousands of everyday business-as-usual decisions. It was a culmination of having profits as the top priority, ahead of everything else. Syndicate decision-makers felt they had to obey the dictates of the market. If they didn't—if they put the big picture ahead of profits and tried to do the best thing environmentally—the system would eliminate them, weed them out mercilessly, to be replaced by others who would play the game without limiting scruples.

It was a matter of survival. Grow, maximize profits—or die. That spirit permeated the culture, down to the lowest classes. Millions of individual decisions were adding up, coming together to accumulate a potent, toxic synergy.

The system thrived on a chronic sense of insecurity. Working people rarely had the time or breathing room needed for clear thinking. They were too busy for that.

Health insurance syndicates often dropped clients as soon as they got expensive. Many people, especially those that needed it the most, had no coverage at all. Cancer treatments, heart trouble, any number of medical conditions could, and often did mean financial ruin. Glort had a heart problem. It wasn't a good idea to get into heated discussions around her.

When Mott paused, Zilla had to say something. "Dad, what if the government had the right of preferred-purchase for farmland?"

"Yeah? Okay, go on," Mott said.

"Instead of being paved over for another damn shopping center, we could set up big cooperative farms where people could work a whole lot less than they'd have to as individual farmers. They could have time off, take vacations, and get away. And we'd be saving the land instead of burying it under concrete. Concrete doesn't clean the air, Dad. And it sure as hell doesn't produce food."

"Sounds good, but…" Mott started.

"Can we change the subject? " Zyzz injected, squeezing Zilla's hand under the table.

"It's been so hot!" Glort said. "And they're cutting down so many trees that it's getting hard to find any shade to cool off. I'm so glad that we kept some trees around our place. At least the animals can get a break from the heat." She paused a moment. "You know, we really need to get rid of these damn developers."

Glort usually came down on the liberal side, which vexed her husband. They enjoyed a loving but frequently flustering marriage. She knew she should avoid blood pressure-raising situations, but kept getting into them.

"You and your eco-agitator friends are a joke, girl," Mott said, his spiracles hissing. "To hell with the government. Politicians bugger up everything they touch. They're in bed with the same damn syndicates you're railing against! Supply and demand, son; that's the answer." He tapped Zyzz on the chest. "That's the only answer. Rising food prices will stop this. Sooner or later, it'll make farming worth the bother again. We need to depend on the free market."

"Can we talk about something else for a while? Please?" Zyzz asked, with a pleading gesture.

Zilla asked him, "How are your classes going, dear?"

They talked about school and other less antagonistic matters as they finished their krill soup. When the bill came, both Mott and Zyzz grabbed for it. Zyzz won. "I'll get it this time, Dad."

The four sat and talked some more, as they preened themselves in the Drelbi way. First, you take a drink of water and swish it around in your mouth to clean your maxillae (teeth). Then you bend your antennae and pulled them through your mouth—all the while chatting about this and that. Or, in more formal occasions, you'd go to the washroom and rinse off your antennae, face, and hands at a sink.

Mott left some change on the table for a tip. They got up, and slowly headed toward the door, chatting away. When they got to the register, Zyzz reached into his shoulder pack, found some money, and paid up.

Outside, they all hugged. Zilla invited her parents over for supper soon. "One these days, come over for a walk in the park or something. We'll play some Bogundo, have a nice time." They agreed, but set nothing firm.

"I'm sorry, Zyzzles," Zilla sighed as her parents walked away. "Dad likes you; he really does, as long as we can keep away from politics."

He turned his head to look at her and laughed. "We? I wasn't having much trouble. It was *you* that couldn't keep away from politics!"

"Yeah."

"Hey, your dad's okay. I think he likes that governmental preferred-purchase idea and co-op farms. Let him chew on that awhile."

"Oh, you know, they want to do the best thing. But, I mean, what are their real options? If they willed it to me, we could set up a co-op maybe, but the developers are offering them a much better deal than we ever could, and they've worked so hard. They deserve a nice retirement; how else can they get it?"

"Your dad's on target. This current government is a nest of syndicate roaches. If we could get Thromm in there, and more progressives like her, we might be able to turn this mess around. Most of this current crop isn't worth a damn."

Zilla glanced at him. *He's making progress*, she thought. He was right about Thromm, a third-party politician and perennial candidate for senator from the Northeast Coast of Ishtar, and an avowed environmentalist. Thromm was building up a sizeable following that loved her rabble-rousing populist speeches.

Zilla and Zyzz soon discovered they shared another common interest. When they saw a yard sale sign, they couldn't pass by. They had to "just to take a look" and often ended up carrying something home. It took both of them to carry a big table home from a rummage sale a few blocks away. They slowly furnished their place with antique furniture and a growing collection of books and music.

Chapter 6
Early Symptoms

The important thing
is not what you look at,
but what you see.

—A Proverb from the *Book of Drell*

Bayview was a picturesque town on Belisama Bay with the Ausra Mountains as a photogenic backdrop.

The city wrapped itself around three hills; the University campus was up on North Hill.

The colorful coral reefs in Belisama Bay, once so rich, were long gone among the first victims of industrial pollution. The once-timbered slopes had been cut long ago for ship-building, and the city had grown to sprawl over the hills.

Even at its coldest periods, glaciers on Venus were never as large as those of Earth. Restricted to the polar regions and the tops of the highest mountains of Venus—Alpha Regio, Beta Regio, and Maxwell Montes—all glaciers were now shrinking in full retreat.

Fossil fuel companies wanted the Drelbi to use as much coal, oil, and natural gas as possible, as fast as they could. Zoom companies promoted big petrol-guzzlers and governments—both federal and local—neglected mass public transit that could have conserved fuel. That way, the companies netted more profits. It was stockholder-driven with the primary fiduciary responsibility to maximize profits or get sued. Woe to the manager that tried to do the right thing: she would be replaced by the less scrupulous.

Carbon, stored in coal, petroleum, and natural gas that had accumulated over millions of years, was released into the atmosphere with thoughtless abandon.

The average carbon dioxide (CO_2) content in Earth's atmosphere was, as of September 2009, 390 ppm. Earth's safe level is 350 ppm, above which serious changes, such as polar ice and alpine glacier melt, is initiated. The CO_2 reacts with sea water to form carbonic acid. The Earth's average ocean water is 30% more acidic now than historically, due to carbonic acid. Venus, because of its location nearer the sun, had a lower tipping point than Earth's. When the CO_2 reached 300 ppm, things started to go seriously wrong.

The forests, farmland, meadows, and marshes that filtered the CO_2 from the air, sequestered the carbon into biomass, supported wildlife, and released oxygen, were scalped willy-nilly, wherever and whenever a profit could be made. This crippled Venus' means of filtering CO_2 out of the air.

At first, some farra and other low-lying islands lost some land to rising sea levels. After devastating storms, many Drelbi left their seaside homes for higher ground on both Ishtar and Aphrodite. In the planet's temperate zones, rainfall came less and less predictably, adding to farmers' insecurity. When it did rain, it often came down in torrents, washing away precious soil from deforested slopes. Storms were more violent than they used to be, winds more fierce, blowing more bare soil away. It was growing noticeably hotter and drier. Some crops were ruined; some harvests failed. Hunger was growing, and famine loomed.

A few Venusians understood what was happening. Even fewer put the pieces together and got a glimpse of the bigger picture.

Some scientists—if you could call them that—received hefty salaries from energy companies. Their articles appeared regularly in the major (syndicate) press. One stated:

The proposition that the planet is warming is based on spurious science. If there is anything to it, carbon dioxide and water vapor will put the brakes on any warming. It will act as a shield, a parasol that will shade the planet.

Most in the scientific community were perplexed. How could anybody believe such nonsense? Why didn't the major media print articles submitted by real scientists? Why the lack of balance?

Most working people were too busy to read the non- and anti-syndicate "alternative" press. Even if they were curious and would have liked to read it, people hesitated to buy a copy from a street vendor or stop at an information table. Many were afraid they might be seen as a "radical" if somebody saw them with a copy of one of "those" papers.

A few scientists joined the Ecology Party (EP) and worked overtime to get the word out to educate people about the crisis and possible solutions. A physicist named Gorrzz was interviewed on an alternative radio news show, and said, "The system is running out of options. How can we hope to deal with the problems we're facing—the climate crisis and the problem of labor-displacing technology, to name just two of the many problems—with the old syndicate system? Syndicate rule created these problems. We need new answers."

Pundits on the big syndicate media seized every opportunity to use wedge issues and make progressives appear irrelevant and ridiculous, all the while making flacks of the fossil-fuel syndicates appear as the font of all knowledge and reason. Progressives were marginalized.

Those working in the media had to be careful. Journalists who took their jobs seriously, who honestly reported syndicate abuses, had been terminated—in one way or another. Self-censorship was the norm. A few alternative newspapers circulated here and there. Some college radio stations tried to get the truth out, but their allowed wattage was miniscule compared to that allowed the syndicate propaganda mills, and so reached comparatively few.

Some politicians were beginning to speak out about the climate and environmental problems. However, without syndicate financial backing, they rarely had any realistic chance of being elected. Political campaigns were expensive. They timidly couched their language with phrases like "market solutions", "free enterprise", and "business-friendly approaches to our problems". A few came out and honestly admitted that the market system and business-as-usual were causes of the problems, not solutions. The syndicates didn't like that sort of talk. Those who did speak out risked losing any major funding, so rarely got more than a few percent of the votes.

Some prominent clergy were also speaking out. Zilla and Zyzz attended a mainstream temple in the university district that had a large congregation. The head priestess, Sister Boff, very outgoing and amiable, often spoke out against injustice and the abuse of creation. Her sermons were peppered with things like, "When employers don't pay their workers enough to lift them out of poverty, that is a violation, not only against working people, but it is a crime against our Creator who calls upon us to treat each other as our sisters and brothers.

"When syndicates pollute the living waters we all depend upon, when they pollute our air and the breath of life… this is a crime against the Goddess and Drell, the Greatest Prophet… may her holy name be forever sacred. The Goddess, creator of all things seen and unseen, calls upon us to be good stewards over Creation and the gifts she has given us."

Some criticized her for mixing religion with politics. In one of her homilies, she preached:

> Remember the parable of the old lady on the roof? No?
>
> There was once an elderly lady that lived in a village not far from here. She lived in the floodplain of the river. One day, she heard an announcement on the radio warning that a storm that was raging was creating a flood danger and advised people to vacate their houses and move up to higher ground until the danger passed.
>
> Not long after, a second warning came over the radio. The riverbanks would soon overflow and flood the nearby homes. The Ministry of Public Safety ordered everyone in the town to evacuate immediately.
>
> Well, this lady stayed put. A neighbor drove over, knocked on the lady's door, told her they had room in their zoom, and asked her to pack some essentials and come with them. Well, this gal would have nothing to do with that, and told her, 'Thanks, but I'm not worried. The Goddess will save me.' "

Her neighbor left without her, and it started to rain even heavier. Looking out her window toward the river, she could see the water rising.

Then, some other neighbors came by her house and said to her, “We’re leaving and we have room for you in our zoom; please come with us!” But she declined, saying, “I have faith that The Goddess will save me.”

As the lady stood on her porch watching the water rise up the steps, a man in a canoe paddled by and called to her, “Hurry and come into my canoe. The waters are rising fast!”

But again, she said, “No thanks, The Goddess will save me.”

The floodwaters rose higher, pouring water into her living room, and the woman had to retreat to the second floor. A police boat came by and saw her at the window. “We will come up and rescue you!” they shouted. But again, she refused, waving them off, saying, “Use your time to save someone else! I have faith that The Goddess will save me!”

The flood waters rose higher and higher and the lady had to climb up to her rooftop.

A rescue-patrol chopper-zoom spotted her and dropped a rope ladder. A rescue officer came down the ladder and pleaded with her, "Grab my hand and I will pull you up!" But she STILL refused, folding all four of her arms tightly to her body. “No thank you! The Goddess will save me!”

Shortly afterward, the house broke up and the floodwaters swept her away, and she drowned.

When she got to Heaven, the lady stood before The Goddess and asked, “I put all of my faith in You. Why didn’t You come and save me?”

> And the Goddess replied, "Girl, I sent you two warnings via radio. Twice, I sent you neighbors with zooms to help you. I sent you a canoe, I sent you a motorboat, and I even sent you a chopper-zoom. What more were you looking for?"

Laughter broke out throughout the temple.

"Truly I say unto you, my brothers and sisters. We are the voices, the arms, and the legs of the Goddess. Each and every one of us can be used by Drell and our Creator.

"Who were the prophets of previous generations, the prophets whose writings are in our Holy Book of Drell? They were seen as the radicals of their time. And who are the prophets of our time? Are they not the socialists and ecologists, who the fat and pampered disparage as the *radicals* of our time?"

After the service, Zilla and Zyzz stopped to chat with Sister Boff, standing outside the main entryway, shaking hands and chatting with her parishioners as they left the temple.

"I've been meaning to ask you, Sister. Have you ever thought about running for public office?" Zilla asked the priestess.

"Yes. For about three seconds." Sister Boff smiled. "No, my job is here in our temple. This keeps me busy enough. Too busy!"

CHAPTER 7
THE BACK-TO-THE-LANDERS

After speaking with a Drelb,
count your fingers.

—Thlarg proverb

In those days of mounting unrest, one tendency that rejected politics as any solution was the "Back to the Land" ("BTL") movement.

BTLers advocated dropping out from the mainstream culture to set up model communes as living examples of how to live simple, sustainable lifestyles and tread lightly upon the planet.

One of their slogans, often appearing as graffiti, was "Industry is the Problem—Be Part of the Solution!" It was a loose, anarchistic group that had no formal organization or leadership, and made its decisions by consensus in assemblies.

Many subscribed to journals that espoused Thlargian philosophy, wore caps with Thlarg designs and pendants around their necks with Thlarg insignia, and listened to Thlargian music: tribal drumming and chanting. Thlarg chic. Most were college students.

A few dozen BTLers from the Bayview area caravanned down to Mumphara, the reservation that was home to the largest concentration of Thlargi on Ishtar. Mumphara is Thlargian for "shimmering waters". They set up their tents in a circle around their central meeting area, an encampment outside the main gate, where they drummed, played their instruments, and sang songs around a campfire. One day at an assembly, they selected three from their group to go into the reservation and meet with the Thlargi.

After discussing it for a while, the three left their encampment and walked across the parking lot to the main gate, where they soon encountered their first obstacle: the outer gatehouse staffed by Drelbi police. They went in.

"Purpose of your visit?" asked Grrzz, the duty sergeant of the day.

"We'd like to meet with the chief council," answered Tenas, the designated "non-leader" leader of the three. Moorv and Zhtipp, the other two, nodded in agreement.

"Okay, let's try this again," Grrzz said. "Purpose of your visit?" she repeated, her antennae standing up straight as arrows.

"We'd like to establish diplomatic relations between the Thlargi and the Back-to-the-Land Movement," Tenas replied.

"Under whose authority?"

"We have been elected to represent the Back-to-the-Land Movement to establish relations with the people of Mumphara."

"Movement, schmoovement. You kids having fun partying out there?"

None of them responded.

"Well," Grrzz said, tapping her pen on the desk. "You are aware that I can't guarantee your safety once you're on the reserve?"

"Yes, ma'am. We're aware of that."

"Have you contacted anybody on the reserve yet?"

The three quickly glanced at each other, then Tenas said, "No; this will be our first formal contact."

Grrzz' eyes quickly shot to those of the corporal standing by the three, shaking her head in exaggerated disgust, and said, "I should just kick your mangy asses out of here."

Tenas said nothing.

"But," she said with a smirk, "I'll let you pass. This might be a little education for you. Any weapons?"

"No, ma'am," Tenas answered, all three spreading their arms. No clothing, no concealed weapons.

"Okay, you may proceed. Just stay on the road," she said, thumbing a quick gesture toward the back entrance.

"Sergeant Hardass, at your service!" Moorv said outside. The other two hissed in agreement, laughed, then walked the short distance ahead to the Thlarg gate where they were questioned by another officer, a Thlarg this time.

"Purpose of your visit?"

"We request an audience with the president of Mumphara and her council."

"Who in the hell... uhh, do you have an appointment, miss?"

"My name is Tenas."

"T-e-n-a-s-s?" she asked, spelling it out.

"Just one ess."

"And your names?" she asked Moorv and Zhtipp, and logged them in.

"I don't see any of you on the appointment calendar, miss."

"No; not yet. We'd like to make an appointment."

The Thlarg officer went over to pick up the phone, pushed a few buttons, and chatted with somebody for a few minutes, then came back to them.

"Okay. Come back at 3400 hours. The president won't be available. You'll be meeting with a couple members of her council."

On their way out, the Drelbi sergeant acted a little surprised that they had even gotten as far as making an appointment.

In what was equivalent to a span of two earth-days later, the three were back. The Thlarg gate officer told the corporal on duty to walk them over to the administration office.

"Okay, let's go then," said Corporal Zuski as he picked up his walking stick and led them down a dusty gravel street into Mumphara townsite.

The village was well populated with gaunt snarfs freely ranging for food and fighting each other for any choice morsels they might chance upon. The visitors soon attracted the attention of a pack of a half-dozen, who surrounded the group too close for comfort, bristling, snarling, and baring their fangs menacingly.

"Scat!" The corporal swung his stick at the snarfs, and they backed off enough to allow them to pass, still growling with eyes glaring in hostility. The ruckus attracted the attention of a few Thlargi who stopped and watched in silent disapproval as the strangers passed by.

In a few blocks, they came to a building that had seen better days. The sign said "Community Center".

Inside, the receptionist spoke fluent Drelbian, with a strong Thlarg accent. No surprise. Although an effort was being made by traditionalists to preserve the Thlargi language and teach it in reservation schools, it was proving to be a losing battle. Not one TV or radio station on the planet broadcast programming in Thlarg, and everyday business was conducted in Drelbian. Most young Thlargi weren't interested in learning a dying language.

The receptionist picked up the desk phone, pushed a button, and said, "Ms Tenas and her friends are here." To them he said, "Okay, you can go in now. Second door on your right." He jerked his chin toward the hallway.

They walked down to the open door and went in. Behind a table sat three Thlargs. The one in the middle stood up and said, "Good afternoon. I'm Councilor Muff; this is Councilor Frumm," she indicated the Thlarg to her right, "and this is Councilor Schmunn."

The three extended their upper arms, spreading them wide, palms facing the Drelbs, then reached across the table to touch palms with them; the traditional Thlargian welcome and peace greeting.

"On behalf of the people of Mumphara, I'd like to welcome you to our home," Muff said.

"Thank you," the three nodded.

"Now, how can we help you?" Schmunn asked, glancing at her wrist watch and thinking, *why couldn't you kids just go through PR instead of bothering us?*

"We come in peace," said Tenas. The other two nodded.

Muff turned her head, did a quick-glance eye contact with the other two councilors, and said, "Please; cut the dramatics. This isn't TV. What can we do for you?"

Tenas looked at her two friends, flustered. "We three are from our group at the Encampment. Our group is a detachment of the Back to The Land movement. We reject the ways of the Drelbi; and we honor the Thlargi way. We ask that you allow us to move onto Mumphara, so we can better learn your ways."

The three councilors had seen TV coverage, read the printed articles and books, and talked about this BTL movement. Muff shook her head and said, "Thank you, but we'll have to decline your kind offer."

Tenas said, "We understand. Please understand us. We come to learn from you, not to take from you. We only want to learn from your wisdom. Your ways have proven better than the Drelbi way."

"You wish only to learn from us?" Schmunn asked, slowly nodding her head.

"Yes, ma'am."

"Like the missionaries you have sent us?"

"Your Drelbi missionaries tell us the same thing," added Councilor Frumm. "And the next thing you know, they're telling us our ways are backward and holding us back. Huh! That their one goddess is better than all our gods. No thank you."

"You misunderstand us," said Tenas.

Muff said, "Look, we're not here to argue with you. If you truly want to learn more about our ways, that can easily be arranged. You could have done that without us. Go to our Public Relations department. The receptionist will be happy to give you information on how to get there."

"But…," Tenas said.

"Listen, please, and understand," Muff said. "Our ways are nothing mysterious, and really not all that much to learn. Don't they teach you any of this in your schools? Is it so difficult for you to understand that our planet is not just here to make you rich? Is it so hard to see that all species have a right to exist for their own sake, and that we must learn to live in balance with the needs of nature?"

"Yes. We can see that, ma'am. The Drelbi way is ruining the world."

"Our struggle to save the forests has been a trail of tears and broken promises, Frumm said. "You Drelbi have destroyed our land and culture, and lock us up on these reservations with TVs. Ghettos!"

"We—our movement—reject the way of the exploiters and spoilers who have hurt you, and misled us. Greed is not good," Tenas said.

"Yes, yes. Good luck with that. So how many of you are there in your "movement" anyway? You clearly speak not for the majority of your people."

"We are few, but we are strong in our commitment to breaking with the destructive ways of the Drelbi," Zhtipp said.

"Good; that is good," Muff said. "Go back to your friends. Then, after your… camping trip, go back and change your society. Stop the destroyers before it's too late."

"We have dropped out from all that," Tenas said. "Politics is futile. We will change our society by living example. Many Drelbs are starting to realize that the Drelbi way is bankrupt. It's destructive and needs changing."

"Good. Now, can we get serious for a moment? And this is important for you to understand. You won't change a damn thing by 'dropping out', as you put it, " Frumm said. "It never has and never will. No. This will take much work. Do you really want to help us… and yourselves?"

"Yes," the three nodded.

"If you expect to harvest your garden, first you need to sow. Then you need to nourish, mulch, compost your plants. You need to pull out all the weeds. Get your fingers dirty," Councilor Frumm said.

"If you seriously want to help, then get involved with changing your practices. That means persistent political activity," Muff said. "And that 'Industry is the Problem' stuff?"

"Yes?"

"You guys are on the wrong track with that. Industry isn't the problem. Industry is just a tool. The problem is how it's used."

"Well, we would disagree with that…" Tenas started.

"Now, hold on; just bear me out on this," Muff continued. "Take a hammer. It's a tool. Now, in the hands of a skilled carpenter that hammer can be used to build a nice house, eh?"

"Okay."

"Okay. Now take that very same hammer. Put it in the hands of a Drelbi-cidal maniac, or a vandal. You could get some very different results, no?"

"Yes, but… "

Muff continued, "All I'm trying to say is this. The tool of industry is too often used to rape our Venus Mother and screw working people. It doesn't have to be that way. Industry doesn't have to be the enemy of nature. We have shown that we can live in harmony with our Mother."

Councilor Schmunn added, "You may drink from the fountains of nature and come back again and again to satisfy your thirst. But if you destroy the fountain, you destroy the stream that the fountain feeds. All of us—Drelbi and Thlargi—live downstream. When we say that if you continue fouling your nest, you will wake up in a bed full of your waste, this isn't just poetry. It's real. Now, go to the PR office and set up a few classes on Thlargian ways. But promise us that you and your friends will *use* this knowledge. Put it to practical use, or you're just wasting your time. Your time and ours. Can you promise us that?"

The three looked at each other, then looked at Muff and nodded in agreement. "Yes. We will."

"I notice that you're wearing a Thlarg medallion on your necklace, Miss Tenas," Schmunn said. "Where did you get it?"

Tenas reached down and held it up. "At the Bayview fair."

"Could I ask what you paid for it?"

"Ten kecks."

The three councilors looked at each other with raised eyebrows. Frumm said, "We sold them to the trader for two and a half kecks each. Nice markup, eh?"

"Yes, I guess so."

"Drelbi have been making money from us for a long time," Frumm said.

"Sorry. What can I say?" Tenas answered. "Maybe we can work out something on this. Maybe set up a Fair Trade arrangement that would bring in more money to the tribe and help the reservation."

"Yes, we've heard that before too."

Tenas raised her palms up, in the "hopeless" gesture.

Muff said, "You've told us what you want. Now, may I tell you what we want?"

"Yes, ma'am?" Tenas asked.

"A law has been proposed by the Mossbacks in the World Senate. It will be coming to a vote soon."

"Hmmm. It can't be much good if it comes from them! Which proposal are you referring to, ma'am?"

"The one that would allow Thlargs to sell reserve land to Drelbs. This would be a terrible thing."

"Yes?"

"Yes. Many of us live in poverty. Many of our people would feel forced to sell their allotment for a short-term apparent benefit, but this would end Mumphara and the entire reservation system, with nothing better to replace it. This would kill our communal system and undermine the very basis of our survival and traditional practices."

"I see."

"Please. Give me your word that when you get back, you will do all you can to stop this. Talk to Drelbi. Write letters to the editors of papers. Organize. This is something you can do."

"I give you my word, ma'am. I will do all I can."

"Me too," said the other two Drelbi.

"All we Thlargi really want is simple. I mean, what part of "Leave us alone" don't you Drelbi understand? That is what the Drelbi can do to help us. Leave us alone. Why is that so difficult for you people to get? You Drelbi have burned us so often. All we want now is to be left in peace."

The councilors stood up and Muff said, "The receptionist will direct you to our Public Relations office. We'll give them the okay to set up a few classes for your group."

"Thanks," Tenas said, getting up off her chair.

"Now, good day. It's been a pleasure."

"Kids!" Muff tsssked after they left the room. The three Thlargs looked at each other and shook their heads.

"Who knows? Something might come of this," said Schmunn. "I kinda liked her, uhh… them."

"Hey: at least they're not trying to talk us into drilling for oil or digging up coal, like those other swindlers."

As they had been directed, the three BTLers stopped at the Public Relations office and made arrangements for a teacher to come to their encampment for a series of classes. Then they returned to their encampment to discuss their experience inside the gates.

All the BTLers in camp came to the classes. The Thlarg teacher took a seat on a hilltop, talk about history, creation, restoring harmony with each other and nature, while the Drelbi listened attentively.

"The Drelbi see the land and what she holds as a thing that they can own and divide among themselves for profit. But how can you buy and sell the air you breathe? The water you drink? We Thlargi see things differently. We love our planetary mother, share all, and live in harmony with each other as her children, as sisters and brothers." Then she asked questions and the group engaged in discussion.

"Are we to believe that all is calm and happy among the Thlargi?"

"Not at all. Is everything peaceful and wonderful among your brothers and sisters? No. Sometimes you don't get along. Sometimes you fight. But if you have any common sense at all, you remain family, and I hope you don't rob and kill each other."

The group laughed.

"When you see each other as family, you learn to share and learn to get along in more or less harmony. Do you let your sister starve while your belly is full? Now, take that idea and apply it to all in your society. While some Drelbi have grown fabulously wealthy by gouging resources out of our Great Mother, others of you live in abject poverty and starvation. That is the Drelbi way. We share what we have as family, respect our Mother, and all rise together. That is the way of the Thlargi.

"Now, part of being a family is thinking about your children and grandchildren, eh?"

There was unanimous nodding and agreement on that point.

"We are only here for a short while," she continued. "We must not only think of the here and now. You Drelbi seem to have a very limited horizon. For the Thlargi, all we do, all the decisions we make, are guided by the here and now, but also by what good or bad it will do for our children and grandchildren and ahead ten generations when we who are living now will be long gone. This is the responsibility of a good family."

Soon after the last session with the Thlarg guru, the Back-to-the Landers encampment broke up. Some went back home and did little or nothing. Others followed up on the ideas raised at the Encampment. Some started working on projects to build solar installations and wind turbines. Some started bicycle co-ops and tool-lending libraries.

A few, like Moorv and Tenas, took what they learned from the experience seriously and got involved in politics.

Chapter 8
Health Care Meeting

Thunder is not yet rain.

—Thlargi proverb

Increasing social unrest was polarizing Drelbi society.

By the time he got back from the Back-to-the-Landers' encampment up in Mumphara, Moorv had made up his mind to follow up on the advice of the Thlargi Council. The two major parties disgusted him; no way would he ever join either of them. He checked out some groups and found that the Ecology Party (EP) was closest to his views on most of the main issues. The EPers welcomed him and, true to form, he became an active member.

Now he stood behind the literature table near the entrance at the back of the meeting room, wondering how the EP could draw in more people. Ecology and Socialist forums tended to draw the same familiar faces, the "usual suspects". Most people seemed either apathetic, too busy to get involved, or couldn't imagine any practical alternative to syndicate domination and business-as-usual. *If our membership doesn't grow, we'll never be able to turn things around,* he thought.

The party had just published his new pamphlet, "Save the Trees!" and he had it displayed at the center of the table. His heart thumped an extra beat when somebody picked up a copy.

"Some interesting data in there about how much carbon trees filter out of the air," he suggested. "Might come in useful in your science classes." The girl nodded silently, glanced through it, and then put the copy down. She did buy a copy of the latest issue of "*Wake-Up Call*" though. She looked nice, her antennae curving beautifully above her big blue eyes. Moorv's heart skipped a beat.

Just as the meeting was being called to order, two guys stopped and bought copies of Moorv's booklet and some other pamphlets, then sat down, as did Moorv.

"Thank you for finding the time to come to this presentation," the host began. "We're pleased to have Doctor Bonza, secretary of Physicians for Health Care Reform, with us to speak on recent developments in the struggle for better health care. Doctor Bonza is in town for the PHCR's world conference, so we're fortunate that she could take some time from her busy schedule to spend with us tonight. Now, let's give the doctor a warm, Bayview welcome!" The small audience applauded enthusiastically.

"Thank you. It's good to be here. You know, Bayview is one of my favorite places. Just before I came in, I was talking with a friend about how far ahead you are on the health care issue. Speaking with you is a little like preaching to the choir."

This gal blathers like a politician, thought Moorv. He rolled his eyes and looked sideways around the audience, who seemed to be enjoying her.

The girl Moorv had spoken with a few minutes earlier sat in the second row from the speaker, up ahead of Moorv. Paying more attention to her than to Doctor Bonza, he wondered how he could speak to her and still cover his literature table.

It was a good turnout, about thirty. Not surprising; this topic was a big one. He hoped at least this many would come to his talk next month about global warming.

He would've preferred to give his presentation right now. He was already prepared and wanted to impress this girl. Putting it off for two weeks risked low attendance, since many people would be winding down by then, getting ready for a good, long sleep. *Giving a presentation to sleepy people, when you're tired yourself? Not good,* he thought. *How can I make my talk more exciting?*

In one way, the thought of the coming night was comforting. It would put most polluting activities on hold and stop clear-cutting for a while.

A "day" on Venus, from sunrise to sunrise, is 117 Earth days long. There are two days per year. And, compared to the other planets in this solar system, Venus has a "retrograde" rotation. On Venus, the sun "rises" in the west and "sets" in the east. The Venusian calendar has ten months of about twenty-five terrestrial days each. Summer on Venus isn't very different than winter. Due to its 23° axis tilt, seasons on Earth are much more extreme than on Venus.

Although technology and electricity allowed the Drelbi to extend their activities somewhat, their biological clocks were set for sleep about one third of the time during the day, and to hibernate for most of the long nights. Just before sunset, mothers usually lay eggs, and babies hatch hungry in the morning.

As Moorv thought about his coming presentation, Doctor Bonza was saying, "Now, the insurance syndicates are putting together a stiff pushback against healthcare reform. During the break from parliament, when senators go back to their home ridings" (a *riding* on Venus was an electoral district, considered the distance you could conveniently ride to attend town hall meetings), "companies are bringing in bus-loads of syndicate-financed hoodlums to pack meetings, start shouting contests, disrupt things, and raise hell in general. Nothing new; you've probably read or heard about all this."

Several in the audience hissed sharply in agreement, expelling air from their spiracles when the speaker talked about the tactics of the insurance corporations. Moorv snapped out of his ruminating.

"They have nothing to add, nothing constructive anyway. They just want to derail the whole process and keep gouging the public. They know they can't compete against any half-decent public health plan.

"We health care providers are there for you when you need us. That's our job. That's why we went to medical school and nursing school. Now, make it your job to be there for us. We want to practice medicine, not waste our time wading through the paperwork jungle created by having a dozen competing insurance companies, each with their own forms and special rules, each one trying to shift the expenses on to somebody else. Help free us to do what we do best—medicine—not playing games with the insurance syndicate. Your medical decisions should be up to you, the patient. You shouldn't be rationed and limited by some profit-gouging company telling you how sorry they are that they won't cover this or that medical procedure. Who gave *them* the right to intervene between a patient and her doctor?"

"Nobody!" somebody shouted.

"Will somebody please tell me, who gave them the right to act as death panels? Get these paper-pushing, meddlesome, bureaucratic boobs out of the way!"

The audience erupted into loud cheering.

"That's why it is crucial to get to your local town hall meetings. The insurance rackets are killing people. Stand up to these racketeers! Don't let them suffocate democracy!" Bonza pounded the podium with her fist, hammering home her last points above the boisterous whistling and clapping.

There were some questions and a short discussion, but nearly everybody was in strong agreement on this issue. When the meeting was over, people drifted off, some in small groups, to continue the discussion at local pubs and muncho stands.

CHAPTER 9
BIRTH, DRELBI STYLE

There are too many fatherless children.
Eateth not thy mate's head;
it is a waste of a male. It is Thlarg.

—Proverb from the Book of Drell

A year quickly passed. Zilla was pregnant.

Venusians come into the world somewhat differently than humans do. Barring complications, they're usually born in the home. There were several birthing aids stores that sold a wide line of merchandise, from hardware to music and incense. Zilla and Zyzz shopped around, picking out the best of the essentials for their nursery that they set up next to their bedroom.

When Zilla felt the contractions starting, she went to a corner of the nursery and started excreting a white froth onto a branch of their borhgel, a miniature tree-shaped scaffolding device. Then she whipped it into a foam with circular movements of the tip of her abdomen.

"Can I help?" Zyzz asked.

"Yes. Get the hell away from me! Can't you find something to do? Aaargh!" she screamed from the pain of her contractions. "Just leave me alone, will you?"

Bitchiness was an accepted part of the mantid birthing process, from time immemorial. Zyzz expected it. "Want the window open?" he asked.

"Yesss, a little. Thanks. Now, please, just go away!"

Zyzz walked over to the window, slid it open about half way, took a deep whiff of the fresh incoming air, and backed out of the room. He went to the kitchen, turned on the radio, and picked up the latest *Ishtar Times*. On the radio, a song was fading out, and a jingle for a retail chain store started: "Be a smart shopper, shop from your home, with your Schmunkle's catalog and your telephone!"

He kept the volume down so he could hear Zilla if she wanted him.

"You've got the hot sounds of VJZX 99.5, where we be playin' smash hits! We even be gettin' some smash hits in the temperatures here in ZX-ville! The weather for College-land and Southwest Ishtar: Today in Bayview, you'll be getting 32 Centigrade, Gimli 34 degrees; Guzz will be the hot spot at 40, and you highlanders up around Schtilt will be getting a nice, cool 27."

Yeah, it's getting hotter. Its happening, thought Zyzz. *Now tell us why, dammit!*

Big media, both in print and on the airwaves was great at headlines, but once they got your attention, they just went on to the next headline with no depth or analysis.

Discussion? Hardly. The talk radio stations were dominated by pro-syndicate pundits that used call-screeners to eliminate intelligent-sounding callers who might oppose the syndicate line. Those who made it past the screeners and got on the air were usually in the syndicate echo-chamber choir that sang various songs of denial, like: "Yeah, we've had some high temperatures, but that's normal. We'll flip back into a sequence of cold years again; nothing to worry about."

Zyzz thought about the upland ecosystems filled with plant and animal species adapted to cool conditions. When they run out of "uphill", they'd die out. Already, several species of Alpine Clorms, Ice-flies, and Mountain Fly-Trap plants had been declared extinct by the Wildlife Management section of the Ministry of Natural Resources. The Mother of all Mass Extinctions loomed on the horizon.

"Now here's the Lowballs with 'Zingle Me One More Time, Daddy!' on 99.5, where the hits just keep on comin'!" The radio announcer cut into his thinking.

Zyzz shook his head at the moronic lyrics and the computer-generated music. Mother Drell, is this what kids are listening to these days?

College radio stations had programming worth listening to, but were allowed only such weak signal strength that hardly anybody off-campus could tune them in.

Over in their maternity room, Zilla was squeezing three eggs into the foamy mass. As each egg passed through her ovipositor, it united with a sperm cell that had been deposited during their love-making. Then she shaped the froth some more, making narrow passageways for the babies' emergence. The foam hardened and darkened into a brownish hue.

Zyzz shut off the radio, turned on the TV, and watched the Roy Roach show for a while. He was another conservative pundit blathering about how ecologists were threatening traditional values. He got up, turned it off, and went over to the window. Night was descending like a thick blanket. Across the hills of

Bayview, lights were blinking off. Over the hills, the stars were starting to put on their show.

Her birthing ordeal accomplished, Zilla staggered out of the nursery. Zyzz got up, hugged her and asked, "How ya feelin'?"

"Shot. Totally. Drell, I'm so tired," she said, half-moaning, half-yawning. "I'm gonna go take a shower."

Zyzz walked her to the shower, then went to prep their bed, putting a towel on Zilla's side to absorb any residual trickle from her egg-laying.

"Time for bed," he said when she came back, toweling off.

She was already half-asleep. "Yeah; a good, long sleep."

When he woke up, Zyzz was alone. He got up and went over to join Zilla in the nursery. Her mother's instinct told her that when the nymphs hatched and ate their way through the hardened froth, she had better be there for them with something to eat, or they might eat each other. She apparently woke up in time, but wondered what had happened to that third egg.

"Look at these girls," she said beaming and giggling while feeding them from the aphid-pack from the fridge. "Just look at 'em!"

"They're so tiny. And so pale!" Zyzz had grown up as an only child, and had rarely been around babies.

"Yes, yes. White almost. That's normal. They'll get more color."

"You are one lovely lady," he said, giving her a hug and a kiss on the forehead.

As Drelbi children, called *nymphs*, grow, they go through seven molts before becoming adults, each time emerging from their old skins with a larger brain and increased communication and other skills. The growth in brain size triggers molting. The time between molts is referred to as an *instar*.

"Wow; look at that!" Zyzz said, pointing at nothing over in the corner to distract Zilla. When she looked away, he reached in and picked up a few aphids squirming in a bowl and munched them. "Mmm; these ain't bad. Kinda sweet."

"Help yourself, silly. Why don't you go make us some breakfast?"

"Yeah; I'm starving. Anything in particular?"

"See what's in the fridge. And clean it out a bit while you're at it."

Zyzz set about his task. The carton of splorff, a milk-like liquid from caterpillar-like clorms, was sour. No surprise; he poured it down the drain. Then he took some bread out of the freezer and popped a couple slices into the toaster. When they were done, he spread them with clorm butter—*still good, a bit funny tasting*, he thought. When he brought them to Zilla, he said, "I'm going over to get a few groceries."

She took a bite of the toast, and quickly spit it out. "Yucch! This butter's spoiled!"

He added butter to his mental list.

On his way out, he glanced at the yard. They would need to get the girls outside one of these days soon. The backyard and garden had a healthy population of aphids and other goodies, so it also had occasional predatory visitors that had a taste for aphids—and baby mantises.

Zyzz went down to a hardware store and inspected the different kinds of line, rope, and netting that hung in big spools along the walls. He pulled off enough netting from the roll to cover their backyard play area, then added a little extra. In the store's center aisles, he hefted a hammer, screwdrivers, picked out what he figured would be the best tools for securing the anti-raptor netting. Then, waiting in the checkout line, he picked up some plush toys that looked like comical characters from a kids' TV show, placed there to stimulate impulse-buying.

When he got home and was unpacking his goodies, Zilla picked up the toy snarfs and clorms and said, "Oh, now these are very practical!"

Zyzz just grinned and gave her a palms-up shrug. "Yup. They'll do the hammering and help us hold the netting in place!"

"Cute," she said.

They tacked the netting up to some trees, making a safer play area for the kids.

Zilla named the girls Callibia and Cilnia, after two famous warriors and trusted officers of Drell. Cilnia had gone down in the history books as the Liberator of the North (the continent of Ishtar), and Callibia as the Liberator of the South (Aphrodite).

Both girls were healthy and very active, soon exploring and crawling over everything, including their mom and dad. That tickled mom and dad, and made them laugh.

The girls grew quickly. After just a week, they went through their first molt. A crack appeared at the top of Callibia's head, and split downward along her body. Zyzz held her as she crawled out of the old, faded dry husk of a skin, greener, with a bigger head, and prettier than ever. In a couple hours, Cilnia went through the process.

Zilla asked Zyzz, "Should we get a snarf? It'd be good to have one in the back yard, help keep an eye on the girls."

"I haven't had one since I was a kid," he answered. Yep, it'd be nice. Something to scare off a nasty maybe."

They packed up the babies and walked down to the Central District in "Old Town", where the animal shelter was located to see what they had. They could tell when they got close to the shelter by its pervasive essence-of-snarf odor, produced when so many were confined in such a small place. It was a tough decision. There were some nice adults that would make good pets, but they wanted a fifth or sixth instar juvenile. Knowing what would happen to those that weren't adopted made the decision even tougher. They finally chose a big-eyed male puppy.

"Yah, we'll give this one a try," Zyzz said. The snarf-let wagged its tail enthusiastically and licked him when he rubbed its head.

The bouncy six-legger was playful and rambunctious walking to its new home, curious and sniffing at everything. It didn't bother him to be on a leash. Wagging its tail and acting exuberantly, it seemed happy to be out of the pound. When they got home and opened the door, the snarf hesitated, as if he was afraid to go in.

"It'll be a while before this guy is any good as a watch-snarf," Zilla said, laughing.

"Maybe he thinks we took him back to the pound. It's okay boy. You're home now." Zyzz picked him up and carried him inside.

When he set down the new pet, it barked. "Well, at least he can make some noise! Ain't that right, fella?"

It yipped in agreement.

They named him Kamari, after a ruggedly scenic peninsula on Ishtar's northeast coast.

Zyzz phoned down to the Forestry Department and talked with Tayla, his receptionist.

"How are things going up there?" he asked her.

"Well, looks like you have thirty students signed up for Botany 101, and seventeen for Bot 201. Will you be in today?"

"Not unless you really need me."

"Not really. You need more time there at home now. How are the kids?"

"Just fine. We brought home a snarf today. Feisty little guy. Gets along great with the babies."

They arranged for Tayla to stop by for lunch, see the girls, and drop off any paperwork that needed his signature. He'd have to go in to his office for a couple hours tomorrow.

Chapter 10
On the Beach

Time spent in laziness will later reap vain regrets.

—Proverb from the *Book of Drell*

Moorv's presentation was coming up soon.

He wanted to—needed to—get away by himself for a while to clear his head and do some thinking. Thoughts and ideas are up there in the free wind, accessible to anybody with a mind open enough to catch them. Out here in the fresh air, he might catch one or two. He kept a notebook in his pack so he could jot down a good idea before something came up and pfffft! It was gone.

One of his favorite drives was west from Bayview along the south coast road. There was still some unlogged land, lush with tree ferns, club moss, and scale trees; the view down the coast was stunning. He pulled onto the shoulder, parked, and got out. He reached down to his hip, tapped and snugged up his zapper, an old, dependable standard model secure in its holster, and walked down onto the swash.

Transparent, glassy water fleas jumped around on the piles of flotsam washed in by the surf. Dragonflies flittered in the wind above, and there were probably some centipedes, scorpions, and who knows what else crawling around on the shore. No raptors in sight. Moorv took out his zapper and bumped it up a few notches as a precaution, then put it back into its holster. It could easily knock out a dragonfly at 10 meters, but he resisted an urge to blow one out of the sky just for target practice.

Moorv squinted as he looked down the beach. The sunshine reflecting off the white sand was blinding bright. He had seen megaraptors swooping along this stretch before, so he kept a wary eye on the sky as he walked along the narrow beach. Venus has no moon, and the solar-tides are paltry compared to the lunar tides of Earth, so salt-tolerant plants grew nearly down to the shoreline.

Behind him, the coastal Danu Mountains reared up abruptly from the sea edge. This beach lay at the foot of terrain too steep for logging, so it was still pristine.

He breathed in deeply, savoring the fresh pungency of the stiff sea breeze blowing in. Surf slammed and sprayed into the rocky headlands on either side of the beach. He looked out over the waves and could barely see the hazy outlines of the barrier Ut Islands in the distance. Beyond the islands, out where the waves met the skyline, lay the Sedna Sea.

Moorv thought about the sea. Lobster, crab, ammonites, squid, and other essentials made up a big part of the Drelbi diet. The industry provided a lot of jobs for those who could tough out the hazards and time requirements inherent in that lifestyle. He had worked on a fishing crew between school terms. The pay was good, but it was a tough life out there, buffeted by the wind and rain. "The sea is a harsh mistress,"the saying went.

In the sea, coral reefs played a similar role as forests did on land, filtering carbon dioxide from the air and producing life-sustaining oxygen. But when the slopes were logged, there was little left to hold the hillside soil from washing away, and that was choking the reefs. Rising water temperatures were bleaching and often killing coral, and spawning more severe storms, which increased the number of lightning strikes, which, in turn, caused more fires. The various parts of the natural system were all so intricately tied together, developed over millions of years. Pluck a thread in the fabric anywhere; tip one domino, and the rest fall in succession. Disturb the balance at any point, and repercussions trembled through the entire living network.

That was happening too frequently now, and it wasn't pretty.

The rich diversity of life on the reefs—the keystone link in the chain of aquatic life that supported the shrimp, lobster, and sea-scorpion fisheries—was being impoverished. The reefs provided food and shelter for the young of all the species harvested for seafood; they were the base of the marine food chain. Boats had to go farther and farther out and away to get decent catches.

Even with the latest, expensive remote-sensing equipment, catches were still down, and food prices were going up. Moorv shook his head, thinking about it. Were the timber and fossil fuel companies too blinded by their profit mania to see what they were doing? What would it take to wake them up to start seeing the big picture?

And could the syndicate system survive that awakening?

He walked along the beach, heading toward some pools below a rocky point, wondering what he might find here today. With luck, he might get some ammonite watching in, but he'd have to keep quiet and move slowly. He was entranced by the creatures: octopus with big, intelligent eyes that would quickly rush back into the shelter of their big, snail-like shells to hide when something scared them.

A sudden crackly rustling noise snapped him out of his meditation. He looked up in time to see big trouble plummeting out of the sky and aimed right at him.

"Holy shit!" he gasped, grabbed his gun and popped off a quick beam at the huge dragonfly rushing toward him. Missed. It kept coming, grappling-hook arms extended, reaching down for him. He fired again and scored a direct hit right in the middle of the megaraptor's thorax. It shrieked loudly in agony, quivering Moorv's antennae, and fell with a sizzling crash a scant couple of meters from his feet. Shaking, with his heart pounding in his throat, the sharp pungency of burnt raptor stung his nose as he looked it over. He nudged one of its legs with his foot. *Drell,* he thought, and looked up and around at the sky above him. *That was way too close.*

Its head alone, with huge, piercing mandibles and short, bristly antennae, was bigger than Moorv. Most of it was taken up by its wrap-around bulging, iridescent eyes reflecting a rainbow of colors. A beautiful specimen, blue-bodied with black stripes and red-striped wings.

I've gotta tell the guys at the Zoology lab about this first thing when I get back. They'll probably want to come out and pull this in to work on.

Chapter 11
Incident at Onatah Bayou

It is better to be comfortable alone,
than be miserable in the company of others.

—Proverb from the *Book of Drell*

Zyzz's field work frequently took him away from Zilla and the girls.

He was often torn between field and family. Occasionally he brought them along, but only to places he felt certain were safe.

This wasn't one of those places. When he packed his gear for this trip, he paid special attention to the tools on his utility belt. Zapper: fully charged. He pulled his knife out of its sheath, sat down on the front step, and gave it a quick sharpening on the cement.

Today, he was out on his own again in an area he had visited once before, down in the bayou country near Lake Onatah at the southern tip of Ishtar. Being alone didn't bother him. His senses, dulled from being indoors, came back alive out here. His botanist's curiosity fed his growing knowledge, and that knowledge of the wild country kept him in good company. Confidence and a healthy respect for what could happen out here flowed from that knowledge. Conditions were optimal here for healthy populations of carnivorous plants.

The mighty Thongnorff, a species of predatory giant spider seen rarely these days, had been reported in this area. Some would eat you on the spot; others would sting, paralyzing you with the venom. Then they'd carry you home to their nests to feed their young. Even megaraptors left them alone.

If a raptor or mega-spider didn't get you, a plant might. On Venus, carnivorous plants had evolved a diabolical variety of ways to snag a meal. Tendrils to sense, grasp, and pull in prey. Some leaves were snap-traps that consumed victims. Other plants used the fatal attraction principle: food or pheromone fragrances that many species found irresistible. Prey was enticed into rolled leaves down into pools of sticky mucous, where all comers were ensnared by the goo and digested.

Out here, death could come quickly.

Zyzz walked down a shady trail in the forest. Several big trees had fallen over from old age across the trail; the mossy logs were decomposing in the moisture. These warm, muddy swamplands with their rich sour smell, the hums and whirrings of crickets, the whining of locusts, and a hundred other sounds all came together to create a feast for the senses.

Most of the vegetation in the more accessible highlands had already been catalogued; these low wetlands, not so much. Although he preferred hiking the high-country, where tumbling white-water streams ran laughing and dipping over rapids and waterfalls, Zyzz concentrated his efforts on the swamplands.

To most, the forests and swamps all looked the same: boring and monotonous. But the more Zyzz learned about these places where nature had her way, the more he saw. The more he saw, the more he learned. Most considered him an expert in his field, but Zyzz realized just how ignorant he really was.

Long ago, Zyzz had noticed there were two distinct types of cricket calls. When it was warm, the clicking was compressed into a smooth whirring. When they felt cold, cricket-calls were a staccato series of individual clicks. He rarely heard those cooler calls these days.

The trees, similar to the ferns, club mosses, scouring rushes, and horsetails of Earth, towered above him. He was treading potentially dangerous ground. Some people, Zilla included, said he was crazy for venturing alone into places like this. He reached down for his sidearm zapper, took it out of the holster, and checked the charge indicator. With his thumb, he flipped off the safety lever and took a quick shot at a mayfly. He fried it on the second try. Satisfied with that, he clicked the safety back on and re-holstered it.

Overhead, the leafy branches weaved together to form a tight, shadowing canopy. Where most people saw a forest or meadow as just a mass of greenery, Zyzz saw a fascinating assortment of unique individual species, each as different to his eye as grasshoppers were from mayflies. He had never outgrown his awe of the beauty and intricacies of the wild country. If anything, his awe and wonder of how things fit together were growing; there was always something new out here.

He heard a slithering noise, then something grabbed his leg. He tried to shake it off, but whatever it was, it was fastened on securely. Looking down, he saw a rubbery tendril. At the moment he reached down to try to pry it off, it suddenly yanked him off his feet, pitching him forward. As he fell on his face in the mud, Zyzz could feel the tugging at his leg that was pulling him backwards through the undergrowth.

Damn widow-maker, he thought, about the same second it stung him. The venom paralysis would set in soon. He didn't have much time now.

His zapper was useless at such close quarters. He reached down for his knife, unsnapped the sheath, grabbed it, and stabbed the snaky tentacle over and over. It gushed a green viscous fluid, relaxed its grip enough to free Zyzz, and then continued its way through the foliage in the same direction. From studying these things, Zyzz knew it was withdrawing into the plant body.

He lay there on his back for a while, holding his knife, catching his breath, heart pounding hard. He felt down to where the thing had stung him. There was a big numb area between his knee and ankle. He was helpless just lying there and knew he had to get up. He took his time to slowly stand up, testing his leg. Wobbly. He tried to walk, but the leg felt like dead weight and wouldn't cooperate. He brushed off some leaves and dirt and tried again.

He had to get a look at this thing. Widow-maker plants were a focus species Zyzz was studying. He thought they were superbly adapted to their ecological niche and he even had a poster of one on his office wall. They had no need for eyes. Tendrils radiated out from the plant, hunting by sensing body heat and exhaling carbon dioxide of its prey. When a tentacle secured a victim, it dragged its prey back to the plant where it was stuffed into its mouth.

Still holding his knife in his right forearm, he reached down to grab his sidearm with his left, his thumb flicking the control to sub-lethal level. He didn't want to kill this thing.

Limping, he followed the retreating tendril. He could see the plant now, and the scattering of bones that littered the ground around it. He reached down with one of his two free hands and picked up a hairy caterpillar that happened to be wriggling by. He gave the plant a light, numbing zap with his gun, then limped over and peered down at the red mouth deep inside, at the base of the frill of tendrils. The mouth emitted a sweet, rotten odor that flies found irresistible. Once they started down into the throat of this plant, insects were trapped; the backwards-pointing bristles prevented them from getting any traction to crawl back out. Ordinarily, Zyzz would have munched it himself, but this time he dropped the caterpillar into the mouth and watched the orifice close around it.

This was an outstanding specimen. With its fat stem nearly as tall as he was, it had obviously been feeding itself well. He took out his notebook to log some field data on the species and location of the plant. He'd need to teach more on field safety to prep his students, but this would be a good place for a class outing.

He was getting hungry. He finished his field notes, tucked his notebook into his backpack, then went down to the pond's shoreline to build a fire. He took out his waterproof matchbox, crumpled up some old newspaper from his home recycling bin, and started it with a match. He added some dry twigs, then a few small chunks of club-moss wood. The fire was soon snapping quite nicely. He pulled some clorm sausages out of his pack, impaled them on a stick he broke off from a calamites tree, and cooked them over the fire. The aroma made his mouth water. When he figured they were cooked enough, he took a couple slices of bread from his pack and wrapped them around the sausages. Then he sat down with his back to a tree trunk and munched them while he looked out over the pond.

Tree trunks, crusted with lichens in shades of red, orange, and purple supported feathery foliage, reflected in the calm water gently lapping the shore. Sometimes Zyzz wished he could paint scenes like this. His artistic ability was limited to rough sketches in his field notebooks, so he got help from arts students to get them into presentable shape for publishing in his field guidebooks. He was working on three new guides for areas that had no good coverage yet. He doubted that he'd ever be truly "finished" with them. All his books were works in progress. Each time he went out in the field, he found something new.

By the time he finished lunch, a pack of scrounge bugs had shown up, attracted by the smell. He was tired, and felt like stretching out for a nap, but if he did, they'd soon be all over him. He had to stay alert.

Time. Out here in the wild country, it always sped by too quickly. He got up, stretched, then stepped down to the pond, dragging his numb leg. He splashed his face with the cool water, scooped up some with his cap and drank. He drowned the fire; it was time to go.

Zyzz' field work gave Zilla some welcome space for herself. She soon noticed one frequent side effect. Usually, he came back horny.

By the time he got home, the spot where he had gotten stung was puffed up and itching intensely.

"What the hell happened to you?" Zilla asked when he came in. She pulled up a stool and sat down facing him, pointing to the scratches on his legs, face, and arms. "We gotta get something on these."

"Oh, I had a little disagreement with a widow-maker."

"Oh?"

"Yeah. It invited me to lunch, but I had other plans."

"Honey, you look awful. Go take a shower. Lots of soap. Then I'll get some Whiz on you." Whiz was a popular brand of fairly effective antiseptic in those days.

"Sure—if you wash my back," Zyzz said.

Chapter 12
Ecosystem Services

She that speaks, sows; she that hears, reaps.

– Ancient Drelbi proverb

The turnout at Moorv's presentation was slim.

He half expected that, but was still disappointed. He had made the rounds with a few friends, taping and tacking up flyers on bulletin boards, walls, and other high-visibility spots. Many had already started their night's hibernation. This is what he got for scheduling a late afternoon talk.

Oh, well, he shrugged. This will be the first time he'd given it in front of a group; the practice wouldn't hurt. After a trial run in front of a few people, it would be better next time. Zilla, Zyzz, and a dozen others were there. He and his slide projector were ready to go.

"Many wetlands, forests, and other lands have been classified as *non-significant* under the Global Environmental Policy Act (GEPA), due to the property not meeting criteria such as the presence of potentially important archeological findings or other features," Moorv began his slide show.

He had picked out the most powerful and compelling images he could find for this. Some photos he had taken himself, beautiful pristine scenery that contrasted with images of spoiled, polluted places.

"The absence of such historically important findings has often been enough to allow the land to be developed. But, if you look at it through the lens of climate change, we can see that much of this land truly becomes significant. Therefore, it may be appropriate to revise the GEPA process of determining significance to include essential environmental services, and require mitigation for significant long-term effects on climate.

"Now, as you know, there are two primary forces propelling the impending climate crisis: increasing levels of greenhouse gas emissions, especially CO_2, and the destruction of photosynthetically active, carbon-sequestering ecosystems, both on land and in the sea.

"Tons of carbon dioxide are being dumped into the air by burning fossils fuels, so reducing these greenhouse gas emissions is an obvious part of any effective strategy.

"But, at the same time the lungs of our planet, nature's ability to filter out the CO_2, is being crippled. Forests, meadows, coral reefs, and other carbon-sequestering ecosystems are under assault. Mining operations are scraping plant life off the land. Forests are being clear-cut. And run-off from erosion of the exposed land is smothering coral reefs."

As he spoke, Moorv got out from behind the podium, walked the front of the room from side to side, then came down and worked the aisles, slowly progressing through the slides he had put together.

"So, protecting and enhancing carbon-sequestration is another part, inter-related. Successfully meeting the challenge of climate change will require coordination and progress on both fronts.

"Ecosystem services of these threatened lands are significant and valuable. They should not be destroyed via suburban sprawl (*developed*) for narrow, short-term economic reasons. These services include…"

Here he changed slides with his remote, and a list appeared up on the screen):

Flood control
Oxygen production
Carbon sequestration
Wildlife habitat maintenance
Soil erosion control

"Now, we all depend upon these environmental services, but often act as if they're unlimited. More accurate valuation of carbon sequestration, oxygen production, and other services as part of the GEPA process will provide us with a much more effective tool that will be useful in making better decisions about applications to develop land.

"I recommend that the GEPA Threshold Determination of Significance process be amended to include consideration of the environmental services provided by at-risk lands.

"The values of some of these services have been calculated by environmental economists. My attempt to plug in numbers for the value of intact ecosystems, based on primary ecosystem productivity values found in most introductory ecology textbooks, follows in these charts below."

He then screened a series of slides with table and numbers, showing how much carbon various ecosystems filter out of the air and how much oxygen they produce annually. The current monetary valuations seemed outrageously expensive, but were accurate.

Moorv heard a few yawns.

"The crisis of global climate change is bringing our dependency upon natural services into sharper focus. The lives of millions of people living in low-lying coastal areas and islands are put at risk by rising sea levels. Around the world, glaciers are in retreat, including sources of rivers that are used to irrigate agricultural lands that feed millions.

"Carbon sequestration is crucial in combating climate change. Oxygen production is critical in maintaining a life-sustaining atmosphere. Both are parts of the public commons. They rightfully belong to us all; they're not private property. In my opinion, those who willfully harm or destroy either of these ecological services—especially those who destroy large acreage of carbon-sequestering ecosystems—disable our planet's ability to stabilize climate. This is taking from the commons that degrades our climate and air quality. Objectively, this amounts to ecological vandalism.

"It is time for government agencies that allow the disruption of these eco-system services, via so-called *development*, to re-examine their sprawl-friendly policies that are impoverishing the commons.

"To get a clearer picture of where we stand in our efforts to bring climate change under control, we need information re: the amount of acreage being lost to development. This information is now being collected by most local governments through their permitting departments. This data is already being collected," he stressed. "It should be used to accurately measure how much carbon sequestration is being lost to development."

Moorv switched slides and went on to the next section of his talk. This was the important part, where he switched from griping to offering real solutions.

"Possible goals – A pro-active approach that values and sharply reduces ecosystem loss. No net loss." Moorv explained. "Starting at a threshold of three hectares, developers should be required to plant the same amount of acreage of the carbon-sequestering ecosystem that they destroy, on land reclaimed from sprawl, preferably within the same riding or county nearby."

"Accurate monetary values of ecosystem services should be employed. For example: Say Syndicate X applies for a permit to develop three hectares of land in, say, the Lakshmi Plains to build a shopping center and parking lot. The land currently is under one hectare of meadow, and two hectares of agricultural land…"

He used the blackboard, showing the arithmetic involved. Hopefully, this would gel some of the points he was trying to make.

He heard more yawns, and stopped to look out over the audience. "How we doing out there?" he asked.

People smiled and nodded. One asked, "How much longer?"

"I'll make it quick," he answered, thinking, *nobody sleeping yet. Good.*

"So, a syndicate would apply to the County Planning Department for permission to proceed on the project. Now, currently, the company would get easy approval. That results in the rampant sprawl that's becoming so obvious.

"With my proposal, the company would have two basic options: either proceed with the project, and pay for the annual damages resulting from the project until the damage is repaired and the land restored, or decline to proceed, without damaging the land. I think if this was enacted, there'd be a dramatic reduction in sprawl—and it would put some brakes on global warming."

This brought him to his conclusion. Wanting to have them engaged for his finale, Moorv went back to the podium and squarely faced his audience.

"Now, yes: this is a new approach. It may need some refinement; it probably does. My main purpose is to get us to start looking at this, considering this, get it on our radar screen. Hopefully, this proactive approach and financial accountability will tend to slow ecosystem service loss, with its corollary benefits to climate, wildlife habitat, sprawl reduction, and overall quality of life."

He paused a moment, then said, "Thank you," and asked, "Any questions?"

A few more people had drifted in, so about twenty people clapped loudly, as if to make up for their small numbers. The group included several of his friends. A few hands shot up immediately. He called on a middle-aged lady toward the back of the room.

"Okay," the woman began tentatively, searching for the right words. "Okay… if we were to start pricing carbon filtration and these other at-risk 'ecological services'… or is it 'ecosystem services'?… whatever… You know this would stop or slow down a lot of projects that provide jobs for many people. Wouldn't this put a lot of people out of work? I mean, what do we do with all the unemployed?"

"Good question, thank you," Moorv replied. "Doing this in isolation might cause some problems. True enough. But converting to a solar economy will provide thousands of jobs. Replanting forests will create many more jobs. With re-training, new skills can be learned. We don't need to burn coal and petroleum. There is so much solar energy we could be using. And solar panels don't create greenhouse gases."

"But manufacturing them sure does!" one guy said.

"We can retrofit and remodel industrial processes to lessen the impact of manufacturing," Moorv answered. "This is fixable—with technology that's available right now."

"But where's all the money going to come from?" asked a female voice this time.

"We need government financing to prime the pump and get this started. To do that, we'll need to elect some better politicians in government, people who can see that this thing is more important than syndicate profits. Many see this as a core problem. To say that Big Business exerts a lot of influence over governmental policy is an understatement. More accurately, the syndicates are, for all practical purposes, the only way anything can be done. That is where the real money is."

He pointed at another woman. "You, ma'am? front row?".

"Yes, thank you. In this week's issue of the *Ishtar Times*, it discusses several technological solutions that we could use to combat climate change, like cloud-brightening technology and cooling the planet with sun-blocking particles or shades. What do you think about those ideas?"

"Well, the simple fact is, to put it bluntly, ma'am, that nature knows best."

This got a few chuckles.

"…and nature sequesters carbon best, " Moorv continued. "Plus, natural photosynthesis produces oxygen as a waste product. Not for tons of money—these projects you mention would be terribly expensive. Somebody already made that point, pretty clearly. Indeed: where would the money come from for these projects? The point is, natural sequestration doesn't cost us anything—it's free. Pretty neat trick, eh? None—not one of the bio-engineering proposals discussed in that *Times* article can create oxygen. I agree: this money issue is relevant. Where are we going to find the money to pay for these massive, complex, global geo-engineering projects?"

At that point, a girl—the same one that Moorv had his eyes on at a prior meeting—raised her hand. Moorv smiled and said, "Yes?"

"They're not only expensive, but they don't work!" she said. "Things like sun-blocking technologies are bogus schemes dreamed up by the energy syndicates. 'Everything's okay; don't worry, just keep burning fossil fuels', they say. Even they don't take them seriously," she finished, and there was nodding and a general murmur of agreement around the room.

"Right you are," he said, smiling at her. "In my opinion, we need to start with the best technical solutions first. Those begin with a moratorium on new, unnecessary *developments* (he made the quotation gesture with his hands), which has become a euphemism for sprawl. I would define *sprawl* as ecological destruction destroying nature via conversion of photosynthetic surface to non- or less-photosynthetic surface.

"And, we need to restore natural eco-systems by replanting forests. (Tree farms of just a few, commercially important species are not real forests!) And safeguard agricultural land. If you think that food prices are rising now, you ain't seen nothin' yet. Keep on destroying farmland, and see what happens!"

At this point, Zilla stood up and said, "I think we can draw an interesting parallel here. Now, I think most of us here can agree that a socialized, universal-access medical care system free at the point of service, is in the vast majority's best interest, right? Yet the health insurance syndicates are dominating and distorting the decision-making process, and could end up totally derailing it."

Several people looked at her curiously, wondering if she had stumbled into the wrong meeting. *Where was she going with this?* Moorv wondered.

"Well, we can expect even more opposition from the syndicates when it comes to this issue. They're in it for the money. They will try to con us into spending billions of taxpayer kecks on climate engineering projects if they think they can make a profit out of it.

"We know what works; we know that it's simple: stop clear-cutting forests! Stop destroying stable, natural eco-systems. Enough with this sprawl already! People can understand this. We should start with that before attempting some convoluted, complex approach that could easily go awry, and curse the day we ever considered it."

Somebody else chimed in, waving a copy of the paper, "In this same issue of the *Times*, it quotes a Professor Schmunk of the University of Aphrodite as saying, 'The idea of even testing such a system scares many people, and some scientists argue that climate-engineering research should remain theoretical.'"

"Work it out for yourself," Moorv broke in. "Open up a general ecology textbook. Look up the primary productivities of various ecosystems. Take net primary productivity values of various ecosystem types and crunch the numbers. You'll find that the amount of carbon that forests, meadows, coral reefs, and so on, sequester is much higher than any artificial bio-engineering boondoggle."

There were still a few hands in the air. People were clearly interested in this topic.

"Okay, I'm getting tired. It's getting late, let's make this the last question." Moorv pointed to a guy in the second row. "Yes, you sir."

"How about the timber industry? If you had your way, woodcutters would be an endangered species. Hell, so would miners and oilmen. How about working families?"

"Like I said before, sir," Moorv was getting tired. "We need to—and we *can* put people to work—replanting and restoring forests. There is a ton of work to do there. And building a solar energy grid would create thousands hell… millions of jobs. Just because something might not make mega-profits for Ishtar Forest Resources doesn't mean it's not worth doing."

That got him a scattering of positive clicking and whistling. He'd have to remember that line for his next presentation, hopefully to a bigger audience.

"For every hectare that is clear-cut, a hectare should be restored. Selective cutting—leaving some trees behind for natural re-seeding—isn't as easy and isn't as cheap for IFR, but it's much less destructive. We're talking about thousands of jobs here."

"Okay, I'd like to thank you once more for coming and listening, and for your questions. I'm sure you will be hearing more about this topic in the times ahead," Moorv said, drawing a polite round of applause.

As he and a friend named Schlong were packing up his slide projector and notes, Moorv was approached by Zilla and Zyzz who came up to compliment him for a great talk. They chatted a bit before leaving for home.

Then a girl—the same one that Moorv had his eyes on at a prior meeting—came up and said, "I dunno, Moorv. I like what you're saying. These are good ideas, but how can we do this? "

"What's your name?" Moorv asked. He had some questions for her as well.

"Majanga," she replied. They shook forehands.

"So good to meet you, Majanga." He looked into her eyes. Deep and beautiful. She was the best looking female he had ever seen. Beautiful face from her vertex down to her lips, nicely proportioned arms, legs, thorax, and abdomen. *Mmm-mm, she looks good,* he thought.

"Where do you want these?" asked Schlong.

"Uhh, there in the blue box. Might as well start loading up. I'll be with you in a minute."

When he turned back to her, he said, "Majanga, these are important questions. Really good questions, but no quick, easy answers. This will take a while. Could I… uhh… could we go out for supper somewhere and take some time to really discuss this stuff? I really want to talk with you."

After his talk, Moorv had a bad case of the yawns. He had blown off his adrenalin; the anxiety he had built up for the talk was over and he was relaxing. He would sleep well tonight.

"Well, I'm about ready for some serious sleep. I'm getting sooo sleepy…", she responded, yawning.

Really nice mandibles and very kissable maxillae, Moorv thought. "Me too. But, yes, I'd love to talk with you in the morning."

He wished he could crawl into bed with her now. "What's your phone number?"

She told him.

"When would be the best time to call you?"

"Just call me when you wake up."

"Great. I'll do that," he said.

"Okay. See you," she said and started to walk toward the door, stopped and turned around and looked at Moorv for a moment. She walked right up to him, looked down into his eyes, put her forehand around his neck and gently pulled his head toward hers. She kissed him right on his lips, and walked away, saying "See ya!"

"Happy Hibernation!" he replied, and turned back to finish packing up the equipment.

"I think she likes you," Schlong said.

Moorv fell asleep quickly that night and dreamed about Majanga.

Chapter 13
Spring Fest

He who wants to build high must dig deep.

—Thlargi proverb

Like all arthropods, the body temperature of Venusians is dependent upon the ambient temperature.

With the oncoming of the cool night, a Drelb gets sleepy and goes into a dormant period of hibernation until the sun returns again.

The differences between day and night take on seasonal characteristics when a day, from sunrise to sunset lasts two Earth-months. With a two Earth-month long night on Venus, morning is spring.

The stars faded, the long dawn came, and the sun rose in the west. Life stirred into wakefulness.

Moorv rang Majanga on the phone, and they agreed to meet down at the main gate of Riverside Park and take in Spring Fest, a free music festival. After a breakfast of cereal, splorff, and gungkel, a fermented drink similar to the kefir of Earth, he walked a few blocks to the park gate. The fresh fragrances of opening buds filled the air.

Several Drelbi were jogging along the track that wound into and around the park, through the fresh spring breeze. Some were out getting their pets some exercise.

Moorv watched a woman sitting near a pond and throwing a ball into the water. She told her snarf, "No, wait." It whined plaintively, straining to hold itself back; this snarf was itching to run. "Wait… now… Get it!" The snarf bounded down the bank, splashed into the water, swam out, snatched up the ball, swam back to shore, ran up to the woman, and dropped the ball at her feet, giving her a quick shake-off shower. They played until the snarf lay panting, exhausted, at her feet.

Farther along, Moorv saw the tiniest snarf he had ever seen. Snarfs always walk on all six legs, but not this one. Moorv laughed as he watched as a guy held out a ball, and his miniature snarf danced around on its hind legs in eager anticipation. He laughed so hard his sides started to cramp. He was feeling good.

"Hi!" He turned, and there was Majanga, looking better than ever. "Good morning, Moorv."

"Hi."

They hugged, and he kissed her lightly on her soft cheek. They walked on into the park. Moorv reached out to hold her lower hand. They slowly strolled past the ponds and toward the stage.

"I dreamed about you," Moorv said.

"Hmmm. Good or bad?"

"Oh, horrible. Just frightful!" he said with a laugh.

"Gosh, really?" She had a smile that he found captivating.

"Nah. Actually very nice." He smiled back. "A little, uhh… erotic though."

"Uh-oh." She was glowing this morning.

When they got close enough to the stage, Moorv unrolled his blanket on the mossy ground and they sat down. Niko and the Nonggs were just finishing a song. When the band started playing the first notes of their next song, Moorv said, "Mmm, I love this one." He stood up, reached out, took her hand, and led her out on the lawn where about twenty Drelbi were dancing to the smooth rhythm.

She expected him to just do the same free-style moving around to the music like everybody else, so she was pleasantly surprised and a little embarrassed when he took her in his arms and led her through some old-fashioned couple-dancing.

"I can't do this too well," she said, embarrassed at her stiffness.

"Nothing to it. Just follow; you'll catch on in a few minutes, I promise."

The steps fit well with the relaxing, sensual groove that the Nonggs were laying down. They stayed up and danced through the rest of the set. Before long, she was really getting into it. A fast learner.

A bluesy group called What the Funk was up next. After the band had all its gear set up, they started playing some good, danceable music, thlargy and primitive with a strong beat. Dozens of people danced on the lawns, while farther away from the stage others played catch with discs or balls.

The next song was a schnuzz, a dance with roots in prehistoric ancient mantid mating-swarm orgies. Moorv and ten other guys got up and started a traditional, stylized pattern dance. There was something instinctive about this dance; the steps seemed to come easy and naturally, from somewhere inside.

Females got up, laughing, and stepped expectantly, rhythmically toward a male, then they all danced closely together, weaving intricate spin patterns. They danced until they were tired, then danced some more. After a while, Majanga and Moorv sat down and relaxed on the moss, just listening to the band play.

They saw an occasional familiar face, and made light conversation with an acquaintance, nothing serious.

After several hours of partying, they went to get something to eat at a muncho stand, then walked down to the bay. Neither felt much like talking. They stood at the water's edge and looked out to sea. In the distance was the ridge of the Sigrun Islands, looking like a sleeping giant in shades of misty gray-blue. The waves reflected the sky with an exquisite interplay of incredible hues of cobalt blue, flecked with the golden sunshine.

Standing there together, arms around each other, felt like a dream to Moorv. He turned to look into her deep eyes and felt himself falling into them. He moved his face closer to hers, then stopped a few millimeters way. She closed the gap, and the connection was magic. She curled her antennae around to wrap and caress his, and they kissed long and deeply.

CHAPTER 14
TOWN HALL MEETING

Experience teacheth fools.

—Ancient Drelbi proverb

Health Care reform was a contentious issue throughout the Empire.

The campus child-care center was well utilized by both students and faculty. Kids usually liked to go there. After checking Callibia and Cilnia in, Zilla and Zyzz joined Majanga, Moorv, and several others to walk down to the campus stadium. They arrived about a half-hour early.

Things were already busy. Several literature tables—some of these groups were for socialized medicine, some opposed—were set up along both sides of the hall's entryway and people were talking, some heatedly. They ambled along, stopping now and then to listen to the banter.

They talked for a while with some people they knew who were staffing the Ecology Party table. One was arguing with an elderly guy who was objecting strongly to a piece of EP literature he was holding and waving it threateningly. Zilla thanked the other staffers for volunteering for table duty, and they moved on.

The literature on the table of People for Free Choice looked very professional.

"Damn, I wish we could afford to publish slick stuff like this," Zilla said quietly. Moorv picked up and looked through several papers that opposed socialized medicine.

This group was apparently an insurance company front group pretending to be a grassroots organization.

"Nice looking poison," Moorv mumbled to Zilla. "Astro-turf."

From the signs and banners in the bleachers, they could see how folks were polarized on this issue. They sat down just before Senator Smada began his opening. He welcomed the crowd, made a brief statement, and then invited questions. Some raised their hands, and the senator's aides worked the crowd, handing the microphone to people as the senator pointed to them.

Each comment was punctuated by a rowdy mixture of boos and applause.

When it was her turn, one woman said, "We are letting the lies of the insurance and pharmaceutical syndicates con us into working against ourselves—against our own best interests. This is ridiculous! Please everyone, get out there, speak up, write letters—whatever it takes to get real health care reform!"

The next Drelb who was handed the mike made a comment against reform. "Our way of life is based on free choice and letting the marketplace work things out. Government bureaucrats have no place in deciding what medical care you should or should not have!"

She was countered by the next one, who said, "Bureaucrats in charge? Yes, I'm afraid so. The real question is, what kind of bureaucrat do you want to be in charge of your health care? Will it be a government bureaucrat or a syndicate bureaucrat? At least a government bureaucrat isn't aiming to increase her bonus by denying coverage to people who need medical care! Health insurance companies make more money when they deny coverage. Power over life-and-death decisions is in the hands of the insurance companies. Decisions over your medical care should be between you and your doctor, not with some protection syndicate! Only the government is big enough and powerful enough to protect us from syndicate tyranny."

Then it was Zilla's turn. "Here's the blunt truth," she said, when she was handed the mike. "The truth is, the syndicate is a powerful tool, invented and developed to do two things—maximize profit and limit liability. This makes it a very dangerous tool, destructive of anything that gets in the way of maximizing profit."

At that point, there was a clamor of derisive hisses and shouts of agreement.

She continued. "The time has come to hang up this tool in the museum of history! Even then, we need to warn our children to watch out. Keep an eye on this thing. And don't ever, ever forget that syndicates can bite."

All in all, things were pretty civilized. No shoving, no hooliganism from either side at this meeting. But, this was a college town; debate over controversial topics was nothing new here.

Chapter 15
Wrangle at a Muncho

Wealth is like dung;
it does good only when it is spread.

—From the *Book of Drell*

Zyzz and Zilla lunch at a munch stand with friends.

They sat at a table with Moorv and Majanga sharing lunch before going to a concert. As a rule, they preferred these small, family owned and operated places over restaurants. There were a few bad muncho stands; but when they were good, they were very good.

They talked about forest policy. Majanga was saying, "Ishtar Forest Resources aren't re-planting. They're over-harvesting, way beyond sustainable levels before moving on to the next clear-cut. Hillsides, for Drell's sake! Then the soil washes away. Why are they doing this? It's stupid! Don't they know better?" she asked, shaking her head slowly. "It's just not logical."

The thought of clear-cuts made Zyzz feel sick in his stomach. "IFR land managers aren't dummies," he said. "Hell, quite a few have taken my classes, and they've done pretty well. They're really not bad guys. Then they go out, scalp the hills, and leave them to gully-wash away. Just doesn't make sense. I mean, can't they see that they'd have more trees in a few years if they re-planted?"

"So, whoever said syndicates are logical?" asked Moorv. "There are no villains in this. The system itself is criminal. If you're going to succeed in this system, you have to maximize profit. They're so damn focused on short-term profit, that's all they can see. Everything else is way down their priority list. Sustainability? That's not even on their radar screen."

"Or is it just Drelbi nature?" asked Majanga. "I mean, it's people that run the system, right? And it's people who would operate your new system, so..."

"We're basically animals. Just dumb animals with a few extra tricks," said Zyzz.

Zilla looked over at him. *Back-sliding fearlessly again,* she thought. "Drell!" said Zilla. "What Drelbi nature is or is not might make an interesting philosophical discussion, but it's beside the point. Totally irrelevant to this. Let's get real, can we?"

"Okay, go for it," Zyzz shrugged.

"Come on... clearcutting? Drelbi nature? Catching so many lobsters and squid that whole species are going extinct? Screwing up the reefs? You think this is Drelbi nature? Or how about dumping food in the ocean while people are starving, just to keep prices up? Do you really think that these are...what?... unfortunate manifestations of *Drelbi nature*?" she asked, holding up her forehands and making quotation signs with her fingers. "Come on, now. That's a pile of clorm-swill, and you know it. Thlargi and Drelbi lived in more or less harmony with nature for thousands of years."

"Millions," Moorv said.

"Yeah," Zilla went on. "Then the syndicates come along and... pffft... in just a hundred years or so, everything quickly starts going to hell. Pollution. Clear-cutting. Think all this is just a coincidence? *Drelbi nature,* my royal ass!"

A breeze gusted by, whisking up some papers and blowing them on down the street.

Then Moorv said, "These aren't illogical results of a sane system. No. These are the logical results of a screwed-up system. Profit is its number-one priority. This system was never designed to be sustainable. I mean, what the hell do you expect when nature and labor are treated as commodities for making profits?"

"Hell, putting profit first is guaranteed to mess things up. The surprise would be if this kind of crap *didn't* happen!" Zilla thumped the table with the bottom of her glass.

"So the system makes good people do terrible things. What is this… terminal profitosis?" Majanga asked. That was good for a chuckle.

"Not bad," Zilla smiled. "Or is it profit-itis?"

"Whatever the hell it is, it's awful," Zyzz said. "But I've got a question. Economics wasn't my best subject… never has been, so help me on this."

"Yeah?" Moorv said.

"Okay. *Commodity*. I've heard the word, but what's the difference between a commodity and a… uhh… product, anyway?"

"A commodity is anything—any product or service—that's produced to be sold to make a profit," Moorv said. "Its defining purpose is for making a profit, not for use. It probably has a use, but it's not produced for use, it's produced to make a profit. That's why so many commodities are produced that they can't be marketed, and have to be warehoused somewhere, eh?"

"Okay…"Zyzz said tentatively.

"Now, labor is people, with needs and rights," said Moorv. "But syndicates treat them as commodities too. The syndicates make huge profits by paying workers less than the value they create by their labor."

"Whew, you're losin' me," said Zyzz. "Wanna back up and run over that again?"

"Okay. Say you work in a mine, okay? Or on a logging crew... or anywhere, as far as that goes. How long do you think you'd have your job if you didn't produce more value for the boss than she paid you in your paycheck?" Moorv asked.

"Well, not very long, I suppose. If you're in business, you have to make a profit. How else are you going to pay the bills, support your family, meet payroll, and all that? Business isn't charity, y'know."

"Exactly. And stockholders want a good return on their investment. The best possible return, or why would they risk their money investing in your company?"

"That's just the way it is," Majanga said.

"And that's why things are getting so messed up!" said Moorv. A car drove noisily down the street, spluttering and coughing as if it had a cold.

"So what do you propose?" Majanga asked.

"Think. What produces all wealth?" Zilla asked.

"Hmm..."

"All real wealth is created by... what?" Zilla asked again.

"Okay, labor, capital, and nature," Majanga said. "That's what they taught us in high school. Seems pretty basic."

"Well, you're right about nature and labor. Those create wealth," Zilla said. "But capital? No, capital is just a catalyst."

Zyzz looked perplexed, then asked, "A catalyst, eh?"

Zilla nodded.

"Okay," Zyzz said. "Chlorophyll is a catalyst. It doesn't actually take part in any solar-chemical reaction, but if it ain't there, nothing happens. It's gotta be there, or sunlight, water, and carbon dioxide won't combine. No chlorophyll, no food," he said.

"Right," Moorv said. "Well, capital is the catalyst that brings labor and natural resources together to produce wealth. It enables wealth production in the same way chlorophyll enables photosynthesis and food production."

Zyzz nodded. "Okay, I'm with you so far."

"The problem," Moorv said, "is that it's the syndicates that get the most out of it. Workers and nature are undervalued, systemically. The game is rigged. These things don't just happen; the system is based on organized theft of value from the producers. We need to start treating both workers and nature with the respect they deserve. We need to liberate capital from the capitalists and use it… democratically decide to use it for real needs, not just to make the already rich even richer!"

Majanga, Zilla, and Zyzz were all nodding in agreement.

"Okay, but who would hire anybody if they couldn't make a profit? I mean, why would they even bother?" asked Majanga. "What's your alternative?"

"If we're going to survive—if our kids are going to have any kind of decent future—we have to stop treating natural resources as just something to use up and make money from. We need to recognize that there's no such thing as an infinite supply of anything," Zilla said.

"And labor should get back all the wealth it creates. *All* of it, directly and indirectly," added Moorv.

"So... what do you mean by 'indirectly'?"

"Well," Zilla said, "Some money would have to be invested back into equipment, machinery, that sort of thing. The main thing is that businesses should be run democratically by the people working in them—as cooperatives, not as dictatorships. Cooperatives, responsible and responsive to the communities where they operate. You can't have a democratic society when a syndicate dictatorship is at the top of it all. It's a sham."

"And you can't have a democracy where one percent of the population owns more wealth than the bottom ninety-five percent...," Moorv said, "...and when that top one percent makes all the command decisions that affect all our lives."

Majanga and Zyzz nodded.

Zilla went on. "Take medicine, for example. Health care resources are public resources, but the syndicate hospitals and insurance rackets are using them to make millions out of people's suffering."

"So, yippee! Let's go out and shoot all the capitalists!" said Zyzz sarcastically. When he got agitated, like he was now, he tended to speak too loudly.

Zyzz felt a foot bump his under the table. "Ssshhh! Not so freakin' loud," Zilla said, barely above a whisper.

People had turned to look at this guy with the coarse backwoods drawl, and she felt uncomfortable with the stares. "Damn, Zyzzles, we're sitting right here, not a mile away," she said. "And don't talk with your mouth full."

He swallowed, took a drink, and went on, his volume lowered a few notches. "Well, if that's what you're sayin', then no thanks!"

"Now, hold on a second, good buddy," Moorv said. "That's not what I'm saying. Listen, dammit! Seriously! This is where the anarchists run off the track. Those clowns go and smash some windows and then swagger about it. Or they kidnap somebody; maybe even kill some syndicate officer. Then what? The system has plenty of replacements eager to step in and take over. Terrorist tactics do more harm than good. They're fools. They just make the syndicate honchos look like victims… and then *they* get sympathy."

Zilla chimed in, "The only way to change this system—or *replace* it… that's really what we're talking about here… is to educate people. Educate, agitate, and organize for peaceful change. The better the organization, the less violence. Violence is a symptom of poor organization. Non-violent tactics. If there's going to be any violence, let them—the syndicates—start it. We want *peaceful* change."

"Clormshit. I'll fight back!" Zyzz said.

"Any violence—even self-defense—coming from our side gets so twisted in the media that it makes us look like the bad guys," Moorv said. "It might be too slow for some, but building public opinion for positive change is really the only sure way."

"But how much time do we have?" Majanga asked.

"The planet can't take much more of this," Zyzz said. "That's for sure. Things are starting seriously to go to hell. Our life-support system is already breaking down. We need serious action now or it will be too damn late," Zyzz said. "It's always been either too soon to worry, or too late to do anything."

"Yep," Moorv said. "That's all true. But hot-headed, ill-planned tactics are just plain wrong. Stupid. They slow down building public opinion for change. It doesn't help our side; it hurts us."

"Because it makes the syndicates look like victims, huh?" Majanga asked.

"That's right." Moorv and Zilla nodded.

"These syndicate execs are people… with families," Zilla said. "They might do shitty things on the job—make horrible decisions as far as the ecology goes, nasty, abusive labor decisions—but they have families. On a personal level, they might make good friends. They might be wonderful, warm, loving people. They might give generously to charities and good causes."

"Like they have to get right with the Goddess somehow?" Majanga said.

"If they even think of it that way. On the job, this crazy system forces them to make these rotten decisions. And the media supports them. 'Oh, well: that's just the way things are', and 'there is no alternative'. It's the way this wacky system works that creates the problems, well, most of them anyway," Moorv said.

"The media has people befuddled," Majanga said.

Moorv responded, "What is the purpose of Big Media anyway?"

Majanga shrugged.

"Well," he said. "It's owned by the ultra-wealthy. So, is it to educate people? Ha! It's for promoting ruling class fears and priorities. They are very aware that they're a tiny minority trying to keep a huge working class under their control."

"So they try to discredit anybody and any ideas opposed to them!" Zilla added.

"Yep. Thought control. So the bastards can stay in power and money. And they're succeeding quite well at that. The syndicates ridicule the notion that a runaway greenhouse effect is imminent. They reject the science, belittle the messengers, and use their control over the major media to disseminate their doctrine of denial."

"Don't forget to have a home base," said a husky male voice from behind them.

They turned around and looked at a guy who was sitting at a table behind them.

"Huh?" Zyzz asked.

"Sorry; I couldn't help but overhear. You guys have some good ideas, but there's something I learned years ago as a union organizer."

"Whuzzat?" Zyzz asked him.

"Yes, peaceful tactics. Yes, be prepared, but let *them* start any rough stuff, not you."

"Yeah?"

"Yeah. And, when you take some action, a demonstration, or whatever, don't all of you go."

"Okay. Why not?"

"Always pick one of you to stay home, out of the action, by the phone. If there's any trouble, you need somebody that will be there when you call, somebody who's not in jail or holding pen or whatever. Somebody who can go to the bank, raise some bail money. If you're all in the slammer, who'll help you get out?"

The four of them chatted some more with this guy as they finished their munch. Zyzz covered the union organizer's tab, and they continued their discussion on their way down the street and got into line for the concert of the Bayview Symphony.

"So how does the Ecology Party take power?" asked Majanga.

"It's not about power." Moorv shook his head. "Or being the new boss. It's about building a better system with no slaves and no bosses."

"If all we wanted was power, we'd have gone into one of the big establishment parties a long time ago," Zilla added.

"So, the only way out of this swamp is education. People have got to understand that gouging maximum profits out of workers and nature is messing up the world we'll leave our kids," Majanga said.

It looked like Majanga might be experiencing some sort of break-through. Zilla loved it when she saw the light bulb switch on in somebody's eyes. "This is the only world we have. Education; that's task number one," she said. "And keep building public opinion until we reach a critical mass, a tipping point, when enough people will finally see that a better world is possible."

"Yeah, yeah. But do you really think there's enough time left for that?" Zyzz asked.

"How the hell do I know?" asked Moorv. "Do I have a crystal ball? All I know is that this is going to be one helluva struggle. But if we don't try, things will never get any better."

Their conversation had gotten the attention of some people near them in line. A few nodded in agreement; some shook their heads in disapproval.

Chapter 16
The Space Program

There are those who walk through the forest but see no trees.

—From the *Book of Drell*

The stars had long beckoned Venusians.

Space exploration was a popular theme of books, TV, and movies. The space program was in the hands of a few companies that combined to form a syndicate dubbed the Space Development Consortium.

Massive infusions of financing from willing, enthusiastic taxpayers helped jump-start the space program, and, even though it was now reaping mega-profits, the Consortium was still feeding at the public trough. Two things mattered to the Consortium: money, and the science that could make them money.

Space exploration fired the imaginations of many young people and spurred advances in mathematics and technology. The Space Consortium founded an Academy of Interplanetary Development and Commerce. There were far more applicants than seats at the Academy, and applicants were required to take loyalty oaths to the Empire and were subject to intensive background checks.

The Consortium first sent unmanned fly-bys and atmospheric probes to explore Mercury, Earth, and Mars, and was happy with what they found. Automated orbiters and robotic landers followed. Precious metals and other elements rare on Venus suggested possibilities of incredible profits to be made. The cartel's shareholders had struck it rich. And they found life on Earth, perhaps even intelligent life! This was a jolt that had more than business possibilities. This affected everybody. The Drelbi were not alone!

On Mercury, Earth, and Mars, the syndicate started bases to develop their discoveries. On Earth, they found a treasure-trove of seeds, spices, perfumes, and other botanical materials that they shipped back home to lucrative markets. This increased popular support for space exploration.

There was a Flower Bubble. Life on Venus was comparable to life on Earth during the Carboniferous Era, before there were any flowers, nor pollinators. Venus had a thousand shades of green, but little color. When the first robotic missions returned from Earth with seeds, it created a sensation.

The Flower Bubble began with an advertising blitz from the Space Consortium's commercial wing: *A rainbow of color in your garden! Buy now! Be the envy of your neighborhood! Easy Terms!*

Those who could afford to pay astronomical prices did so; the colors and scents were amazing. Because no bees or other natural pollinators had ever evolved on Venus, the alien plants could set no seed, so it was a seller's market and a lucrative investment. Some got very rich. When artificial pollination techniques spread, the Great Flower Bubble popped and investors lost millions of kecks. There were some suicides.

The Grass Bubble lasted longer. Grass seeds from Earth revolutionized agriculture on Venus. Grasses are wind-pollinated, so propagation was easy. Wheat, barley, rye, and other grass seeds rapidly became staples of the

Venusian diet. In the vast interior upland barren-lands that were too dry for forests, syndicates bought lands that could be profitably "dry-farmed" and consolidated them into extensive New Agricultural Zones. The plains of Lakshmi, formerly useless wastelands, became the "breadbasket" of Venus.

Because there were no natural controls, grasses soon proliferated. They hybridized and then spread like wildfire, out-competing and displacing many native plant species. The grasses invaded and overran ecosystems. Many animals that had co-evolved over the millennia to become dependent upon native plants, and vice-versa soon became endangered. There was an epidemic of native plant extinctions. The ecology of the entire planet became impoverished.

The Space Consortium could expand its profit margins if it were not for one problem. There was a severe labor shortage at its off-Venus mining operations. The Consortium needed more workers. In spite of an ongoing recruitment campaign, very few were signing up for those jobs.

CHAPTER 17
UNITY!

I was with you in our long days of struggle,
and many long days lie ahead of you.
Victory will come.
My sole lament is that I could behold our
united Holy Empire only in my dreams.

—From the *Last Testament of Drell*

The results of the most recent elections had been good.

For the syndicate-financed parties. Not so good for the progressive parties.

The lineup: The two "majors"—The conservative Grand Empire Party, also known as the "Mossbacks", who some referred to as "reactionary hirelings of the developers-polluters," and the Liberal Party, referred to by some as "mossback lights" or "deceitful middle-roaders".

There were several left-of-center, "third party" also-rans who never received more than single-digit results. After several financially ruinous efforts, two facts were becoming painfully obvious: no single third party had any chance of becoming a major party.

Some gave up, saying that the whole effort was hopeless. Others, including the leaderships of the third parties, started talking about uniting their forces. They made plans for a "Unity Convention", realizing that until they stopped competing with each other and focused on the common enemy, none of them would ever get anywhere.

Although the anarchist-oriented Back-to-the-Landers theoretically rejected the concept of leadership as elitist, those who had the energy, initiative, and drive tended to take on the duties of de-facto leaders.

Tenas and Zhtipp followed through on their promises to Muff and the Mumphara Reservation Council. Soon after the last session with the Thlarg guru, the Back-to-the Landers' encampment broke up. When Tenas and Zhtipp showed up at a meeting of the Ecology Party, still wearing their Thlarg caps and medallions, determined to work for preserving traditional rights for the Thlargi, they found strong support. Perhaps politics might not be irrelevant after all.

Tenas went through the prescribed channels to get representatives from the major Thlarg reserves to speak at the Convention, but they were allowed to attend only as non-voting observers.

Just short of a thousand delegates from around the planet showed up in Bayview for the Unity Conference. Many stayed with friends and family, but hotels still did a very brisk business that week.

In the opening speech, Thromm, a leader of the Ecology Party, said:

"After still another massacre at the polls, one thing should be clear by now. We are at a crossroads. We stand on the razor's edge between hope and catastrophe.

"The syndicate system is destroying the life-support systems of this planet. Due to high-tech computers and automation, productivity has never been higher. Yet unemployment and homelessness are soaring, while other people are being worked so many hours that accident and fatality rates are growing significantly. It doesn't have to be this way.

"We have two choices. Each of our parties can continue to run their own candidates. You know how much that costs in money, energy, and time. And what do we have to show for it? Yes, we could continue to split the progressive vote and hope that your own little party can grow and win. That road has proven to be a dead end; it is taking us nowhere!"

There was mixed applause and muttering around the convention floor.

"Do we want to continue this foolish factionalism?"

"No!"

"Shall we continue fighting each other for third, or fourth place?"

"No!"

"Shall we continue helping the syndicates laugh all the way to the bank by helping their parties keep a monopoly of power?"

"No way!"

Thromm was a lively speaker and had a knack of stirring up a gathering. She loved this back-and-forth with the crowd.

"Shall we allow the syndicate hacks to continue their same old shit and wreck our planet?"

"No way!" they shouted again. A couple dozen Drelbi standing near Ecology Party signs got on their feet and starting chanting "Save our planet! Save our Planet!"

Thromm smiled and held up her hands to quiet the crowd, then continued. "We are here to explore a different option. I suggest that it's time for a tactical readjustment. Shall we at long last finally get serious and combine our forces?"

"Yes!" shouted the crowd.

"Now make no mistake about this. We are up against powerful foes with buckets of money. If we want to stand up toe-to-toe to these leeches, this job will take our time, energy, and yes, money—and lots of it."

"We're with you!" "Let's go!" and a mixture of other enthusiastic responses came from around the hall.

"We share a lot of common ground. Let's focus on that. Can we set our disagreements aside for a while? Can we work together to form a united electoral front?"

This brought the hall full of delegates to their feet with loud applause, whistling, cheering, and shouts of "Yes We Can!"

The unity convention was barely controlled chaos. Each party had its share of sectarians who tried to dredge up old controversies and wedge issues, but the leaders of the major constituent groups came together and agreed on a short list of ground rules:

1. Current issues were to be given priority. People should leave old, divisive issues aside.

2. Emphasize common ground, agree to disagree on some points, and put those aside for the time being.

This was to be a coalition, not a merger. The participating parties weren't asked to liquidate to form one united party, but would each maintain their individual organizational integrity.

There were other bones of contention. Who would lead this Coalition?

Leadership of the coalition was chosen after a long session in which candidates nominated to be chair by at least twenty-five delegates fielded questions from the delegates on various issues, and debated points of difference. After several votes, Thromm won on the final ballot, and gave a rousing acceptance speech.

What to call this outfit now became the question.

The name would have to encapsulate and summarize the basic ideas the delegates could all agree upon. It had to combine ecological principles with socialist principles. Some wanted ecology principles to come first; others insisted that socialist principles should take top priority. After heated debate to narrow the wide field of suggestions, the choices on the ballot were:

Socialist Green Party
Eco-Socialist Coalition
Eco-Socialist Party
Social-Ecology Labor Party

After all the votes were counted, the third option was the clear winner. The "ESP" double entendre helped.

Delegates from the Workers' League (WL), the political action committee of the central labor union federation, made a proposal to the platform committee. First, some background information is necessary for understanding this challenge.

The government of Venus at all levels was "unicameral", run by one house, i.e. the Senate. The chair of the party winning a majority of seats became the President of the Empire. Drelbi residents of both continents, Ishtar and Aphrodite, and the islands elected senators to their respective Regional and Continental Senates and to the Senate of the Empire. Senators represented geographical districts called "ridings".

The WL proposed creating a two-house government (bicameral) at all levels. The new house would be based not on where one lived, but where one worked—what she did for a living. It would be a continental and world coordinating union center.

The chair called Sister Hass, a WL delegate, to the podium to explain her proposal to the convention. The WL had been planning for this. As Hass walked to the podium, two huge banners were unfurled from the upper balconies on both sides of the convention hall bearing WL slogans: *All Power to the Workers!*, *A Union for All*, and *All in a Union!*, and *For a Worker's and Farmer's Government!*. The hall erupted in boisterous approval.

"Sister and brother delegates," Hass began. "The Empire has had its day. Its day is over! It is now time to make democracy *real*. It is time to have a People's Democratic Planetary Republic!" The assembly cheered loudly.

"The WL proposal is simple," she continued. "Voting in the plants and shops, workers will elect their supervisors, administrative committees, and representatives to local, regional, and continental industrial councils, and, finally, to the All-Industrial Union Congress. Representation will run from the bottom up, and power will flow up from the grassroots, not from the top down.

"The qualifications of these representatives elected to the All-Industrial Congress will be a good working knowledge and understanding of the processes of production and distribution, ability to coordinate and direct those processes, and dedication to the duties and responsibilities with which they are charged.

"The workers who operate the industries today for the bosses are the workers who will operate them tomorrow under Democracy, for themselves and the good of society, plus, of course, those millions who are ruthlessly thrown into the scrap heap—the unemployed and so-called *unemployables*. They, the organized workers in the factories, mills, mines, stores, farms, ships, and railroads of the land, will constitute the basis of a Workers' Democracy—the most complete democracy the world has ever achieved."

Hass' proposal generated a lot of excitement and questions from the floor. There was a motion to accept the proposal and add it to the platform. The motion lost. Then somebody proposed to have the WL choose a delegate to work with the ESP platform committee. That motion carried and passed with only a couple scattered "Nays" heard after a roar of "Yays".

Now came the hard part. Could the convention draw up a platform that all could agree with?

It was contentious. Some advocated nationalizing essential industries, like energy, communication, transportation, and space. Government ownership, they said, is the only way to phase out fossil fuels and build a clean energy grid.

Others said that nationalization under a syndicate-dominated government would do no good at all.

Over several Earth-day equivalents of heated wrangling, the ESP had its ten-point platform. Thromm read it from the podium:

• No more clearcutting; replant forests.

• Make polluters pay to clean up their messes.

• Sharply cut greenhouse gases and build a solar and wind-based, not fossil-fuel-based energy system.

• Build a socialized Empire-wide health care system.

• End syndicate domination of society.

• Convert syndicates into a network of democratic, worker-owned and community responsive cooperatives.

• Reduce the work week by 10% with no reduction in pay to logically apportion the work.

• Build a coordinated network of wall-to-wall industrial unions for all workers.

• Full voting rights and self-determination for Thlargi.

• Change Venus only with non-violent methods and elections.

Applause and whistling accompanied each point. When the cheering had quieted down after Point Ten, Thromm said, "On this platform, I and all other Eco-Socialist candidates proudly stand in our run for public offices! And when we win, we pledge to vigorously carry out this program!"

Delegates stood up, clapping and cheering loudly; some stood on their chairs. Prolonged cheers and whistles reverberated around the hall. Many hugged each other, cheeks wet with tears of joy.

An important compromise was reached when the delegates decided that each piece of campaign literature that bore the name "Eco-Socialist" had to be approved by each member party, via delegates to a special review committee. The committee was to use the latest cyber-technology to quickly approve, reject, edit, or revise campaign materials.

The delegates voted to register the Eco-Socialist coalition as a legal political party and run candidates in the next regional and global elections.

Members of the Revolutionary Party (RP) played an obstructionist role in the Convention. RP delegates said that elections were just so much foolishness, and that voting just encouraged the syndicate oppressor class. Instead, they advocated mass armed uprising to overthrow the syndicate system.

Most labor unionists tended to regard RP members as spoiled brats from upper-class families, with little or no experience in the real struggles of working people. Many dismissed them as window-smashing provocateurs.

Delegates discussed key issues in break-out workshops which often became heated. Zyzz and Zilla went to the workshop on "Strategy: Reform or Revolution?" that drew a crowd of about a hundred.

It's hard enough to stand up to your enemies and take a principled stand. But people were starting to realize that it's even harder to stand up to your friends or allies, point out where they're wrong, and keep them as friends. In the latter case, it's important to be able to disagree without getting disagreeable, and Zyzz had that going for him. In his down-home drawl, he asked delegates from the RP, "Are you kidding? Where will you get your weapons? You'll need a whole lot of 'em. And where will you drill and practice? You'll have the law down on you faster than flies on clormshit."

RPers looked at each other and shook their heads. One responded, "I hope you can understand why we can't share any details concerning weapons training."

"And as far as armed uprising goes," another delegate said, "most people just aren't interested in that. It's hard enough to get people to get out and vote. How are you going to get them to pick up a zapper and maybe get killed?"

An RP delegate countered, "Now, why do so few people bother voting? I'll tell you why. Because they see, correctly see, that voting doesn't do any good, that's why! We need radical change now! People are ready to join an uprising when they see some real leadership. We need action, *now*. The time for talk is over."

Another delegate said "But if you pick up the gun first, you'll lose all popular support. People just aren't ready for that yet. What we need is to fight for meaningful reforms now, that people can agree with. That's the only way we can grow and organize to make real change."

"I can agree with our RP comrades," another delegate said. "Yes, revolution is needed. Badly! But it's got to be a peaceful revolution. If you get violent you'll never attract the support that we'll need to have any chance of success. You'd just have a premature insurrection. You'll get stomped; guaranteed."

"*Peaceful revolution*? Hah! You expect the syndicates to say, 'Oh, we're sorry. We were wrong', and just hand over all their power and wealth? Voluntarily? Are you crazy?" asked an RPer.

"What I'm trying to say is, if there's going to be any violence, let the syndicate goons start it," the non-RP delegate answered. "If you start it, you'll lose all public support. Use non-violent tactics as long as possible, then use force only when absolutely necessary—and then for self-defense. Otherwise you'll lose all support."

Another non-RPer chimed in. "Change isn't easy. Never has been. And there are no shortcuts in building up mass support. This is where the RP is making a strategic error. They are failing to relate to the real, on-the-ground, concrete struggles of workers. Instead, they're proposing a fantasy, a glorious workers' armed uprising. Well, wake up; that ain't never gonna happen!"

The wrap-up by the chair reflected the consensus. "What is the point here? Is it to pose the most radical-sounding slogans and say 'I'm more radical than you?' Or do we want to bring as many people as possible into the struggle? Clearly, we need to connect with people where they are now, not where we wish they were. The goal should be to fight for reforms to help people realize limitations of this system and move beyond its narrow restrictions. People are nowhere near picking up guns and jumping into armed street battles. Not yet, if ever."

The Revolutionary Party was clearly outnumbered. They staged a dramatic exit and sent no delegates to other sessions.

Coverage of the Unity Convention in the syndicate media and press was scanty, limited to ridiculing and snide comments of a "radical, chaotic, gab-fest."

Chapter 18
The Campaign

She who telleth the truth doth not sin,
but causeth many inconveniences.

—From the *Book of Drell*

The Liberals were notorious for shifting their message.

Throughout the campaign, Liberal Party (LP) candidates asserted that voting for the Eco-Socialist Party (ESP) would be wasting your vote, and that splitting the center-left vote would help the Mossbacks.

They changed their message to fit different audiences. Candidates told more liberal audiences that the LP was the only practical way forward to real change, albeit a little more gradual than the ESP. To more conservative gatherings, they pledged that they were loyal to "free enterprise incentives" (code for syndicate domination), and they would implement reforms only where needed to promote stability and prosperity (for the syndicates).

One LP leader was quoted as saying, "Look: if we don't give them (working classes) something, we risk a revolution. If that happens, we could wind up losing everything!"

The Grand Empire Party's (aka "Mossbacks") main talking points: The Empire was in a cultural war against wicked radical change, and the ESP were devils incarnate that wanted to foment class hatred and war. Thlargs were secretly conspiring with ESP operatives in an evil secret conspiracy to take society back to the Stone Age.

And, yes: even a few Liberals were involved in this conspiracy! According to the Mossbacks, the LP was just "ESP Light".

The two major parties (usually abbreviated to simply *the Majors*) pressured the media to include only "serious candidates" (code for *exclude the ESP*) from campaign coverage and any televised debates.

The Eco-Socialist coalition organized demonstrations and rallies in front of the major media syndicate offices, demanding that all three parties should be fairly represented in any debates. Demonstrators carried signs that read. "Let All Three Parties Speak!" Their chants of hundreds of followers reached the syndicate offices. There was too much public outcry to be ignored, and the debates commission yielded to public demand.

ESP activists staffed information tables at festivals and flea markets around the world. While working their shifts at farmers' markets in their riding, Zilla and Zyzz talked to hundreds of people across the political spectrum about the campaign. Many just ignored them. Others walked by and shook their heads in disapproval. A few made nasty comments. But many snatched up campaign literature and bought bumper stickers for their zooms and buttons for their caps. ESP tablers often ran out of campaign materials; it was a challenge to meet the demand.

When she was tabling, Zilla usually succeeded in projecting a friendly attitude to everybody, whether friendly or not.

"You guys are making a big mistake," said one guy who stopped at their literature table. "All you'll do is split the left vote and help the Mossbacks win."

"What's the difference?" asked Zilla. "The LP and Mossbacks both support syndicate rule."

"The LP isn't perfect," he said. "But they're a helluva lot better than the Mossbacks!"

Many took this "lesser of two evils" line. The prospect of breaking with the LP was just too risky for many veteran labor unionists.

Both of the two Majors got most of their funding from the syndicates. Organized labor supported the Liberals, and that got them some lip service from candidates when they spoke at union halls. Senators with strong labor or "green" constituencies proposed some good legislation that would improve public health, on-the-job safety, pollution control, or otherwise better workers' lives. But time after time after time, when it came down to voting, a proposal would be defeated by the Mossbacks and the pro-syndicate LP majority.

The Eco-Socialists managed to get some air time on the major media. One day during the campaign, the popular Borgus Zymphal Show featured a lively exchange between two of the three candidates running for Bayview's seat in the World Senate. Borgus had asked them about one the top issues in the campaign, energy policy.

Schnuzz, the Mossback candidate, answered, "Yes, we need to develop alternative energy sources. The energy companies, indeed, are studying this issue and developing solar and wind power."

Karz, the ESP candidate countered, "Ms. Schnuzz is obviously repeating the syndicate deceptions. Look at the facts. Behind the façade of *studying*, the energy companies are going full steam ahead drilling for oil and removing mountain tops to get at the coal. They're not making any real progress on developing alternative energy."

Schnuzz countered, "That is a lie. Energy Corp alone is spending millions of kecks on research and development of solar power."

Karz returned, "That might sound like a lot, but it's a miniscule fraction of their budget. Eyewash. We already have the technology to make real advances in solar energy and gravity-neutralization, but the energy companies are just sitting on these plans, figuring out ways to profit by them. That's what they mean when they say *research and development*: profits first! Well, how about our planet's health?"

Zilla and Zyzz were sitting on the couch, munching on some Crunchies and enjoying the show at home on TV.

"Okay, ladies: let's move on to a related question. What is your opinion on government subsidy of alternative energy development? Ms. Karz, you go first this time."

Karz began, "The government is providing millions of kecks in subsidies to the fossil fuel syndicates. That money comes from the pockets of taxpayers. Why? These are very profitable companies; they don't need that money. We need to fund start-up solar and wind companies. Level the playing field so they have a fair chance. Put some of that money to work to create a clean energy grid. That's how we can wean ourselves off fossil fuels."

Schnuzz came back with, "Utopian dreaming!" raising laughter from the studio audience. Most were clearly on Schnuzz's side. "Sorry, but this doesn't pass the reality test. We just can't do it yet. If we did, industry would grind to a halt. Thousands of people would lose their jobs. Do you really want that?" The audience made a rumbling sound.

Then Schnuzz said, "It's time for the solar and wind industries to stand on their own. We need to stop subsidizing these failures. Taxpayers can no longer afford it."

"Sure," said Zyzz. "Take two tax cuts for the oil syndicates and call me in the morning, says Doctor Schnuzz."

Karz chimed in, her laid-back antennae displaying combat-ready anger, "Cut subsidies for clean energy while fossil-fuel companies continue feeding at the public trough? They get millions of kecks in tax breaks and lavish subsidies from hard-working taxpayers and you want to stop a modest subsidy for clean energy development? Ms. Schnuzz, do you want to kill thousands of jobs? Good, green jobs. Jobs that will clean up our air and water, and pull our planet back from the brink?"

Schnuzz answered, "Can I be honest here? The demand for energy is increasing. That is a fact. Fossil fuels are a proven technology; they will continue to be the primary way to meet this demand, at least for several decades."

"Again, it's obvious that Ms. Schnuzz is reading from the script prepared for her by her syndicate backers. The fossil fuel companies don't want to talk about how their pollution is adding to the climate crisis. They don't want us to know! All they can say is that they're *working on it*, with their 'research." Karz made quotation gestures. "My question to you, Ms. Schnuzz is this: How much more of your pollution do you think our planet can take?"

"What should be obvious by now is that my friend is spewing radical junk-science again," said M. Schnuzz. "There you go again: 'Oh, the sky is falling! Oh, run and hide!'" (More laughter from the audience. It was becoming obvious that the hall had been packed with anti-ESPers.) Still, she continued, "Many scientists agree that the climate change we are seeing is natural and that we play no role in climate change. Other reputable scientists say that nothing can be done about it. That's the reality."

Karz cocked her antennae at an incredulous angle before she responded. "Which *reputable scientists* are you referring to? The ones on syndicate payrolls?" Boos erupted from the audience. "Most reputable scientists would take issue with my friend. The broad consensus among the scientific community is that climate change is indeed real and not natural. And, yes, we can and must do something about it. The best route to create more jobs—more green, clean jobs—is a massive restructuring of the energy system away from coal and oil to solar and wind power."

Schnuzz cut in, "The fossil fuel companies pay a lot of taxes too, my friend. Much more than our radical friends pay. Way too much, according to many economists. Now, one of the demands these radicals are making… these radicals are really good at making demands, aren't they?" More laughter. "These radicals are now demanding government-funded health care. Now, if you implement your ideas about phasing out energy companies and put them out of business with all these regulations you're advocating, you will cripple industry. That would bring on massive unemployment and homelessness. Ms. Karz, if you put the energy companies out of business, who will pay for your proposed socialist health care boondoggle?" She accepted the loud applause from the audience. "Where will you get the money to pay for all your cockamamie schemes? And, if you're so sure that climate change is real, well, shouldn't you start adapting to it?"

"Sarcastic bitch, isn't she?" Zyzz said.

Schnuzz wasn't finished yet. "What we need to understand is that these ESPers are just noise-makers. They have no good ideas. Their agenda is just to disrupt business and prosperity, by stirring up class envy and hatred, and for what? Much of this so-called *global warming...*" She held up her fore-arms and made quotation signs with her fingers. "...stuff is a hoax!" That brought a mixed reaction from the audience, some boos, and some applause.

"Screw you, Schnuzz," Zilla said.

Karz, who had been trying to get a word in while Schnuzz was blathering, said, "No, it's not about envying your wealth, Ms. Schnuzz. The syndicate class and its parties are indeed waging a cruel class war against working people and this planet. That's reality. And it's about time we woke up to that and started fighting back. What you need to understand is that your system is based upon destroying nature and brutally exploiting labor for your own private profits. You and your cronies are ruining the real wealth of this planet. How much more of your greed can the planet stand? Where does your wealth come from? Labor! Your system is built upon theft!" The audience went wild, with both boos and cheers.

Zilla said, "Woo-hoo! Getting a bit worked up, aren't they?"

"About time somebody told that bitch off. Did you notice that Schnuzz didn't just blow away the whole idea of health reform?" Zyzz asked.

"Hmm. The insurance rackets ain't gonna like that," Zilla said.

Sure enough, soon after that debate some Public Relations representatives from insurance companies met with the Mossback and LP leaderships in closed meetings to discuss "messaging".

At a press conference about twenty hours later, Schnuzz answered a reporter's question by saying "Yes, let's be perfectly clear about this. Government health care would be a disaster. A one-size-fits-all approach would lower the high standards of the great health care that we all enjoy. We need less government meddling with business, not more. A government that controls your health care controls you. I, for one, don't want some government bureaucrat getting between me and my doctor!"

"But it's okay for some insurance company to tell people 'No, you can't have your operation'?" Zilla asked. "What a buncha crap!"

"Profits first, baby," Zyzz said.

Mossback talking-points were picked up and repeated by popular talk show hosts and pundits, who added dashes or buckets of vitriol to their diatribes assailing climatologists and advocates of clean energy.

Some took off on ad-mantisem, personal attacks against ESP and LP candidates.

A few earth-day equivalents later, Zyzz and Zilla were watching another debate, this one between a Liberal and an Eco-Socialist candidate named Zorra, televised from a city hall auditorium.

LP: "Windmills, solar energy plants, are proven failures. They aren't economically viable, and won't be for a long time."

"You bet. They'll see to that!" Zyzz said.

ESP: "What my opponent doesn't want to admit are the reasons why solar and wind power haven't lived up to their potential. Lack of funding! While the fossil fuel companies get lavish government support, solar and wind companies have to hold bake sales to generate funding."

"Amen. You tell 'em, sister!" said Zilla.

The ESP candidate continued, "We know that the fastest way to create decent paying jobs is to rebuild our roads, bridges, airports, and schools. We know that we can create thousands of jobs by getting us off coal and oil and into wind, solar, geo-thermal, and other clean technologies. Not only must we oppose those who deny the reality of global warming, we must demand the transformation of our energy system to a solar and wind-generated energy grid and electric zooms!"

That got a smattering of applause from the audience.

"Give people a choice," she continued. "Make low-carbon pollution choices easier and more accessible for all people, and I can guarantee that you will see a dramatic reduction in global warming!"

"A campaign promise, Ms. Zorra?" the moderator asked.

"Yes. And it will be an easy one to keep—but only if we switch from fossil fuels to renewable energy!" she responded.

LP: "On the contrary, my friend, we need to develop more proven, effective resources like clean coal and oil. More, not less. *That* is a proven job creator."

ESP: "Smart energy policy will make a big difference and create solid social and economic benefits. Green jobs; thousands of them! And we need to hold the polluters responsible for the damage they're inflicting on our world!"

LP: "There you go again. Doomsday is coming! Oh No! Run for your life!"

That got another round of snickering from the studio audience. Ridicule was becoming a default tactic of the Majors.

"Drell, what an asshole!" said Zilla.

ESP: "Are you disagreeing with reality? Or do you believe that the facts have an Eco-Socialist bias?"

LP: "Neither!"

ESP: "Well, then stop using the bogus facts generated by the pseudo-scientists on the syndicate payrolls! The fact is that temperature records are being broken. The fact, ma'am, is that climate change is real. Could be the biggest threat to our survival. While the syndicates are focused on increasing their profits and paying their flack teams to provide bogus scientific support, the majority of real scientists tell us that these are very serious issues."

This got a spattering of applause from the studio audience, and a "You tell her, sister!" from Zilla from the couch audience.

On the financial end of the campaign, there was no contest. Thousands of people gave modest donations to the ESP campaign, and many small, family run businesses sent in checks, while the big syndicates supported the Majors, easily dwarfing the ESP's campaign funds.

But the ESP had other resources. An army of energetic, enthusiastic supporters made a difference. Going door-to-door to talk with voters, waving signs, calling talk shows, writing letters to the editors of major papers, and showing up at campaign events presented fresh and lively faces. That broadened the appeal of the ESP over the stodgier Majors.

Some ESP supporters in the film industry put together a powerful movie that made a compelling case for the ESP, but it had a disappointingly limited distribution. Those who were already convinced came to see it, but few beside the "usual suspects" showed up.

The ESP did best in college towns and industrial ridings. The goal of uniting the two target support groups, labor and greens, appeared to be panning out.

When the election wrap-up began, things were festive at the election-watch party as results came in. When it was clear that Thromm had won her seat in the Senate, the crowd went ecstatic.

Tenas narrowly lost her race for a seat in the lower, continental senate. In her concession speech, she said, "We're clearly on the right track. Our alliance not only won seats in the lower senates of Ishtar and Aphrodite, we won a seat in the World Senate! Wherever we ran, we did better than the pundits predicted. Even in the most conservative ridings. We are now recognized as a real contender. We have proved without a doubt that the sum of all of us working together is far greater than each of us working separately. We can only grow from this point. We'll do better next time. Yes, there is light at the end of this tunnel!" The crowd gathered at the "victory party" down at the Union Center cheered. Tenas was learning how to push the right buttons.

"Now, I'd like to introduce somebody you already know," she said. "Our first ESP senator-elect, Thromm !" It took a minute for the uproarious cheering to subside. Some wept in joy.

Thromm held up her arms asking for quiet, and began. "First, I'd like to say Thank You to all of you who put in so much work and gave so much of your time into this effort. All the tabling, door-knocking, leafleting, talking to so many folks, all your hard work. You made this happen! Thanks to you, we now have some voices in the continental and islander senates, and my voice in the Senate of the Empire."

As she hit her rhetorical stride, her voice boomed. "We have some crucial work ahead of us. Working people are being cruelly exploited. Our planet is not just dying. It's being killed! And the killers have names and addresses: SteelCo! Ishtar Forest Resources! United Energy! We will now go forward to get a fair deal for the working people, hold the syndicate destroyers accountable, and save our planet!"

The applause was sustained and loud. Thromm waited patiently. When she held up her hands the crowd quieted a little and she continued. "Considering that this was our first combined effort as the new United Eco-Socialist coalition, this is one helluva breakthrough." More applause. "It's been a struggle. We have made a great start. We are now on the political map!"

She waited for the applause to ebb, then said, "Now, if you want to cool off for a while, I can understand that. Go take a vacation, you've earned it. Then come back and keep fighting! Maintain this momentum! Keep making noise: I'll need you out there when the Senate is in session. Never forget: politics is a long story, and elections are merely the punctuation marks. Yes, elections are important, but it's what happens between elections that really counts. Make your voices heard in the Senate! Keep educating and organizing!" She held up all four of her arms high in the air, making a four-fisted salute.

A few voices started, and soon loud chants of "Educate! Agitate! Organize!" reverberated throughout the ballroom.

Some felt that if the ESP had reached out just a little more to moderate voters, the coalition could have built a broader base and become a mass center-left party. Others felt that if they had watered down their campaign and abandoned their core principles, many voters would have stayed home and the coalition would have gotten fewer votes.

As it was, several LP members dropped out and joined the ESP. A few senators announced that they were leaving the Liberal Party to caucus with the Eco-Socialists.

And, some powerful people were starting to get nervous.

CHAPTER 19
ISHTAR FOREST RESOURCES

The one who throws the stone forgets;
the one who is hit remembers forever.

—Thlargian proverb

IFR tended to see timber as a "one-time crop."

Sustainable land management wasn't Ishtar Forest Resources' strong suit. Ishtar Forest Resources (IFR) was a cluster of companies that had combined like big raptors gobbling up smaller ones. It was the monopoly lumber and paper power of the planet. Its combined holdings made it the largest landowner on the planet, and it had secured "harvesting rights" to many more hectares.

The company planted a few tree plantations after clear-cutting flat land. They used them as showcases for their "IFR: the Tree-Planting People" advertisements. But land with any slope was abandoned to erode into ugly, gullied badlands when scraped clean of its protective cover. The wind blew in spores that could have restored the stripped land, but then blew most away again before they could take root and grow. Rain washed away the rest. Only sheltered, low spots re-greened, often with alien grasses.

A big, beat-up old logging truck about thirty centimeters long, bearing a large IFR logo careened down the winding, narrow mountain road, filling the air with clouds of choking dust.

It had been a long, hot day, and Borl, the driver, was anxious to get to the mill, unload his logs and go home.

He was hungry and tired from putting in too much overtime. He reached down to his crotch where he had a bag of Crunchies that he munched on as he drove.

Winding around the sharp corner, Borl didn't see the two hikers until he was nearly on top of them. The truck had so much downhill momentum that he couldn't stop if he had wanted to. He pushed hard on the steering wheel's horn-pad.

Kobe and Porm, walking up the logging road, heard the oncoming noise and jumped into the ditch with only micro-seconds to spare.

"You asshole!" Kobe stood up in the ditch and shouted after the truck. Coughing and dusting himself off, he reached out with an obscene gesture toward the dust-cloud. "Think you own the bloody road?"

"Well they do own the frigging road. That's the problem!" Porm said, coughing, trying to wave the dust away from his face as he adjusted his backpack.

The two of them were up for a hike, enjoying the view and looking for whatever wildlife might remain in the last few pockets of what had recently been lush forest. Where just a few weeks ago, the wind sighed through stands of lycopods, horsetails, and tree ferns, now only desolate slash, stubble, and stumps remained. IFR's land-use policies, or more accurately, land-abuse policies, were creating short-term profits for a few and wasteland for everybody else.

Mushrooms had quickly sprouted from the stubble, and up through the naked rocky soil from occult secretive underground tangles of mycelia. Not plants, they were more like slow-motion animals. Some red ones, some blue, others tan-colored, fungi towered over them. That was about all that was left that had any height. If their trunks had been woody, they would probably have been clear-cut as well. But once they shed their spores, mushrooms quickly melt down into slimy, fly-infested goo, which added even more to the scene's ugliness.

"Stupid jerks. IFR: Ignorant Friggin' Morons," Porm said. The damp sweet smell of a thousand things growing was gone. His antennae drooped. The memories of all the life that had been here brought tears to his eyes as he looked over the scalped hills, shaking his head in disbelief.

"Moron starts with an 'M', not an 'R', you idiot," Kobe said.

"So? Make it 'Retard' then. Yeah: Ignorant Friggin' Retards!" Porm wiped the tears from his eyes, and they both laughed, antennae standing upright again.

A dust devil swirled by, peppering them with grit the wind had plucked up from the loose dirt and swirled across the barren slash-field. Just last week, this had been a forest, alive and singing with a hundred different kinds of critters. Now it was empty except for slash and mushrooms, ripped and torn apart to the bleak horizon, silent but for the wind. The damp, organic essence that smelled so sweet just a few days ago was gone.

Dead tree roots couldn't hold soil. The coral reefs and kelp forests in the seas were being smothered by soil erosion and runoff.

"So what can we do about it? Maybe their gas tanks need some sand. Let the air out of all their tires? Somebody's gotta do something," Kobe said, peeing at the side of the road.

Their pulses soon returned to normal, but their anger level increased. They continued their hike.

And, they started making a plan.

CHAPTER 20
THE OUTLAWS

The prince that is feared by many must of necessity fear many.

—From the *Book of Drell*

Bufo was the CEO of Ishtar Forest Resources.

As the chief executive, he liked to come in to work on weekends. He could get a lot done when he had the place to himself. And, you never knew what you might find snooping through your employees' desk drawers.

Kobe and Porm patiently watched his comings and goings closely for a while. (NOTE: a day on Venus is months long.)

One day, he had a surprise when he arrived at work. He parked his zippy red compact in his space in the IFR's executive lot, as usual, and had just gotten out, heading toward the entrance when two guys pulled up and got out of their zoom. They wore masks, and one carried a gun.

"Just hold it right there, Bufo", Porm, the one pointing the zapper at him, said. "Don't be afraid. Do exactly what we say, and you won't get hurt. Don't do anything stupid. Now…" he said, pointing with his weapon, "…get in. You're going to come stay with us for a little while."

Kobe opened the back door and grabbed Bufo by the upper forearm.

"What the hell do you think you're doing? Why are you doing this?" Bufo was obese and easily broke into a sweat. His antennae quivered nervously.

"Just calm down, big guy," Kobe said through his mask and quickly bound all four of Bufo's arms together behind him with twine.

"You'll never get away with th-th-this!" Bufo said.

Kobe grabbed Bufo by his shoulder, walked him to the zoom, opened the door, and threw him into the back seat. He stuffed a rag into Bufo's mouth and wrapped a blindfold around his head, then pulled the door shut. "Lay down, and shut the fuck up!" Kobe sat next to Bufo, stun gun pressed against his belly, and took off his bandana mask.

Porm pulled his mask off, quickly got behind the steering wheel, and drove away, resisting the urge to floor the gas pedal. This would not be a good time to get pulled over for speeding. A twenty-minute drive took them to a suburban garage. He drove in and pushed the button to close the garage door.

After they brought Bufo inside, Kobe walked about a mile to a payphone to place a call to the *Ishtar Times* to tell them their demands, then took a circuitous route home.

The next day, the headlines on the *Ishtar Times* read:

> Chief Exec of Ishtar Forest Products Kidnapped!
>
> An eco-anarchist group going by the name "Nature Defense Front" is taking credit for the abduction. The terrorists demand an end to clear-cutting and full funding for reforestation projects.

> Gorm, acting CEO of IFR, says: "We're working closely with the police on the matter." Chief of Police Fuzzodo calls for calm.

Throughout his ordeal, his two captors kept Bufo tied up, except for potty breaks, treated him politely, and fed him well. They followed the coverage on TV, but it wasn't easy to track just what was happening out there. After the first day, no mention was made of their demands. In the media, it became a cops-and-robbers melodrama in which no issues were discussed.

On the news, they watched the police department's press secretary announce that negotiating with terrorists was against agency policy, and that all those responsible would be apprehended and dealt with severely.

Kobe and Porm were afraid to use the phone or even go out much, so they had no clear idea of what was going on. From all indications, their demands were just being ignored, and it was business as usual.

It didn't take long for the police to track them down.

They heard the loudspeakers. "You are surrounded. Resistance is futile. Release Mr. Bufo unharmed and you will be fairly dealt with." Neither of them had been getting much sleep, and they were sorry for ever concocting such a stupid idea.

"Well, shit. This is it," Kobe said. He untied Bufo's legs so he could walk, and told him, "Go on out. Don't worry. Sorry, man."

Bufo was shaky, but went through the doorway and walked outside and down the stairs to the waiting police. The whole thing had lasted only a week. That was about a week too long.

"So what now?" asked Porm.

"I don't bloody know," said Kobe. "It could be bad, but we didn't harm him. Not a scratch on Bufo. He's not hurt, for what that's worth. A few months in jail? A year? Shit. I don't know."

Then it was the loudspeakers again, telling them to come out slowly, hands held high and empty. They did as directed, nervous as hell. Porm stumbled on the edge of a step and nearly fell on his face, but caught himself. That was the wrong move. A rookie cop, nervous himself, had Porm in his sights. He pulled the trigger and squeezed off a jolt that caught the already off-balance Porm square in the thorax. The jolt threw him back against a wall where he smacked his head and was knocked senseless.

CHAPTER 21
CRACKDOWN

A mob has many heads, but meager brains.

— Ancient Drelbi saying

The misguided escapade had unintended results.

A police ambulance brought Porm into the emergency room where he was examined and pronounced dead on arrival due to brain concussion.

Kobe was taken in to the Department of Public Safety's detention center for booking and locked up in a small holding cell with nothing but a bare cold metal bed, commode, and sink. They questioned him for hours using "enhanced interrogation techniques".

They brought him before the judge an equivalent of four earth-days later. While he was being held, he wrote a statement and was looking forward to using the courtroom as an opportunity to read it and explain their reasons for kidnapping Bufo, describe how clear-cutting was messing things up and why it had to stop.

But things didn't go that way. There was one reporter from the *Ishtar Times*, but no jury. When Kobe tried to make a statement, the judge told him "Be quiet; just answer any questions with a simple yes or no." His antennae drooped, and the photos printed in the *Times* made him look like a criminal.

When Bufo took the witness stand, he testified that he had suffered horribly from the mistreatment he had received at the hands of his captors, and was subjected to anguishing mental torture. After Bufo's testimony, a sergeant named Glitzer drove him home.

Bufo was still seething. "You know, we need a few agents to infiltrate the ranks of these clowns. Pose as converts. Get to know them, and gather enough information to burn their butts and lock them up for good. How else are you ever going to get this situation under control?" he said.

"Thanks, sir. We're way ahead of you on that, sir." Glitzer looked bored.

"Yes, I suppose so. Good. Hopefully we can prevent future incidents like this. I could've been killed! Damn environmental crackpots. Troublemakers, that's all they are. Stirring things up. Well, they picked the wrong guy if they think they're gonna intimidate me!"

Glitzer yawned.

"Well, I'll see to it that the culprits are dealt with severely, believe you me!" Bufo said.

"Yes, sir. I'm sure we'll get to the bottom of this," Glitzer replied.

Bufo was determined to do all he could to bring the hammer down on all these shit-stirring radicals. When he got home, he called some friends at the police department and security bureau. Then he phoned some senators to remind them of his generous campaign contributions. He suggested ways they could help squash the perpetrators and their ESP co-conspirators and bring a final solution to these disturbances.

He had some chits to collect. It was time for his investments to start paying off.

Support demonstrations were held in the major cities. Zilla and Zyzz helped organize speakers for rallies and marched in many, carrying signs. "Free Kobe!", "Stop Syndicate Greed!", "Stop Clear-cuts!", "Save the Planet!" The air was strong with the taste of anger, and the smell of an outrage that grew as it fed upon itself.

Standing on top of a plastic box, a speaker at a rally held up a newspaper ad from Ishtar Forest Resources that declared: "Forestry Workers: A Dying Species!" and shouted, "Look at these lies! This is the kind of crap we're up against! It's time that loggers face the fact that we are not their enemies.

"Loggers: We don't want to take your jobs away! We do want your jobs to be sustainable! It's not us. It's the greedy companies who are mismanaging the forests, not us! Sustained yield is a joke to these companies! These people walk away with huge profits, leave workers jobless, and the environment ravaged! What do we need: more syndicate profits or clean air?"

The crowd shouted, "Clean Air!"

"What do we need: more million-keck bonuses for executives or clean water for our children?"

"Clean water!"

A speaker for the Clean Air Coalition (CAC) said, "We need to get out there to the clear-cuts and plant trees. If everybody went out and planted just a few trees, that would mean thousands—millions—of new trees. That could make a huge difference. We'll be getting hundreds of baby trees, delivered right here. Now, who wants to come and help us plant them?" He waved a clipboard. Zyzz and a few dozen others signed up.

A few Earth-day equivalents later, the CAC had recruited a good crowd of volunteers that included troops of Girl Scouts and Boy Scouts. Zyzz boarded a crowded school bus full of kids with a few scout leaders. It was part of a caravan led by a truck with the slogan "Save Our Planet: Plant Trees!" in big letters hanging on the side. They convoyed out to a site left bare by the IFR after it had gone through on a timber harvest. The crowd, eager to get to work and in a cheery, festive mood, unloaded the seedlings and shovels.

Before anybody could even stick a shovel into the ground, IFR patrol cars and police arrived with a custody wagon. The sergeant of the police detachment got out of her zoom with her bullhorn. It squawked with feedback, then she said,"This is an unauthorized and illegal assembly. You have no permission from Ishtar Forest Resources to be on this private land. You will please cease and desist now! Leave the premises and go home!"

An assortment of moans and shouts of disappointment and anger came from the crowd. Many younger children had come to help their big brothers and sisters who were scouts. Most had no idea why they were being hassled.

The CAC leaders got into a heated discussion with the IFR and police, who advised them that if they wanted to do this, they were to go through proper channels.

"Well, how about these baby trees? If we don't get them into the ground soon, they'll die."

"Kinda late to be thinking about that now, isn't it? You should have thought about that before you started this nonsense," the IFR spokesman said. "Right now, you have to leave these premises."

If looks could kill, the scowls on many faces in the crowd of would-be tree planters would have wiped out the IFR patrolmen and cops on the spot.

A Girl Scout leader spoke up, "Listen: we came out here to plant these trees. If IFR did what was right, what they're supposed to do and *say* they do, we wouldn't have to do this!"

"No, you listen to me!" said the IFR rep. "You are on IFR property illegally and will leave at this time. This is your final warning." She nodded to the IFR lead-sergeant, then walked back to her company zoom, got in, and watched.

The sergeant barked, "Order Arms!", and a dozen troopers in shiny boots and starched uniform caps with IFR badges and carrying stun-batons quickly snapped into formation, shoulder-to-shoulder. Their eyes were concealed behind reflective sunglasses.

Then Sarge shouted, "Stun level three!" followed by a sharp, synchronized click as the squad set their sticks to a butt-kicking level, and snapped the business ends on the palms. "Forward, march!" They started advancing toward the crowd, backing them up toward their zooms, Sarge saying, "Let's go; no sense in resisting. Time to go."

A little girl close to Zyzz tripped on the uneven ground and fell. A cop kicked her and said, "C'mon, get up!"

Zyzz stopped and glanced toward the cop. "Now just hold on a Drell-damned minute, buddy!" as he reached down to help the girl up. Then he felt a sudden, sharp, breath-taking shock, and everything blacked out. Next thing he knew, he was on the ground, flat on his back, and a cop was kicking him saying "Get up! C'mon, let's go!"

Zyzz struggled to get onto his feet, feeling wobbly and seeing stars. Shaking his head to clear away the dizziness, he felt wet. *Drell-damned hot-rod,* he thought, angry and embarrassed for peeing all over himself. Those tazers humiliated as well as hurt. He started taking off his back-pack to get a bandana to clean himself up.

"Don't even try it, buddy! You want more of this? Keep your hands up in plain sight!" the company cop said, as they herded Zyzz with a dozen others onto a paddy–wagon. Most of the others in the crowd got in their vehicles and left peacefully, bringing loads of anger and frustration home with them.

The paddy-wagon pulled into the police station and the door opened. The occupants were escorted into the station under armed guard, where they were asked a few questions, then released after giving their names and addresses.

"Ishtar Forest Resources is letting you people off easy," the desk sergeant said. "Now go clean up, and go home. And stay out of trouble!" They were directed to a washroom, then to a police bus that dropped them off at their homes.

Many saw the official responses to the protests as stupid and arrogant. Instead of calming things down, the authorities were adding more fuel to the fire.

Public outrage grew. Some demonstrators got worked up and threw rocks through windows. Or were they agent provocateurs, planted by the police? Nobody knew for sure, and the para-military detachments and psy-ops squads weren't talking. Police set their shockers down to sub-lethal levels, but they could still "adjust your attitude" quickly and knock you off your feet. Some were injured, and hundreds were rounded up and taken into custody.

At one demonstration, Zilla heard a sergeant order "Don hearing protection!" The shout echoed around several police detachments.

"What the hell is this?" she asked a friend.

Her curiosity was soon answered when the police switched on noise-making devices that generated deafening, high-pitched, ear-splitting, headache-inducing blasts. People dropped their signs to cover their ears. That didn't help. Crowds were reduced to pain-wracked, cowering, helplessness.

For his kidnapping offense, Kobe was convicted of First Degree Unlawful Abduction and Illegal Confinement and sentenced to 10 years in the Ishtar Penitentiary. It didn't matter that the name "Nature Defense Front" had just been a spur-of-the-moment decision, and that no such organization really existed. And it didn't matter that he and Porm were just two friends up for a day hike, and had nearly gotten killed by a speeding IFR truck. The authorities hadn't the time nor the inclination to bother with such "irrelevant trivialities".

Activists' homes were raided, and their literature and computers seized. Hundreds of Drelbi were arrested on charges of criminal conspiracy and disorderly conduct. The jails soon became overcrowded, so crammed that latrines were overwhelmed and plumbing failed. The mess and stench was awful. Drelbi were forced to stand in their own waste, and many got sick.

The mainstream media portrayed the prisoners as less than Drelbi.

The *Wake-Up Call* and other leftist papers called for more, bigger demonstrations and more support for the prisoners and protestors. In response, the police stepped up their search for opposition presses and shut down many, wrecking equipment to prevent future issues from being printed.

A special issue of the *Wake-Up Call* appeared on the streets, trying to rally more public support. With military precision, the police confiscated and burned the papers and tracked down and destroyed more printing presses. Trained detachments of the CSO (Coordination of Security Operations) were stationed at college and industrial towns around the Empire to maintain control.

Seven Drelbi youth were arrested at one place as they were breaking open the bundle and getting ready to deliver the latest issue of the *Call*. They were taken into custody, and driven to police headquarters. Their parents were charged with contributing to the delinquency of minors. In a press conference, Chief of Police Fesdo said, "If we stand by and do nothing, if we allow these children to remain in these homes, they will become radicalized, learn subversive ideas, and become criminals."

Prison authorities were concerned that inmates might be getting too organized and sought to identify any possible leaders, and segregate, isolate, and "remove" them. When word got out that the prisoners weren't going hungry, people rallied to support them and threw them bread over the barricades. The police started harassing and beating those trying to supply any food to the prisoners.

A group of ultra-leftists kidnapped some syndicate and government officials, hoping that it would somehow ignite an armed uprising and revolution among the general population. They misread the public. The syndicate media used the incident to crank up more hysteria and violence against even moderate environmentalists.

Some senators and political operatives held private meetings to discuss how they could prevent Thromm, the only Eco-Socialist candidate to win a seat in the World Senate, from being seated.

Amnesty bonfire parties were organized and ads in the papers, radio, and TV invited people to bring down any "eco-socialist or other subversive" literature for safe disposal. If such material was found as part of a later search, the guilty would face imprisonment and property owners would be held liable for sedition and treason.

Soda and splorff companies got into the act and offered their products as further inducement. One widely broadcast ad finished with "Smile, you're in the Splash generation! Burn your trash and cool off with a Splash!"

Growing numbers of people felt the situation was descending into hopelessness.

Chapter 22
Special Session at the Ishtar Senate

In the forest, a skillet sounds good.

—Thlargi proverb

The forecast predicted a collision of two storms.

Thromm scanned the Ministry of Natural Resources' Personnel Directory for "Marine Biologist", and placed a call.

"Moorv speaking."

"Glad I caught you, Moorv. This is Senator Thromm speaking. I was afraid I'd have to leave a message."

"What can I do for you, ma'am?"

"You may have heard that Emperor-elect Vrrzzle has declared a State of Emergency and the Prime Minister has called for a special session of the Ishtar Continental Senate."

"Yes, I've been listening to the radio."

"That session is scheduled to convene at thirty-seven hours. I'd like to slot you for expert testimony on how warming seawater is affecting our food resources."

"Just a second; let me check my calendar." Moorv opened and quickly inspected his schedule. "I have a meeting then, but I can get out of that. This sounds more important."

"All you'll have is just a few minutes, and there'll be plenty of deniers, so this won't be a very friendly audience. Think you can handle that?"

They spoke a while about the do's and don'ts of Senate protocol, what to bring for a visual aid, then Thromm said, "Get to the Senate Office Building no later than 36:15. Present your ID at reception—can't get in here without that—and somebody'll direct you to my office."

"Sounds good, ma'am. See you then." Well, this should be interesting, Moorv thought, feeling a little intimidated. He hurried down to the Senate Building, his mind racing with ideas. Not much time to plan, but he knew the facts he wanted to present.

Posturing and wrangling at the Special Session was intense. Senator Floonf took the floor, saying, "The mobs are demanding that we adopt some of these… these half-baked Eco-Socialist notions. Over my dead body!"

Many senators hooted their support for Floonf. "These so-called ESP principles are based on very shaky science. If we took this seriously, it would not only be bad for business; it would ruin everything. Unemployment would rise to catastrophic levels. Homelessness and poverty would soon follow. The very foundations of our society would be shaken." More hoots and whistles of support.

"We've already had a taste of what that means," Floonf continued. "Just look at what's happening out on the streets!"

"It tastes rotten!" another senator shouted.

Chair Knux hammered her gavel on the desk. "The assembled will come to order!" After a moment, the turmoil settled down. "The Chair recognizes Senator Schlang from the riding of Ishtar Central."

"Distinguished colleagues, our scientists have clearly shown that the global warming we are seeing is part of a natural cycle. It is not caused by Drelbi activities. The science is clear on this: increased carbon dioxide will be beneficial to plant growth and agriculture. We should not be pushed into making any unsound decisions just because a few radicals are stirring up mobs!" Schlang concluded, to a round of "Hear, Hear!" and applause.

Thromm had her forearm raised so long it was starting to go numb on her.

"The chair recognizes Senator Thromm from the riding of Northeast Ishtar."

Thromm rose, rubbed her shoulder, picked up her desk microphone, and began, "Madame Chair, most honorable sister and fellow colleagues. We indeed face a crisis. The broad consensus among the scientific community is that our planet is warming at an alarming rate, and…"

"Lies!" somebody shouted. An eruption of jeers and hisses, and a light scattering of applause cut her off. Some right-wingers were spreading unflattering rumors that Thromm had Thlarg blood in her ancestry, saying things like "Her wings are just a bit too large, don't you think?"

Knux pounded her gavel, the sound echoing loudly through the chamber. "The assembly WILL maintain order."

"Thank you, Madam Chair," Thromm continued. "The science is indeed clear. These rising temperatures are being caused by industrial activities. Unprecedented levels of carbon dioxide are being added to our air by the over-consumption of oil, coal, and other fossil fuels, and this is causing the global climate to warm, known as the Greenhouse Effect. That is the broad consensus among the scientific community. Now, some scientists that happen to be on syndicate payrolls are telling us that the majority consensus is false."

Scattered hisses and a few cheers burst out around the chamber. The word "syndicate" was obviously a hot button, and Thromm had pushed it. She raised her voice and continued. "These syndicate-scientists tell us that there is no climate problem, that it's all a conspiracy concocted by a few crackpot agitators.

"Our distinguished colleague, Senator Floonf, is repeating the blatant disinformation put forward by these syndicate employees that are calling themselves 'scientists'. They are saying that higher CO_2 levels would actually be a good thing by helping plants to grow. Well, what plants, Senator Floonf? The forests are being replaced by strip malls and parking lots! The meadows are being replaced by sprawl. Oceans and coral reefs, so important to our food supply and to the many jobs that depend upon, are dying!

"If we allow things to continue as they are, we will face unprecedented famine. Conditions on this planet will grow too hot to support life as we know it. I propose that we have a summit conference between a select committee from the senate and representatives from the mainstream scientific community and the Eco-Socialists.

We need to listen to them and come to an understanding."

That sparked a loud hostile outburst from most of the chamber.

When things quieted down again, Thromm continued. "On one hand, we are dumping carbon dioxide into the air at record levels. That CO_2 is reacting with ocean water to form carbonic acid, and that's lowering the pH of the oceans. That is a fact. And you know what effect that is having on the coral reefs! Those reefs are the incubators for all our important foods! The increasing pH is dissolving the shells of oysters, crabs, clams. The larvae can't survive long enough to even get started! Then, by clear-cutting forests, scalping meadows, and draining swamps, we are destroying the only way that our planet can cleanse itself. Why, it's like me hitting you, knocking you down, and then kicking you while you're down. If it were a boxing match, I'd be fouled for using dirty tactics! Well, isn't it about time that we started working with nature instead of against her? Start treating our life-support system sensibly instead of kicking her when she's down?"

Then came another round of razzing. Thromm stood there with all four hands clenched into fists and tucked into her side.

When the noise ebbed, she asked, in a loud voice, "Do I still have the floor, Madam Chair?"

The chairwoman's impatience was starting to show. "Yes, yes. You have, uhh… fourteen minutes remaining. Continue if you must, " she sighed.

"Thank you, Madam Chair. On your schedule, you'll see that the Timekeeper has allotted fifteen minutes to

Moorv, a Marine Ecologist with the Ministry of Natural Resources to give expert testimony on this topic. I will cede the rest of my time to him."

There was a low hubbub around the chamber.

Thromm sat down and spoke quietly to Moorv. "Okay, you're on; remember what I told you."

Moorv made quick eye contact with her, nodded, and stood up.

"Thank you, Madam Chair. Distinguished senators, I'm honored to speak with you today about how climate change is affecting our marine food resources. My presentation will focus on the science, not the politics, of this issue." He filled his water glass from the pitcher, took a drink, and cleared his throat.

"What Senator Thromm says is backed up by most in the academic and scientific community.

"The root of this problem is simple chemistry," he said as he put a transparency on the projector aimed at a large screen at the front of the chamber. He turned it on and it was right-side up. He breathed an inward sigh of relief. "As you can see, CO_2—that's carbon dioxide—plus H_2O—that's water—equals H_2CO_3 . That's carbonic acid. And H_2O plus SO_2 (that's sulfur dioxide) equals sulfuric acid rain. Now, both CO_2 and SO_2 are produced by burning fossil fuels—coal and oil.

"But there's more that you need to be aware of. Rising seawater temperatures are also stressing Eurypterids, one of the largest, most valuable of our food sources, because *their* primary food source—shrimp—doesn't fare well in higher water temperatures. And, furthermore, these higher temperatures are causing the spread of infections that are deadly to many other species we depend on for food."

There were a few low hisses, but most of the senators held back, maintaining decorum.

"Currently, there is a die-off occurring that may be the most extensive marine-disease event ever documented. You may have read about this. This is impoverishing the marine biota. As the food chain's intricate links collapse, the more complex species higher up the food chain will go first, leaving only the simpler species. If this trend is allowed to continue, jellyfish and plankton are all that will be left in a few years. Probably not among your favorite seafoods, eh?

"Increasingly, mainstream scientists are finding that climate change is causing this problem. A hotter world is causing tropical diseases to increase their ranges, infecting Drelbi and spreading on both land and in the sea. Pathogens thrive and become more virulent at warmer temperatures.

"Our seawaters are becoming more acidic—more sour—thanks to the absorption of fossil fuel emissions from the atmosphere. Clearly, action is called for."

The murmuring in the chamber increased in volume and hostility with scattered, loud hisses.

"These are facts, but the syndicate pseudo-scientists are being paid to call it junk science!"

The senate erupted into a clamor. There were shouts of "Shut up, you lousy radical!" and "Thlarg scum!" Decorum was breaking down quickly.

Chair Knux used her gavel again. "Senators, shall we show some respect for our guest?" she asked, shaking her head in disgust at the behavior in her chamber. "Will that be all, Moorv?"

"Yes, ma'am. I notice a few raised hands. Should I take questions?"

"Yes, of course."

One senator asked, "Now, keep this simple. Not all of us are oceanographers here."

"Yes, ma'am," Moorv nodded.

"You suggest that we take action here. Well, what specific action would you advise? "

"Ma'am, I would humbly suggest that, in light of this threat to our food supply, the prudent course of action would be to pass legislation that would effectively reduce burning fossil fuels and transition quickly to sustainable, solar and wind energy sources."

A very few voices rose in support of Moorv, saying "A warmer world is a sicker world!" but most noises from around the chamber were hostile.

"We also need to replant harvested forestlands to recapture the carbon that is driving global warming. We have some laws on the books requiring that, but without any enforcement mechanism those rules are meaningless.

"It would be in all our interests if Ishtar Forest Resources replanted more. It would reduce erosion from slopes, which would benefit the seafood industry, and, in a few years, IFR would be getting more trees that they could harvest and sell."

The next question came from a Liberal senator. "Okay, Mr. Moorv; how much time would you say we have before things start getting really bad?"

There was some grumbling.

"Good question," Moorv said. "Nobody knows for sure."

After some more generalized grumbling from the senators, Moorv continued. "We are currently witnessing a series of quantitative changes. As already mentioned, by burning the 'carbon sinks'—fossil fuels—we are taking carbon out of nature's lock-box and putting carbon oxides into the air. Now, what makes it worse is that the lungs of Venus—the forests, coral reefs, and swamps that filter the carbon out of the air to store as biomass—are being destroyed by clearcutting. There's nowhere near enough replanting to make up for it, and the erosion is smothering the reefs. Unless we stop these practices, these and other changes will cascade into a crucial tipping point, a threshold level that could initiate a runaway greenhouse effect. Then, it would be 'game over' for all of us."

"Do you truly feel that things are really all that urgent?"

"Yes. The majority of the scientific community agrees that we could reach this tipping point within our lifetime. How much time do we have? Who knows? Distinguished Senators, The clock is ticking. Time is running out. I urge you to take decisive corrective action. Now. This isn't a political issue; it's a survival issue."

Such a derisive clamor arose in the hall that Chair Knux decided to cut the question period short. "Thank you very much for your input, Mr. Moorv."

Moorv sat down next to Thromm and whispered, "Whew!"

She patted his hand and reassured him quietly. "Thanks. You did more good than might appear. Can you stick around a while and see what happens?"

"Sure."

"The chair recognizes Senator Mulf from the Meskhent riding."

Mulf started by saying "I think we can all agree that this is a complex problem. It will take some time, probably a long time to figure this all out, and we may never understand it entirely. Today, we have heard from the doomsday lunatic fringe who are trying to rush us into making some hasty decisions based on their pseudo-science."

She waited for a chorus of assorted supporting noises before she continued. "The important thing in my opinion is that scientists have the technology to halt, even reverse climate change. It's available, whenever we need it."

Then she went to her main point: "There is no need to bother speaking with terrorists and crackpots. That is exactly what we must *not* do. We cannot afford to lend these people any credence whatsoever. By the Goddess' blessing, we have enjoyed peace for centuries. Now, it seems there is an uprising brewing. Appeasement is not an option. That would only strengthen those elements that would overthrow our government and destroy our way of life. Anything short of vigorous suppression would invite open rebellion, perhaps a class war!" She slammed the desk with her open hand for dramatic effect.

When Senator Thromm returned home to her husband after the end of that session, she looked tired and beaten. Her antennae were usually up and perky; now they drooped. He hadn't seen her so downcast in years, and he walked over to hold her.

"Was it that bad?" he asked her.

"Schlang, Floonf, and the rest of those jerks…" she shook her head, despair on her face.

"The same ones that tried to keep you from being seated?"

"Yes. Mulf is even talking about class war, for Drell's sake."

They stepped over to the window. In the distance, the waters of the bay reflected the sunshine and glinted silvery. "I tried, honey. Holy Mother of Drell knows; I tried to make them see. What more can I do?"

The Empire had many troops at its disposal, but this was no longer the army of the Great War. With a united planetary Empire, there were no longer any independent nation-states. Any disputes between ridings or provinces were now settled in the world Senate.

The Grand Army and Navy of the Empire now worked hand-in-glove with the syndicates' own security forces. The military had morphed into a tool used to crush any public unrest that the syndicates felt might disrupt the smooth operations of business-as-usual.

The Empire had become a global syndicate-state.

CHAPTER 23
A TRIP TO BRZZT

A barking snarf bites little.

—Drelbi proverb

When flood waters rise, head for higher ground.

Zilla and Zyzz were watching the events unfold via TV news coverage. Things looked bad.

"Sheesh! We better get downtown; at least bring some food in for the prisoners," Zilla said.

"Haven't you been listening? They probably wouldn't get it. Damn cops are blocking stuff," answered Zyzz. "And they're busting people for that. Sounds like they could use some medical help too."

"How can we get some medics in there?"

A few minutes later, Zyzz said, "Drell! Those bastards are using zappers and noise machines against unarmed people! Damn bullies! Okay, that does it. I've gotta get down there."

"No way," countered Zilla. "They'd just throw your tush in jail too. Better cool down some, Zyzzles."

And so it went. First one, then the other would get worked up enough to walk out the door and head downtown to help support the rallies; then the other would come up with a good reason not to.

Finally, they made their decision. Zyzz had wanted to take a trip home for some time. Now that things were starting to turn ugly, this might be a good time. If they stuck around here, both of them would get drawn into the action. The cops had taken his name at the tree-planting fiasco, and getting into more trouble now was the last thing he needed.

But what about Cilnia and Callibia? The children had way too much energy to be confined on a long flight.

Zilla stood in front of the bulletin board at school, looking through the Baby Sitters corner and jotting down some names and numbers. She saw a familiar name and decided to call her.

"Hello?" The voice on the other end was young and sparkly.

"Hey, Shirl, this is Zilla. How are you?"

"Great. I did a whole lot better on that calculus final than I expected. Remember, I was really sweating it?"

"Drell, that's gotta be a relief. Kinda surprised yourself, eh?" Zilla asked.

"Ya! Fer sure. Hey, what do you think of all this stuff that's going on downtown? Looks like the shit is really hitting the fan, eh?" Shirl said.

"Whew! I'll say. It was just a matter of when. This storm has been coming for a long time. Bound to happen sooner or later," Zilla answered. "Shirl, the main reason I'm calling is that I saw your name on the Babysitters Board. I was wondering if you could stay at our place and take care of the girls for a couple days?"

"Yeah. Should be no problem. I'd love to."

They settled the details, and Shirl showed up at their house at breakfast time. Zilla introduced Shirl to the girls. "This one is Cilnia, and this one is named Callibia." The tiny drelblets looked identical at first glance.

"Like Drell's two generals, eh?"

"Them's the ones."

"Yeah, they all look pretty much alike in the first instar, don't they?"

"The fridge is pretty well-stocked," Zilla said, opening the door and looking in. "If you need some other stuff while we're away, just save the receipts, okay? We'll go over 'em when we get back. Just keep a close eye on these two when they're out in the back yard. We put up some netting to keep out raptors, made 'em a play area, but you never know..."

"We'll be just fine; don'cha worry," Shirl assured Zilla. "Have a great trip; see you in a few days," she said, gently picking them up and holding one girl lightly in each arm.

"Oh," Zilla added. "Don't feed Kamari too much. She took a box of snarf-kibbles out of the cupboard, picked up his bowl, and poured some into it. "Fill this up at breakfast time and once more at supper."

"Okay."

"And take him and the kids out for a walk every day, okay? We don't want a fat, lazy snarf."

"Got it," Shirl said with a laugh.

Zyzz put his arm around Zilla and said, "Okay, love. We've got a plane to catch."

Zilla hugged Shirl, who was still holding Callibia and Cilnia, kissed them, and then they were out of there. They caught a flight down to Aphrodite Central and got to Brrzzt in good time. As the old familiar scenery came into view, Zyzz started breathing easier. Soothing decompression. It felt good to come home.

"Well, where are my granddaughters?" Marg asked with keen disappointment. Zyzz and Zilla glanced at each other. Zilla had heard Zyzz when he had told Marg on the phone that just the two of them would be coming this time.

"You know, traveling with kids isn't easy," explained Zilla. "Way too much energy; it would be torture for them. A good friend is taking care of 'em for a while. You'll just have to come up and spend some time with us, Mom."

"Wait a second… yes, yes, I remember. You said you wouldn't be bringing them." But she was remembering less these days. Marg's doctor had told Zyzz that his mother was exhibiting the initial symptoms of something they called Mak's Syndrome. The exact causes were as yet unknown, but the disorder was growing distressingly more common among elderly mantids as Venus' environmental quality deteriorated.

"So why not come back with us for a couple weeks, Mom?" Zyzz asked.

"A couple weeks? Oh, I couldn't."

"Why not?"

"Who's going to take care of the place, get the mail, water the garden? Oh, there's so much to think of."

"Mom, as much as you've helped the neighbors over the years, I'm sure they wouldn't mind looking after the place for a while. Have the post office hold the mail. No problem."

"We've plenty of room at our place, Mom," Zilla added. You won't be in anybody's way, and the girls could get to know Grandma."

"Well… maybe." She had become a real homebody, rarely going anywhere anymore.

They talked awhile over lunch and, when they were about finished, she said, "You know, while you guys are here, we really ought to go out to Uncle Torzz' place. They've been asking about you and would love to see you."

"Sounds good, Mom. How about we get some sleep first?" Zyzz said.

The drive out to his aunt and uncle's place took them over miles of gravel roads, too winding and narrow to engage the zoom's flight option. They drove past hills of rusty brownish-red ore slag that had once been forestlands. Trees were scarce now, tall ones rare. For miles, only stunted, bonsai-like trees remained.

Then they were back in the woods again. A greenbelt had been preserved around this group of homesteads. They saw the lake, shimmering blue down below the cabin. They turned off the dusty road onto the long driveway and drove up to the little house. Aunt Fridzz and Uncle Torzz were sitting out on the front porch.

As they got out of their zoom and walked toward the porch, Torzz said, "Well, look what the schlumff dragged in!" He ambled down to meet them, accompanied by their yippy, tail-wagging snarf.

"Hush, Goldie! Don't you remember Zyzz?" Aunt Fridzz said to their mutt.

"How ya been, Marg?" Torzz hugged his sister-in-law, then they walked up to the porch where they sat down on old wooden chairs and talked awhile, drinking cups of hot, herb-flavored splorff.

With a shifty, mischievous look, Torzz got up, opened a cupboard door, and reached in to take out a bowl of candy. He popped some of the berry-flavored drops into his mouth and set the bowl down on the table for them all to share.

"Not now, you nut. You'll ruin your appetite!" said Fridzz.

"Shit. Can't do nothin' anymore," Torzz said.

"Remember how you used to call me 'Auntie LaLa?" Fridzz asked Zyzz with her giggle. He blushed, smiled, and gave Zilla a quick, furtive glance.

They chatted around the table, and Aunt Fridzz said, "Why don't you guys go outside and find something useful to do? Leave us to get supper and talk about women's stuff?"

"Maybe you guys can catch something for supper," Zilla suggested.

"Probably nothing worth eating," Torzz said.

"And take your crazy yapper with you!" added Fridzz.

They didn't need to be asked twice. "Yeah," Zyzz said. "We'll just go down to the lake for a spell." He kissed Zilla on the forehead and followed his uncle out the screen door.

"And don't slam that door!" Too late. "Oh, those two! When will they ever learn?" Fridzz laughed.

As the three women chatted, the discussion focused on married life. Marg and Auntie Fridzz offered jokes, advice, and insights; Zilla listened politely.

"Enjoy the romantic phase while it lasts," Marg said.

"You know,"Aunt Fridzz added. "If you put a jelly bean in a jar for each time you do it the first year, and take a jelly bean out for each time you do it after the first year, you'll never run out of jelly beans."

Zyzz and Uncle Torzz were gratefully enjoying some relief from the chatter as they walked out into the yard, and down to the shore. The wooden dock, gray and old, creaked as they walked out on it.

"Watch your step," Torzz said as he kicked off a mushroom that had sprouted from the old wood. "I need to get this thing fixed one of these days."

"Get some lumber, nails, stuff like that, and I'll help you next time we're down here," Zyzz said.

"When'll that be?"

"Maybe in a few months. They keep me pretty busy at school."

They walked out on the dock past where Torzz had a boat tied up, and Zyzz looked down into the water. It was full of suspended particulate matter that Torzz just called "gunk".

Torzz said, "The SteelCo pension is good, but just look at what they've done; this lake is all fouled up now." Torzz had tried to make it as a farmer, but took a job at the mines when SteelCo started hiring. A dependable, regular paycheck provided more security than farming ever could.

They looked down into the water, turbid with flakes and ugly floating specks. "The *price of progress,* the company says," Zyzz said.

"Fishin' sure in hell ain't what it used to be. Used to be no problem catchin' my limit. Crabs, all kinds. Trilobites, freshwater squid, snail. Hell, I haven't seen a blue crab for years. About all you can pull out of here anymore is mud-crabs."

"Yuck," Zyzz said.

"You know how to clean a mud-crab?" Torzz asked. "Cleaning" meant preparing something for cooking.

"No, can't say I do," Zyzz answered with a smile; it sounded like a joke might be coming.

"Well," Torzz said. "First you take a board just a little bigger than the mud-crab. Then you take a hammer, crack open the shell, and scoop out the meat."

"Okay, and then?"

"Then you throw away the meat and eat the board," Torzz finished.

Zyzz smiled and shook his head. "Drell-awful stuff, eh?"

"I'll say. This crap here's what done it." Torzz pointed down into the particles suspended in the turbid water. "You used to be able to see the bottom."

"And the Klutz River carries this crap into the bay, where it's fouling up the reefs. What a freakin' mess. How the hell are they ever going to clean this up?" Zyzz asked.

"SteelCo says that nature will clean it up. Yeah, sure. Bastards!"

"What a pile of clormshit. They did this; they should clean it up. That would put a few Drelbi to work, eh?"

"Sure," Torzz said with a disgusted look. "And who's going to make them do it?"

Zyzz had no answer for that one.

After a few more hours visiting over brunch with Torzz and Fridzz, they drove back to Brzzt. They packed their things. Marg packed too much stuff as usual. She had never enjoyed flying much, but had no fear of it either. After a nap, they drove to the airport. The flight back to Bayview was uneventful.

When they got home, they left their stuff just inside the door. Nobody there. They walked through the house to the back door. "Halloo!" Zilla called in a sing-song voice to the back yard. "Anybody home? We're baaack!"

"Back here!" Shirl answered. She and the girls were sitting around the picnic table.

"This is your Grandma," Zilla told the girls. "Your Daddy's mama." They climbed up Mom and Dad's legs.

"Do you like stories?" Grandma asked them. They nodded with big eyes, thumbs in their mouths." Good! I've got sooo many stories to tell you!"

"Shirl, this is Mom." After telling the baby sitter all about the trip and settling financially, Zyzz drove her back to her place.

Chapter 24
Crackdown Deepens

Good, speed, and cheap seldom meet.

—Drelbi proverb

The reaction escalated. Things were changing fast.

Street news spread by word of mouth about how Kobe and Porm and other detainees were being treated. Syndicate-sponsored "news" enraged more people. There was a bomb-throwing incident in which innocent bystanders were killed, but the executives who had been the apparent targets escaped unharmed.

Then a few extremists broke through security at a meeting of the Forest Resource Industry Association and assassinated some high-ranking execs. The reporters didn't read the group's message, nor discuss the group's motives and rationale. The crimes made the news, but with no background analysis. Opportunities to address the underlying issues were ignored.

On prime-time TV, a teary-eyed spokeswoman for Ishtar Forest Resources asked the camera, "Why are they doing this to us? What do these people have to gain? At IFR, we protect our forests. We're the tree-planting company." The narration continued with soothing music and scenes of smiling workers planting seedlings, alternating with scenes of lush forests and wildlife.

"Those liars," said Zilla. "That's old-growth. IFR's replacing it with tree-farms! Talk about junk science!"

Behind the scenes, IFR execs and others pressured the police to consider members of the ESP and allied groups guilty by association and lock them up. The propaganda mills churned out their venom: "Throw the book at the eco-terrorists! Tree-hugging anarchists want to take your jobs away and take us all back to the Stone Age. Eco-socialists are just a pack of neo-Thlargists!"

Anybody deemed guilty of being "politically incorrect" was arraigned for being a member of or offering support to an illegal group; they were locked up, and held without trial. When the jails became too crowded, the Department of Corrections opened concentration camps, which they called Family Protection Centers.

The ESP and allied groups scrubbed their membership lists and records, but they were too late. Much of the information was no longer under ESP control and irretrievable. Over the years, names, addresses, and other information had been collected off petitions and logged into Ministry of Public Safety computers.

A hundred things bounced through Zyzz's mind. *When will they come for us? Should I go underground? Get a fake ID and just disappear and start over again somewhere else? Live as a fugitive? Where would I go? Where can I escape? It's no use. They'd catch me. Maybe not tomorrow or the day after, but soon. And when they do…* he shivered.

Never see Zilla again? Life without her? No good. He decided to take his chances and stay with Zilla and the kids, come what may.

Provisional ordinances were passed forbidding public meetings exceeding five people, at first just in the streets, sidewalks, or alleys, then a general prohibition that included all parks and vacant lots. After a few days, the prohibition was relaxed to allow religious groups to hold non-political public meetings. Then some radical priests were arrested for "preaching class warfare", and the general prohibition was reinstated. People were arrested just for being too close to a rally.

A few politicians like Senator Thromm recognized the importance of the root issues causing the protests and dared to speak openly about them. But most public office-holders sought to out-do each other in advocating harsh treatment for the protestors:

"We need to stop pampering these radicals!"

"We need to put the hammer down on these troublemakers and show others what happens when they pull this kind of nonsense."

"Shall we take a vote to censure Thromm and get rid of her?" Senator Floonf asked.

"No," Bufo replied. "Probably do more harm than good. Her constituents would raise holy hell. We want to tone this thing down, not ratchet it up."

"Maybe its time she had a tragic accident."

In a few weeks, conclusions were starting to jell regarding how to handle "enemies of the state". A purge of all those guilty of being a member of the ESP, any allied party, or "terrorist cell" was to be accomplished by non-lethal means if possible, depending upon the severity of the offense. Some officials openly advocated execution of the "terrorists". Fortunately for the activists, most decision-makers considered that a little too extreme.

As the crackdown deepened, the memberships of "subversive organizations" were rounded up. Entire families were bussed to Family Protection Facilities located outside the cities. These soon became crowded and unsanitary. The food in these camps was inadequate and of poor quality. Inmates were either bored from having nothing to do or worked until they were too weak to stand. Disease, rape, and other abuse were rampant. Some attempting to leave the camps were shot by guards just outside the gates.

"Clear out the jails and the camps," Senator Barz suggested. "They're a public disgrace. Why feed these noise-makers? Send them to the EVBs (Extra-Venusian Bases). Let them rehabilitate themselves via useful work! If we don't get rid of them, they'll just keep on raising hell, maybe start a revolution. Not good for business. And they can take their children with them. Good riddance!"

Barz was considered a moderate and was appointed to lead the Senate's Select Committee for Crisis Management. *Young Thlargs grunt as old Thlargs grunted before them*, as the old saying went.

Up in the executive suites of the Space Development Consortium Building, a Select Sub-Committee met with officers from public security agencies and Consortium executives, with a Mr. Bufo as special advisor.

"We need to get these people out of here for a while, and let things cool down a bit," Senator Barz said.

A Consortium officer said, "So you want to defuse this thing by dumping them on us? No thank you! The Space Consortium isn't part of the Department of Corrections. We have way too much to do already. Just the cost alone of transporting these rabble-rousers to the EVBs would be prohibitive. And what in the hell do you expect us to do with them once we get them there?"

"Their transport expenses will be covered; you'll be compensated generously," Bufo said. "Let Finance work out those details. And those we send, you can use as you see fit. Think of them as free labor."

"Let me get this straight," said one exec. "You want to turn the EVBs into… what… day-care centers for these subversives? Forced-labor camps?"

"Yes," Bufo said. "These bomb-throwers are traitors. You will be free to use them as you will. We understand there may be a few… er… accidents. We accept that."

"They'll have to be fed, both en-route and after they get there. And they'll just stir things up. Our job is already difficult enough without this disruption."

Senator Barz had been watching Bufo with growing disbelief as he made his thinly veiled murderous comments. Finally, he said, "Many… well, to be honest with you… most of these people are not really criminals, not in the normal sense anyway. We'd be surprised if they present any big disciplinary problems. Hell, most of them might make good colonists with skills you can use."

Schrumm, from Public Security, added, "And, we could assign some trained, experienced security personnel as a temporary detachment to ensure that they won't be a problem."

After some tough wrangling, a win-win agreement was reached. The Consortium suffered from a chronic shortage of workers, especially skilled workers. It needed a pool of cheap labor for its ventures. After lengthy training, retention rates at the Mercury bases were too low. Earth, in particular, seemed to eat up Drelbi. The Consortium could easily inflate the expenses and turn a nice profit on this deal. And the government would be paying for their transport.

Those few linked to any violent activity were processed quickly through the courts as "Category One Offenders" and dispatched to labor-camp EVBs on Mercury, Mars, and Earth. Of the three options, Earth was seen as the most desirable, even with the legendary terrors it harbored. Mercury was the most dreaded location.

All too soon, there was a knock on the door. It was the police with subpoenas for both Zilla and Zyzz.

Chapter 25 Schlive, Barrister for Defense

She who is her own lawyer has a fool for a client.

—Proverb from the *Book of Drell*

Schlive's office was in a run-down building

The Public Defender's office was a few blocks from the Hall of Justice. The elevator wasn't working, so they walked up the stairs to the third-story office and knocked on the door with the words "Schlive, Barrister of Law" painted on the glass.

"Yes, come in," a young male voice said.

"We have an appointment with Mr. Schlive at 14:20," Zyzz said as they entered.

"You must be…" The secretary glanced down at his appointment ledger. "…Zilla and Zyzz?"

"Yes."

"Please sit down," he said, indicating the line of chairs along the wall. He pushed a button on his desk phone.

They were alone in the tacky waiting room. After a few minutes, the phone buzzed, the secretary answered it, and said, "Mr. Schlive will see you now."

They went into the office, where a young Drelb with glasses sat behind his desk. After brief introductions, Schlive got to the point. "According to police records and other accounts I've seen, neither of you have done anything seriously wrong. You're guilty of no wrongdoing of any consequence as far as I can see, except that you've been identified as promoting Eco-Socialist propaganda. That's bad enough, these days. A matter of bad timing, I'd say."

"We're guilty of no crime at all, sir," Zyzz said. "In fact, it's me that should be suing the IFR hooligans for unwarranted brutality!"

"Uhh, how's that?" Schlive raised his eyebrows and jerked his head back.

Zyzz related the incidents at the attempted tree planting.

"Were any of you actually arrested for anything?"

"I wasn't charged with anything. Nobody was, far as I know."

"Well," Schlive said. "If I were you, I wouldn't bring it up. Don't even mention it, unless they do."

"And if they do?"

"Then we'll go for a self-defense plea. You were helping the kids… coming to the aid of a friend against overly aggressive private police tactics… that sort of thing."

Zyzz slowly nodded, looked over at Zilla. "And not sue those bastards?" he asked Schlive.

"No."

"Well, why the hell not?"

"For starters, do you have any idea how much that would cost you? You'd have to hire a prosecuting attorney, if you could find one that would even consider taking that case. Then there's be court costs, and IFR would probably win. Besides, all that is a separate case. Don't even mention it at your hearings. After we settle this case, then we can talk about that. Later; not now, okay?"

"Okay, but why not now?"

"One thing at a time, Zyzz. What IFR did and what happened at the tree-planting… that's *not* what this trial is about. Bringing that up won't help you now. That goes for both of you. This case is limited to your trespassing on private IFR property. That's all. After this, we can talk about the other. You can't make a charge and initiate a case, no matter how justified it might be, in the middle of another case. You might have a valid case, but wait until this thing is settled first, okay?"

"Okay."

"Now, have either of you actually joined the ESP?"

"Yes. Both of us," answered Zilla.

"As dues-paying, card-carrying members?"

They both nodded their heads and said, "Yes."

"Hmmm," Schlive sighed and slowly shook his head. "That's not so good. The ESP has been declared an illegal organization, you know. But, maybe we can work around that."

Zilla and Zyzz looked at each other and shrugged.

"Before we go any further, I need to let you know that you have two options," Schlive said. "You can accept me as your court-designated defense attorney at the court's expense, or you could select another attorney at your expense. I'm confident that I can represent you in court on this matter, at least as well as any other attorney you could afford."

Zilla asked, "Are you experienced in this sort of thing?"

"This is basically an unprecedented area. This crisis presents a new situation for all of us. I'm as well-prepared or ill-prepared in this as any defense attorney would be."

The two gave each other the palms-up, *oh-well* gesture. Zilla said, "Well, sir, thanks for leveling with us. Guess we'll stick with you."

"Thanks for your confidence."

They talked about their case and what was likely to happen during the trials, and Schlive coached them on courtroom do's and don'ts. Then he said, "Now, once you're in the stand, you want to establish that you are friendly witnesses. I would advise you to publically denounce the ESP at your first opportunity. Say that the party is wrong and their science is faulty. Say that you were wrong in associating with the group, that you made an error in judgment. Apologize. And name a few names when they ask you."

Zyzz shook his head. "Schlive, what do you take me for? An informer is a traitor, the lowest scum imaginable. Me? Fink on my comrades? Nope, not me. I'd never live it down."

"People; this is serious business! If the judge senses the slightest arrogance or disrespect, he could sentence you to hard labor on Mercury. Permanently. I'm being honest with you. He could order you separated from your family. If you do what I say, hell, you'll be free to go

... most likely. If the judge sees you as cooperative and friendly witnesses, he'll probably decide in your favor. The court will probably require you to pay a nominal fine to cover court costs, and then you'll be out of there."

"Drell! Would they take our children away? Send us to different colonies?" asked Zilla.

"The judge can do whatever he wants to with you. I'm being straight with you."

Zyzz's mouth went dry.

"As your attorney, I need to make you understand that anything could happen. Part of my job is 'surprise prevention'. I strongly advise you to cooperate. Don't say or do anything that even might be seen as hostile. It's all up to the judge. Schrumm will be the presiding judge on the fifteenth, and I would recommend that you not do anything to piss him off. And no speechifying. If you start to expound on any politics, he'll cut you off. Is that clear?"

"Yes. Yes, sir. I... we'll need to think this over some."

"You have until your court appointment. For you, that's 1300 hours on the fifteenth, Zyzz. You're right after him, ma'am. Be there a half-hour before your scheduled appointment, at least. There might be some no-shows. Don't even think about being no-shows. They will find you, and then they'll add contempt and evasion charges onto your initial citation. If you have any questions, call me. Here's my card," he said, handing them one each.

"See you on the fifteenth," Zyzz said.

"At what time?" Schlive asked.

"We'll be here at twelve-thirty," Zyzz answered.

Schlive nodded. Then they left his offices, walked down the hallway and downstairs, and left the courthouse.

When they got home, Zyzz told Zilla, "Listen, we gotta talk."

She wrapped her left arms around him while they talked about the interview, and asked him what he was going to do. He said he wasn't sure.

"What do you mean?" Zilla asked angrily, backing away.

"You heard him, didn't you? If we say the wrong thing, if they decide that we're hostile witnesses, we might not ever see each other again. They could send you and the kids to who-knows-where, and send me to a mine on Mercury. Do you really want to risk that?" He made a pleading gesture.

"My love, they can do anything they want. If you snivel, you'll just humiliate yourself. And me. Do you really think that they'd treat you any better? No bloody way! Stand up to them!"

"Listen. This planet is fucked. The ecology is collapsing. That's sure what it looks like, doesn't it? It's only a matter of time now. And if those we named got deported off this planet, well, wouldn't we be doing them a favor?" Zyzz asked.

"You listen! If you name names, if you turn anybody in, I'll never speak to you again. I mean it! When we get on the stand, we don't turn anybody in. Understand? I would be so ashamed of you if you betrayed anybody—and that's exactly what it would be: *betrayal*!" she said with finality, crossing all four of her arms.

He looked into Zilla's icy glare; her gorgeous antennae were cocked back into combat mode. "Now just... just wait a minute, Zilla. Come on, now. Giving somebody a one-way ticket off this planet, well, wouldn't that be doing them a favor? Thanks to these bastards, staying here is a death sentence! Do you really think we'd gain anything by trying to be heroes? The judge won't allow any grandstanding. It'd just dig our hole deeper."

"But if you name names, you could be sending them to a death camp!"

Zyzz looked into her eyes. She was quiet for a while, and started to cry, saying, "Love, I hear you; I do. Oh, how I hate these fools!"

"Yes, yes," he said and wrapped his arms around her. "I hate them too. But let's not screw up now. If we play this right, we can stay together. With the girls, but probably not here. We're in their hands, like it or not."

"I don't know what's going to happen. Yes, things are going to get worse here. But how fast? How bad will it be? Who knows?" Zilla asked. "How much time does this place have left?"

They went out into the back yard and stood with arms around each other. The clock was ticking. What little time they might still have together was precious.

Chapter 26
Grandma

Age may not bring wisdom – there are many old fools – but it does bring perspective.

– Ancient Thlargi saying

Grandma tried to maintain a cheerful atmosphere.

Zilla and Zyzz tried to keep up a face of normalcy at home, but the sour, bitter smells of stress filled the house. Grandma did her best to help maintain a happy mood and be a presence in Cilnia and Callibia's lives when Zilla and Zyzz were out.

One day, she told them a story that was already old when she had told it to their dad:

> Once upon a time, there was an old lady sort of like your Grandma. She lived on a farm.
>
> One day, when the old lady had just finished splorfing her clorm, she said "There! I'll leave the splorf pail here while I go get some sticks for my fire. Then I'll cook up some fine, fresh splorf."
>
> As soon as the old lady walked away, down flew a grasshopper. "Ahh," said the grasshopper. "Fresh splorf. Mmmm. I'll just drink some of this." But… oops! He tipped over the pail. Over it went, and the splorf was spilled all over the ground. Just as the grasshopper was starting to drink from the puddle, back came the old lady.
>
> "Oh, you rascal!" she said, and caught the grasshopper by the tail.

The grasshopper tried so hard to fly away that snap! his tail broke off. "Oww!" he said. "Old lady, please give me back my tail!"

"Sure," said the old lady. "Just as soon as you bring me some more splorf!"

The grasshopper thought about it for a minute, then walked over to the clorm. "Oh, clorm," he said, please give me some splorf for the old lady. Then she will give me back my tail."

"Certainly," said the clorm. "Just as soon as you bring me some nice fresh leaves to eat. No leaves, no splorf!"

The grasshopper thought about this, and walked over to a tree. "Oh, mighty tree," he said. Please give me a few of your many nice fresh leaves. You'll not miss them. I'll give them to a clorm, so she will give me some splorf, so I can buy my tail back from the old lady."

"Certainly," said the tree. "Just as soon as you bring me some fresh cold water."

The grasshopper thought for a moment. Then he hopped off to find a water bug. "Oh, Mister water bug," he begged, "please give me a pail full of fresh cool water for the tree. Then the tree will give me some leaves to feed the clorm so I can get some splorf to give the old lady so I can get my tail back."

"Certainly," said the water bug. "Just as soon as you bring me a fine fresh grasshopper egg for lunch."

The grasshopper thought about this for a while. Then he walked off to find a lady grasshopper. "Oh, Mrs. Grasshopper," he said. "Please give me an egg, so I can get some water, so I can water a tree, so I can get some leaves, so I can feed a clorm, so I can get some splorf to buy my tail back from the old lady."

She laughed at him. "You sure look funny without a tail! But since you are a grasshopper and I am a grasshopper, I think I will help you. Sit down and wait," she said.

The two grasshoppers sat and they sat. Then Mrs. Grasshopper began chirring. "There you go!" she said. She got up, and there was a fine, fresh egg.

"Oh, thank you!" said the grasshopper, and he took the egg to the water bug. "Here is a fine fresh egg," he said. "Now can I have some fresh cool water?"

Cilnia asked, "Gramma, why didn't the grasshopper just go and fill the pail by himself?"

"I don't know, honey. Grasshoppers are pretty silly, aren't they?"

"Uh-huh."

"So the water bug said, 'Oh, yes. Here is your fresh cool water."

"Oh, thank you," said the grasshopper. And he took the water to the tree, and poured it out. "Here is your fresh cool water," he said. "Now can I have some fresh new leaves?"

Ahh, yes," answered the tree. "Thank you! Here are some nice fresh leaves for you."

"Oh, thank you," the grasshopper said, and took the leaves to the clorm. "Here are some nice fresh leaves," he said. "Now may I have some splorf for the old lady?"

"Oh, yes," said the clorm. "Just splorf me into that pail."

"Oh, thank you," said the grasshopper, and he filled the pail with sweet, foamy splorf. Then he carried the pail over to the old lady..."

"Grasshoppers can't walk on two legs, Grandma. How could he carry a pail?" asked Cilnia.

"That's right, sweetie," said Marg.

"What it did was walk back to the old lady, and say, "Come with me. I have a pail of splorf for you. Now will you give me back my tail?"

"Certainly," said the old lady. And they went to pick up the pail, and she gave him back his tail. He fastened it on again, and flew away to join his friends.

"The old lady settled down to make some splorf shakes for her friends and they all lived happily ever after.

"That was a funny story, Gramma," said Callibia. "Tell us another? Please?"

"Sure, honey. Have you heard the one about the spider and the dragonfly?"

"Mmmm. I like spiders. They're yummy. Tell us!" said Cilnia.

"Okay. Once upon a time there was a dragonfly. He was flying around one day, and..."

CHAPTER 27
THE HEARING

The fly does not talk back to the megaraptor.

—Thlargian proverb

Zilla and Zyzz arrived a half-hour early.

They had expected to watch the proceedings at the District Hall of Justice as observers, but no. These hearings had neither jury nor audience. The only ones allowed in the courtroom were the judge, the prosecuting and defense attorneys, the bailiff, a clerk, and a reporter from the *Ishtar Times.*

They sat holding hands, quietly waiting in the hallway outside the courtroom. Zyzz felt his mouth going dry. He tried to calm himself. *Crap,* he thought. *This won't be much different than teaching a class. What's the worst that could happen, anyway? Deport us off the planet to a goddess-forsaken penal colony? Okay, so be it. Send me somewhere I'll never see Zilla and the kids again? Hmmm… not good…* his heart fluttered and beat faster.

Soon the door opened. The bailiff poked his head out and called Zyzz in. He walked him over to the interrogation box and nodded for him to sit down. Judge Schunk sat up in his seat, old, gaunt, and brown, looking like he had been on the job far too long.

Schunk was getting tired of all this and, finding it difficult at times to maintain his professional objectivity. These people were threatening all he held familiar and dear. *Whatever happened to the days when people had respect for the law, when people had respect for their betters? Why can't they just accept their station in life and follow orders?*

He longed for the good old days, when he settled important cases instead of being used like this. Food tasted better back then. The air smelled better then. People these days have no respect for authority. The business of business is business! Not mollycoddling these radicals belly-aching about some lousy endangered species too stupid to take care of itself.

These people whining about some damn bugs or weeds going extinct. Have they nothing better to do? By the Goddess, I'm sick of them. It would be better if the syndicates just simply took over and ran things as they saw fit. Take the gloves off and do what needed to be done, by Drell!

The judge felt his blood pressure rising. He reached into his haversack and pulled out a pill bottle. Better take a few of these. He was getting too close to retirement to lose control now. When he retired, he would write a book and finally be able to say how he felt about all this.

Zyzz tried to calm himself down by using an old technique he learned in college back when he was still scared of public speaking. It helped him clear his mind and soothe his nerves. He breathed in deeply, filling the bottom of his lungs to the maximum, then the middle, then the top of his lungs. When he couldn't take in any more, he blew it all out, silently. Repeating this a few times usually helped slow his pulse.

The clerk called Zyzz forward and said, "Please state your name, residence, and profession for the court record."

"My name is Zyzz; I live at 237 Ulfrun Street, in Bayview, Ishtar."

"Could you please spell that for the Court?"

"Yes, that's Z-y-z-z."

"Who else lives in your household?"

"I live with my wife Zilla and two daughters. My mother is currently staying with us."

"Ages of your children?"

"Nymphs, both fourth instar."

"And your occupation?"

"I teach Botany at the Bayview campus, University of Ishtar, School of Forestry."

"Thank you, Mr. Zyzz," the clerk said. "Your witness, Mr. Schlive."

Schlive began by asking, "Professor Zyzz, how long have you been in your current position?"

"I've been teaching at the University for seven years now."

"And in that time, have you ever been fined, cited, or arrested for any legal offense?"

"No sir."

"Now, Mr. Zyzz, as a scientist, and respected authority in your field, would it be accurate to say that you have acquired a level of understanding and knowledge of the ecology of Ishtar?"

"Yes, sir."

"In your opinion, sir, are current forestry management practices sound and sustainable?"

"No sir. I find many of these practices to be very destructive..."

Neza, the prosecuting attorney interjected, "Your honor. This line of questioning is irrelevant to the question we have before us. I suggest that this court has more important things to attend to than to serve as a propaganda outlet."

"Your honor," Schlive responded, "It is in the interest of the court to establish credentials and motivations of my client."

"Objection over-ruled. Proceed, Mr. Schlive," Judge Schunk said.

"Mr. Zyzz, how would you characterize the current methods of forest management on Ishtar?"

"Sir, current resource management practices employed by the major companies seek to maximize short-term profits with little or no regard for the preservation or conservation of the resource, nor the welfare of society in general and coming generations. These practices are definitely not sustainable."

"Now, Mr. Zyzz, you've been using this word, *sustainable*. Could you please define this term?"

Zyzz answered, "I would define *sustainable* as resource use that meets current needs while preserving the resource so that these needs can continue to be met for future generations. Current methods tend to be very wasteful and destructive and fail to meet that definition."

"Thank you, Mr. Zyzz. Your witness, Mr. Neza."

The prosecuting attorney cut to the chase. "Mr. Zyzz, are you now or have you ever been a member of the Eco-Socialist Party?"

Zyzz spoke loudly. "Yes sir, and I am proud of that fact. Anybody that has a brain and cares about the state of our world..."

The sharp tapping of Judge Schunk's gavel cut him off.

"You will please simply answer the question with a simple Yes or No."

Neza said, "Okay, let's try this once again, Mr. Zyzz." He got right up within inches of Zyzz's face, so close that Zyzz could smell his bad breath and taste his hostile attitude. "Are you currently a member of the Eco-Socialist Party?"

"Yes," Zyzz answered.

"Thank you, Mr. Zyzz," Neza said, his voice dripping with sarcasm. "That wasn't too hard now, was it?"

Zyzz hated this mock-helpful arrogance.

"Now," Neza continued, "do you recognize the names Moorv and Schlong?"

Zyzz willed himself not to hiss. A loud hiss from one's spiracles was the strongest expletive in the Drelbi language. The trouble is that it's involuntary and largely uncontrollable. He took in a slow, deep breath instead, then answered, "Sir, with all respect," he turned to face Judge Schunk. "And with all respects-s-s-s to your honor and this court, I refuse to answer that question on the grounds that it might incriminate s-s-s-somebody."

Schlive looked Zyzz in the eye and shook his head slowly, clearly disapproving, giving his client a look that said, *well, you dumb shit. You've really blown it now.*

The judge said, "Mr. Zyzz, you have been asked a valid question. For the court to render a fair decision, it is in your best interests to answer all questions."

"With all respect, sir, I will not disclose the names of any people who may or may not be members of any organization."

Judge Schunk asked the two lawyers if either of them had any further questions for the witness.

Neither had.

Then he said, "The court finds Mr. Zyzz as a hostile and uncooperative witness. The court pronounces him guilty of consorting with, and being a member of, an outlawed and criminal organization. By virtue of the authority invested in this court by the Province of Ishtar and the Holy Empire of Drell, bless her sacred name, this court places him under the authority of the Space Development Consortium for a period of twelve years of indentured servitude."

Zyzz felt his mouth going dry and his stomach falling.

Schlive stood and said, "Your honor, Zyzz and his wife have two children. They are a family unit. The defense requests that this family be kept together, not separated."

"The defense's request is for joint domicile?" Schunk asked.

"Yes, your honor."

"The court will take this request under advisement." He called the two attorneys up to the bench and they spoke quietly for about a minute. Everybody in the chamber stood up when the judge stood up to pull a book down from the shelf, and opened it to point out something to the attorneys. Zyzz watched as the judge and the lawyers conferred quietly, then nodded in agreement about something and returned to their chairs. Everybody but the bailiff sat down.

Then the judge said, "The intent of the court is that exile with joint domicile is in harmony with the principles of rehabilitative penitence. Depending on the verdict of this court in the upcoming trial of your spouse, the court may find in favor of your request."

Then the bailiff brought him out to the waiting area.

"Well, how'd it go?" Zilla asked Zyzz.

"Not bad. Don't worry, baby. Just stay cool."

In a couple minutes, the bailiff called her into the courtroom. Same judge, same process.

Zyzz was starting to wonder what was taking so long, when the bailiff called him back in again and walked him up to join Zilla, standing up in front of Schunk for sentencing.

"Zilla and Zyzz, it is the decision of this court that you are guilty of non-violent, political crimes. You have relatively clean records and will be classified and processed as 'Category Two Offenders'. It is the judgment of this court that Joint Domicile is appropriate in this case."

"Thank you, sir," they said. Schunk pounded his gavel and the bailiff walked them down to the clinic, where they had small electronic tracking devices attached to their left legs.

Two police officers drove Zilla and Zyzz home in a squad car and escorted them inside. Zilla wondered what the neighbors were thinking.

Lieutenant Haania sat with them at their kitchen table and explained what they were allowed and not allowed to do while under house arrest. Marg stood by listening; Callibia and Cilnia were wide-eyed and quiet.

"Now, it's important that you understand this clearly. You can work and go about your usual everyday activities, go to school, temple, and medical appointments. You are allowed to leave this place only at authorized times for only pre-approved activities." She scanned between Zyzz and Zilla and asked, "Now, what did I just tell you?"

Zyzz shrugged and asked her "Why don't you tell us, ma'am?"

"Okay, I'll clarify. Authorized times basically means daylight hours. Approved activities include things like grocery shopping, work, temple, et cetera. Do not, I repeat, do not go to any locations that are not on the list that we'll be putting together at this time."

It took a while for the three of them to agree on the list of addresses they'd be allowed to visit, then the lieutenant scanned a copy.

"All your telephone conversations will be monitored. If you try to disable the monitoring equipment..." she nodded at their tracking devices, "...you will be brought in for detention. It's your choice: your home here with our rules, or we can make other arrangements elsewhere. Do you understand all this?"

Zyzz thought about the cold steel toilet in the corner of the holding tank and felt his skin crawl. Penned up in a tiny stinking cell with strange people and no privacy. House arrest would be a luxury compared to that.

"Yes, ma'am," they both said in approximate unison.

"And who is this?" Haania asked.

"This is my mother, Marg," said Zyzz. "She's been staying with us, up from Brzzt, Aphrodite Terra."

"Brzzt? That's a new one on me. Pleased to meet you, ma'am."

Marg nodded. "It's a very small town."

"She'll need to go home, and she can't travel alone," Zyzz said. "May I take her home?"

Haania grinned and shook her head. "Now, that would defeat the whole purpose, wouldn't it? Your choice under house arrest is simple. You stay here and follow order, or you go to jail. Sorry, but you'll have to make other arrangements for getting your mother home, son."

Marg looked concerned.

"Its okay, Mom. We'll get you home. I'll ask around at work. There ought to be somebody that would like a paid vacation on Aphrodite."

"I might have a better idea," Zilla said. "You remember Shirl, Mom?"

Marg was more concerned about the tracking devices and asked, "What are those things for? Do they hurt?"

"Nah. It's okay; just something so they can keep track of where we go. It's an annoyance more than anything," Zyzz said, shaking his leg.

"Do they think you guys are terrorists or something?" Marg asked, laughing. Zyzz shook his head and gave her a *not-now-Mom* look.

"Any questions?" Haania asked.

"Yes. What happens next?" Zilla asked.

"What happens next is you get your things together. You tie up any loose ends, and you say your goodbyes. You'll be going away for a very long time. A bus will be here to pick up you two and your two children at about eight tomorrow morning. That bus will take you to Bayview Intake Station Number Three, where you will report for processing. Bring only the bare essentials, what you'd bring on a business trip, nothing more. Consider yourselves fortunate. You could just as easily have been sent to some Family Protection Center." She had a distasteful expression in her face when she said that.

They nodded.

"Now, you got all that?"

"Yes, ma'am," Zyzz said.

"What time will the bus be here?" Haania asked.

"You said at eight o-clock tomorrow morning, right?"

"Right." Haania gave them three cards. "Call this number if and when you have any questions. Tape one by your phone here and always carry one."

"Right," Zyzz said.

"Well, that's about it. Please don't go anywhere not on your list," Haania said, holding up and tapping her copy with a finger. When she stood up, they walked her to the door. The other cop, who had kept silent during the process, followed closely.

After the cops left, Zilla and Zyzz went out the back door. This was the first chance they had to be alone since their trial. "How was it for you?" Zyzz asked Zilla.

Zilla was silent. Then she started to cry. She told him how Neza had badgered her about Zyzz's involvement and that she had named him as a member. "I figured they knew about that already, so what was the harm?"

"Yeah, they knew that. I already told them I was a member. They were just trying to get you started. Once you named me, then it would be easier for you to go on and give them more names. Did you?"

"No," she said. Then she added "Well, they asked me about Moorv too. But they already knew about him anyway." She felt embarrassed and ashamed. "After that, I clammed up. Neza kept at me, right up to my face with his nasty bullying. I got so upset, I hissed at him! I tried so hard not to, but just couldn't help it."

Zyzz put his arm around her.

"I couldn't help it. It just popped out, like a fart! But it pissed off the judge, and they sentenced me to life in exile." Her tears were flowing now, and she laughed crazily. "If they separate us, they'll pay. The bastards will be so fucking sorry." She kicked the watering can, sending it clanging, tumbling across the yard. "Oh, I feel so fucking powerless!"

"Take it easy, love," he said, gently pulling her closer.

"Daddy, Mommy, what's wrong?" It was Cilnia, with Callibia right behind her. They looked at their mom and dad, bewildered. They had never seen them so upset.

"Oh, honey," they reached down and picked them up. "Mommy and Daddy have had a rough day," she said, sniffling. "But it's going to be all right," she said, drying her eyes.

Kamari, picking up on the vibes, tilted his head, whimpered a bit, and looked at them quizzically. He looked sad and drooped his tail.

"You should have seen Schlive's face when I hissed at Schunk!" Zilla said.

"I hissed too. And you should've seen him when I refused to name names!" Zyzz said.

"Mommy?" said Cilnia.

"Yes, dear?"

"Who's Schlive?"

"Oh, just a Drelb."

"Is he a nice man?"

"Yes, sweetheart. A very nice man doing a tough job."

"Who is Schunk?"

"He's another nice man too. It's just that sometimes good people have to do bad things."

"Why?" asked Callibia.

Zyzz looked at Zilla and said, "Good question, sweetheart. Daddy doesn't know." How can you explain things like this to little ones? They all cuddled.

Next time he was at the school, Zyzz put up a picture and a note that read "Nice snarf—Free to Good Home—Good with Children" on the faculty bulletin board.

Majanga had never gotten around to joining the ESP, nor was she married to Moorv. When he was in the witness box, Moorv named her as a member, and they asked Zilla and Zyzz to be their witnesses at a small civil marriage ceremony. They submitted the paperwork to the Office of Justice, but that didn't work; it was either lost or ignored. She would be staying behind while Moorv was deported.

The last time the two saw each other was when the police bus came to bring Moorv to the Intake Station.

Chapter 28
Last Day on Campus

You never cherish your friends
until the season of farewell.

—From the *Book of Drell*

Members of the Eco-Socialist Party were disappearing.

During the Crackdown, some members of the Eco-Socialist Party and allied groups disappeared with no trace or explanation.

The Ministry of Natural Resource's (MNR) budget was cut. So many lost their jobs at the MNR that the agency could no longer function effectively. The official reason for the staff reductions: budgetary constraints. The real reason: dissent and activism among the staff.

Syndicates tolerated government agencies as long as they remained compliant with syndicate interests. But when staff started to take their agency's mission statement seriously ("To improve and protect the planet's air, water, and other resources for present and future generations"), syndicate execs and their friends in government grew concerned that it might not be good for business.

The Director sent an "All hands message" to everybody in Moorv's program:

Dear Colleagues:

I wish I had better news to share.

This is to inform you that, due to ongoing budget reduction needs at our ministry, the Community

Environmental Education program has been terminated. This will have immediate impacts on this program and our entire agency.

This is not easy for anyone. I expect we'll be using this as an opportunity to celebrate the outstanding work that Moorv and his team have accomplished for the planet and the MNR.

It's also important to recognize all the contributions you have made. Your unit is one of the best in our agency. Thanks to all of you.

Zyzz went in to talk with the head of the University's Forestry Department in her office.

"We hate to lose you, Zyzz, especially over this political foolishness. You don't have to leave, you know. Why don't you just renounce this crackpot Eco-Socialist outfit and disavow your membership in it? Tell the authorities that it was all just a stupid mistake on your part. This would probably all just blow over and you could keep your job."

Zyzz had been listening politely so far. "And stay here while my wife and children are deported? Not likely. Thanks, Zelda, but it's too late for that now anyway."

She looked at Zyzz and slowly shook her head, a pained look on her face. "You're aware that we've nominated you for the University's Educator of the Year award?"

"Thanks, ma'am."

"Drell! I hate to see you go, Zyzz. You've been… hell… you *are* an outstanding teacher. It's been good. Thank you, for all you've done here." She reached out and they shook hands.

Zilla came in with Zyzz to help him clean out his office. Only a very limited number of his things would be picked up by a moving detail from the Space Consortium for shipment to Earth.

"Funny how things can accumulate over a few years," Zyzz said as they were boxing up his stuff. His office was full of plant and insect specimens, fossils, and odds and ends, as well as paintings and posters that covered most of his walls. "What the hell am I going to do with all this stuff?"

"Just take what you need," Zilla said. "There won't be room for much on the ship, they said. It'll be cramped. Leave the rest of it for somebody else."

"Damn, how can I leave this behind?" he asked, picking up his dissecting microscope. It was his access into an otherwise unseen world. He had spent so many hours working with it that it was like on old friend.

"Well, take it. It might make it through to you. Label the box with one of these," she said, handing him a roll of stickers they had been issued, with his name and the words "Fragile: Scientific Equipment".

They continued packing the books, notebooks, and essential equipment Zyzz hoped would survive shipment.

"How can I leave here? So much unfinished work." Zyzz wiped tears from his eyes.

"Well, Zyzzles, they've made that choice for you. It's out of your hands now."

"But, dammit, we're leaving when they need us the most. They're packing us off, along with just about all the opposition to their stupid policies, all the organized opposition, anyway. If they don't change, this whole damn planet is toast."

"So? Do you feel sorry for them? Hey… we're outa here. They've made this stew, now let them cook in it!" Zilla said. "Don't waste your time feeling sorry for those assholes."

"Yes, but… oh, those damn fools."

"I just wonder. Do you think they'll wake up in time?" Zilla asked. "Things are gonna get worse; they'll have to come to their senses at some point. But, then, that's being logical, I guess."

"And then, when it finally dawns on them that we've been telling them the truth, when they finally understand that they need us, we'll be gone."

"They'll know where we are. They'll know how to reach us."

"But they need to make changes now!" Zyzz said. "Or else a whole lot of good people will suffer… die needlessly!"

"No shit. Hey, remember who you're talking to, lover."

They looked out his third-floor office window over the campus below and down over the town to the bay. A few giant, vine-covered, venerable old-growth Lycopod and Calamite trees towered over the buildings and shady lawn. Some children were swinging in the playground. Down on the bay, sailboats were out on the glimmering water.

"Beautiful, isn't it." Zyzz said.

"Yeah. Oh, come on." She put her forearm around him. "Try to look at the bright side. What you... we... need to do is start thinking about Earth. That's the hand we've been dealt, love. Right?" She twined her antennae around his and held him tight.

"Yeah," he said. "Looks like we're outa here."

They finished separating out, boxing and labeling the most important items, before they went home.

The need for fundamental change was glaringly obvious to many, but bad for business. The *profit uber alles system* couldn't cope with the change that was needed. Furthermore, it had imposed such a narrow vision upon the Drelbi that most could see no alternative. Those who offered a better vision were deported. The head, the leadership of the Revolution, was being decapitated. The change that could have saved the planet was being forcibly erased from the agenda.

The last sunset they saw on Venus was on a rare, cloudless evening. From their backyard, they looked to the horizon glowing a brilliant orange-red. Ascending, the arc of the sky imperceptibly changed hue through shades of green until it merged into a dark indigo at zenith. Stars began to appear.

"Which one is Earth?" asked Zilla.

"I dunno. That one? Over there. The bluish one?" Zyzz answered, pointing up at a bright ultramarine star. "I'm not sure. I'm not sure of anything these days," he said.

Zilla wrapped both of her left arms around him and held him close. They stood and watched the sky for a while. One cricket sounded, then another. Soon, a whole chorus was welcoming the night.

Lightning termites were swarming. All termites in a nest are wingless. But, when the population reaches a certain level, it triggers the queen to lay special eggs that hatch into winged reproductives. They leave the nest by the hundreds, seemingly flickering around aimlessly. By emitting pheromones and flickering photo-cells, they seek each other and search for a crack in an old tree or log or a house made of wood acceptable as a place to mate, lay eggs, and start a new colony.

"That's what we're doing, love," said Zilla, gesturing toward them.

"Hmm?"

"We'll be flying away like them. Starting a new home, up there." She pointed up at the bluish star. "I suppose that sounds trite, doesn't it? You do realize that you'll be going to a botanist's dream assignment?"

Standing there quietly, a hundred thoughts bounced through their minds. Zyzz pondered. *Deported. What did that mean, really? Will we ever be able to come back home? I'll never finish my work here. But, then, the way things are going, the way this planet is being trashed, what would there be to come back to? Finishing my projects here? Impossible now.*

"It's time for bed."

"Sweetheart?" she said.

"Yes?"

"I've started taking spermicide pills."

"Yeah?"

"This isn't a very good time to have more children."

Zyzz nodded in agreement and said, "Probably a good idea, Hon." The sunset had them both yawning.

Zilla's mom and dad stopped by to visit with them one last time before they had to leave for the intake station. Mott was looking old and very tired. Zilla had never seen her mother so distraught. Neither looked like they had gotten much sleep. They all knew that this would likely be the last time they'd be together.

Marg kept the girls occupied and out of the way in their playroom.

"You guys just couldn't leave it alone, could you?" Mott said, slowly shaking his head. "Couldn't you be more careful in choosing your battles? You guys have pissed off the wrong people."

"When do you think you might be back?" Glort asked.

Questions with no easy answers. All Zyzz and Zilla could do was shrug, shake their heads slowly, and make palms-up gestures indicating, "Who knows?"

"Wish we could tell you. At least they're giving us joint domicile," Zilla said. "It could've been worse. At least we'll be together."

"Yeah," Mott said. That's something, I guess."

"They're not taking away the kids; they'll be coming with us," Zyzz added.

The four embraced each other; Zilla and her mom were crying. About then, Marg came in and joined the group hug.

"We'll write. We'll send you a letter every week. And you promise to stay in touch too, okay?" Zilla said between sobs.

After Zilla's parents left, Marg, Zilla, and Zyzz sat silently in the living room. "This might be the last time I'll ever see you," Marg said, feeling her tears starting to flow again.

"Yeah. We may never get back," Zyzz said, sighing.

"There's something I need to tell you. Both of you."

"Yes Mom?" Zilla asked.

"Zyzz, your father was Thlarg," Marg said.

"So... why wait until now to tell me?"

"We thought it might be better if you didn't know."

"Why?"

"It might've held you back if you had that to fall back on. 'Well, I'm only a Thlarg, so...' You might have given up when things got tough."

Zilla looked at Zyzz and nodded quietly.

"I always told myself that I'd let you know about it later. And later never came," Marg said.

"Well, thanks, Mom. That might explain a few things."

"Yeah?" she looked into his eyes. "Like, what?"

"Like my tree-hugging ways. Like being so into nature. Yeah. Things like that."

"Hmm-mm. And the Thlargi Education Fund helped cover your college tuition. When you get around to it, you should send them a letter of appreciation or something."

Zyzz nodded in agreement. "Yeah, I hear you. I'll sure do that, Mom."

"I thanked them, but that's not the same as you thanking them directly."

They talked about things Thlargi and Drelbi and family until they were too tired for any more talk, then they went to bed.

Chapter 29
Intake Station

Fire, water, and government know nothing of mercy.

—Old Drelbi saying

When morning came...

Zyzz normally felt fresh and upbeat when morning came, but not this morning.

The sign on the front of the bus read "Bayview Induction Center". They watched through the window as a uniformed Drelb got out and walked up to their front door.

"Damn! They don't waste much time, do they?" Zyzz opened the door before the guy could knock.

"Good morning. We're here for Zilla and Zyzz, with two children?" he asked.

"Yes, that's us," Zyzz said.

"You all ready?"

"Ready as we're ever going to be," Zilla answered.

"Okay, Mom. This is it," Zyzz said quietly to Marg.

The officer waited, watching as they hugged each other for probably the last time. They were all crying. He hated scenes like this and had seen far too many of them. The little girls were holding onto Marg's legs like they would never let go.

"Mom, the taxi will be here soon to take you to the airport. Got your ticket?"

"Yes," Marg said as she held her arms around Zilla and her son and patted their backs.

"I talked with Shirl," Zilla said. "You remember her?"

"Yes, of course," Marg answered.

"She'll be there at the airport where the taxi will drop you off, waiting for you."

"I love you, Mom. Please write," Zyzz said.

"Yes, and you write too," Marg said sniffling. It was hard to break off the hug and let them go. She tried to smile as she said, "Well… you'd better not keep them waiting." Then she turned to the officer and begged him, "Please, sir: take me too."

He'd heard that before too. "Sorry, ma'am. Your name isn't on the passenger manifest. Wish it was."

Kamari came up to Callibia and nuzzled her leg.

"Take good care of Kamari," Zyzz said, fighting back the tears.

"Daddy! Isn't Kamari coming along?" asked Callibia. More tears.

"We've been through that, sweetheart. No, he can't come; he'll have to stay with Gramma."

"I'll take him home with me," Marg said. "We'll get along just fine. Don't worry, honey."

The officer looked at his watch. "Dragging this out won't make it any easier," he said with a sigh. "Let's go."

"Okay. We gotta go," Zilla said.

The four of them went with the officer, got on the bus, and waved to Marg one last time as she stood watching them from the doorway.

At the Intake Station, the deportees' backpacks and other belongings were inspected. Any sharp objects, twine, shoelaces, anything that could possibly be used as a weapon was confiscated. When the corporal asked Zyzz to take off his magnifier and hand it over, he felt like he was losing an old friend.

"What? You really think I could kill somebody with this?"

"Just let 'em have it," Zilla said.

"Keep moving along and shut up," the corporal said. Papers were checked as handprints and retinas were scanned for identification.

When they had finished in-processing, Zilla and Zyzz's group was marched out behind the building to buses that took them to a landing strip, where they boarded a plane. They were to fly south to Cape Salus, located on the equator on the Tinatin Sea on the far western tip of Aphrodite. This was where the Space Consortiums' launch-pad complex was located.

Zilla asked, "Why do we have to go all the way down to Salus, anyway?"

Zyzz and the kids were getting antsy too. "Do you really want to know, or are you just venting?"

"Oh, go for it," she said.

"Well, it's like this," he began, clearing his throat and sounding professorial. "At the equator, the planet's rotation speed is faster. They can make use of the centrifugal force from the spin that way. They can increase payloads by thirty to forty percent and use less fuel. Fuel costs money."

"Okay; go on."

"Well, that's about it. Venus rotates to the west, so they always launch toward the west to use the rotation speed as an extra kicker."

About four hours later, they landed at the Cape, a bustling airport where personnel, equipment, and provisions were transferred to and from the launch pad. They boarded a bus that took them to the base gate, where they stopped and waited while the guard talked with the driver through the window and glanced at the paper the driver handed him. After handing it back, the guard waved them through. In a few minutes, they pulled into a large parking lot ringed by several gray buildings displaying large Space Consortium logos.

"Okay; this is where you get off," barked the driver.

A large, muscular female wearing a blue cap with her rank and the ubiquitous Consortium emblem met the group as it got out of the bus. She wore a mean, cold look on her face and carried herself with a stiff military bearing.

"Toes on the line!" she shouted, pointing to a long yellow line that paralleled the building in front of them. She snapped orders with a steely smile.

"Toes on the line, and shut up!" a few green-capped assistants repeated, shouting.

"Good day," the woman began, and the hubbub quickly quieted. "My name is Lieutenant Schmuck, and on behalf of the Space Consortium, I'd like to welcome you to your Transfer Station."

"Now," she said. "You have a lot to do today. When you hear your name called, step forward to this desk, and be quick about it." She gestured toward a dour, heavy-set Drelb sitting behind a counter piled with a stack of envelopes.

"You will receive a packet from Sergeant Blotz here," she gestured toward him. "This packet is very important. It contains information you will need: your room assignments and other essentials. On the front of the packet is a number. That is your room number. When you get the packet, go directly to your room."

Schmuck continued. "Also in this packet, you will find a schedule of classes and briefings. Do not be late to any of these classes. They're all important. If you need any help finding your way around, ask one of these people with green caps."

Ten uniformed Drelbi in green caps raised their hands.

"You will need to pay very close attention and take notes in your classes. You will find pens and notebooks in your packets.

"Now, for all of you with young children," Schmuck resumed, "the Child Care Center is located in building Number 100, which is that one, right down there." She pointed toward a small building set on a mossy playground behind a fence, uniform gray like all the buildings in the compound. Parents: use the Child Care Center. Your children would be a distraction to yourself and others, and are not allowed in the classrooms. Do you understand?"

All twenty-five of the prisoners nodded or said yes in various ways.

"I can't *hear* you," the lieutenant bellowed, cupping an ear with her left forehand and leaning toward the group.

"Yes!" the inmates said in approximate unison.

"Did you hear something?" Schmuck shouted at her troopers. Some of them were walking importantly among the ranks with their riding crops, thumping anybody whose toes weren't close enough to the line.

"No, ma'am!" the troopers answered, louder than her.

"I said, do you understand?" Schmuck repeated.

"Yes, ma'am!" the group shouted loudly, in tighter unison.

"That's better, thank you," she said. "You people have got to start getting your shit together!"

"One more thing. There's a lot to do here, and we keep pretty busy. You need to select one person from among your group to serve as your spokesperson. We do not have time to deal with each of you on an individual basis, each bringing us your own problems. When you have a problem, you don't bring it to us; you talk with your representative. Take your problems to that person. Then we'll talk with her. Got that?"

The group shouted, "Yes!" in closer unison than before.

"And don't bother her with any picky-ass stuff. No whining! Got that?"

"Yes ma'am!"

"Good. Now, as soon as you select your rep, I want to speak with her. Thank you. Sergeant Blotz." She nodded to the desk sergeant, who started calling out their names and handing out envelopes.

They watched Moorv as his name was called, and he went forward to get his packet. When their names were called, Zyzz and Zilla, each carrying a daughter, stepped forward; Zyzz took the packet that the sergeant gave them. "Room 5-112 is in building Number 5, over there to your right," he said gesturing toward the building's front entrance.

On the way, Zilla quietly asked Zyzz, "Why is everybody around here wearing sunglasses?"

"I dunno," Zyzz shrugged. "To intimidate us, I suppose."

Cilnia asked, "Mommy?"

"Yes, honey?"

"Why is everybody so mean here? I don't like this place."

"I dunno, honey. That's just the way they are."

They went inside, took a right, and walked down the hallway. Just past the bathroom, Zilla whispered, "This place is bugged. Careful what you say." They made quick eye contact, and he nodded.

The door to their room was open. "This looks like a cheap but respectable motel room. Not too bad," Zilla said. She put her backpack and Callibia down on the bed.

"Better than I expected," he agreed.

Zilla rubbed her neck, stiff from the backpack and carrying Callibia, as she took out the schedule. "Whew. We have a class in twenty minutes. They don't waste much time, do they?"

They stopped at the washroom, then walked the kids over to the Child Care Center.

"Can we go with you, Mommy?" Callibia asked.

"No, sorry, honey. You heard the lady. We'll be back soon as we can."

The girls accepted that, but didn't like it.

Zilla and Zyzz got to the class just as it was beginning.

As soon as the instructor was finished with her briefing, Zilla stood up, walked to the front of the classroom, and said to the group, "Okay, listen up. They want us to select a rep. Anybody interested?"

Nobody raised a hand. Zyzz looked at her, and she smiled back at him. Then he shrugged and said, "Guess I'll give it a shot."

"Is there anybody else that would like to represent our group?" Zilla asked. Nobody else said anything.

"Okay, is anybody opposed to Zyzz being our representative?"

Silence.

"Okay, Zyzz. Looks like you're it."

Over the next few hours, they were briefed on a range of topics. There was, indeed, much to learn and remember.

The classes were interesting. In the briefing titled "Earth Time", they learned that it would take two Earth months to get from Venus to Earth orbit. At another class, they were told that they'd be docking directly with

Spacecraft Lena for the flight to the Earth orbital station, then ferried down from there to the colonies via shuttle.

In between classes, they were run through medical exams and vaccinated against diseases that were problems to Drelbi on Earth. The most effective injection sites for Drelbi are in those sensitive spots in their leg or arm joints. Getting or giving a vaccination is never much fun, no matter which side of the needle you were on.

"There are dangers on Earth we can't vaccinate you against," warned a nurse. "Wish we could. It's a dangerous place, full of predators. If they don't get you, some Nasty might,"

"A Nasty?" Zilla asked. "What's that?"

"Parasites," the nurse answered. Lots of those on Earth."

After the last class, they went to pick up the kids and took a walk around the compound. Then they went to the dining facility and got into the long line. Moorv was ahead of them. The food was about what they expected: pretty bad. Moorv, Zilla, Zyzz, and little Callibia and Cilnia sat together at a table with long benches and ate their stew of questionable ingredients.

"This swill is terrible," said Moorv.

"I've had worse," Zyzz said. "You know, the staff here are friendlier than I expected. I was expectin', you know… rougher, colder, meaner."

"Yeah. A few are jerks, but, all in all, most of them don't seem all that bad. I sure wouldn't call 'em friendly, though," Zilla said.

After a few hours' rest period, they went to another building, that looked like it needed a paint job, for their pre-boarding briefing.

"Hello. I'm Technical Sergeant Oxypilus and I'll walk you all through a few things," she began.

"We'll be weightless for a while on the shuttle. You'll have to wear these." The officer walked over to the long racks, picked up a burnished bronze-colored suit, and held it up to show them. "Go ahead and pick out one now. They're all the same, except for the sizes. Starting here on the far left for your children," she said, indicating the smallest ones, "and they go up in size, to your right from there." She made a sweeping gesture. "They're arranged by instar, from children to adult".

"So, what the hell do we do with these things?" somebody asked.

"That's exactly what I'm going to show you," Oxypilus said.

For most of them, clothing was a new and bewildering concept. Uniforms on Venus consisted of merely a cap and boots; that's all the clothing they had ever seen. The nearest most had ever been to a space suit was seeing pictures of astronauts in newspapers, in the movies, or on TV. After a few minutes' shuffling, each had a suit that looked like it might fit.

"Now, you put these on like this," Oxypilus said, and proceeded to show them how it was done.

For the first time in their lives, they strained and tugged to put on clothing. The suit felt constricting and pinched uncomfortably.

"Aagh! I can't breathe. I'm choking!" Zilla hissed. "This thing is plugging my spiracles!"

"Relax, ma'am. Just try to breathe deeply through your mouth. These are required and absolutely necessary on the shuttle. If anything goes wrong between here and the Lena, you will be very glad you have these on. You'll breathe all right, and they'll help keep you warm," she said in a reassuring tone. "If it's any consolation, these suits are a helluva lot better than the old ones."

There was generalized grumbling.

"Now, as soon as you're ready with your suits, pick yourself out some boots." They were all the same gleaming bronze color. After they pulled them on and snapped them to their suit leggings, she asked, "Okay? Good; now, select your headgear, so we can get those on.

While they were getting the right-sized helmets, Oxypilus said, "These are standard issue, used in all the Consortium's inter-planetary operations. They were designed by some of our more creative technicians. They have the faces of some animals that have been discovered on Earth. On the right side, there's a face of a lion, on the left is a cow's face, and that one on the back is an eagle. If you're lucky, you might be seeing the real critters when you get to Earth."

Zyzz and some others had seen pictures of them.

"Now, you put on your head gear like this." She showed them how to put on a helmet, then helped them get theirs on.

The devices scrumpled their antennae uncomfortably, setting off another round of complaining.

"All set? Any problems? Good. I think we're ready to board the shuttle." She led them out the back door and across the tarmac about thirty meters toward the craft that gleamed brightly, copper-brassy in the sunshine.

"Dang, they must really like this amber color," Zilla said quietly.

"Yep. Know why?" Zyzz asked.

"Oh, go ahead professor," Zilla said with a tinge of sarcasm.

Zyzz explained that the material had been found to be superior in reflecting and shielding personnel from dangerous radiation found in space.

Oxypilus heard them, and added, "Yeah, the Consortium's been testing different materials and pigments for years now, and so far, they haven't found anything better than this burnished-brass amalgam. Once you get outside the atmosphere, you'll need this protection."

They went up a few steps, entered, and took seats.

"You attach your air supply like this," she said, exaggerating her movements to show them how to reach up and pull down an air tube from the low ceiling. Now, insert the end into the valve under the helmet's chin-piece, and give it a sharp twist to connect it. Each seat has two of these above it. For those of you with young children, attach your tube first, then attach your kids."

Oxypilus waited a minute while they figured it out, then asked, "Okay, how are you space cadets doing?" Her voice coming through the speaker of the helmet sounded distorted.

Some were grumbling. A few were having trouble, but they were ready soon.

"Now, you with children, help them attach their air-tubes."

They did.

"The first time you put on your gear is always the hardest. It gets easier. Remember, a tight fit is a good fit. Next time, it will be easier."

"Next time? Aaargh!"

"Yes, unless you want to stay aboard the Lena for the rest of your life," she answered. "By Drell, you guys sure bitch a lot, don't you?"

"Now, how are the kids doing?"

In a few seconds they were all set.

"Now, secure yourselves like this." She held up a pair of straps and snapped the two ends of the safety buckles together. "These will hold you down during weightlessness. Otherwise, you could smack your heads. You'll notice that you face backward, toward the rear. Your seat-back will comfortably absorb any pressure from sudden deceleration en route. If you were facing forward, you'd be thrown forward against the straps. Okay. Are there any problems?"

"Everybody okay?" the tech sergeant asked. "Okay," she said. Then she walked up to the cockpit and told the pilot, "All is a go in the passenger compartment."

A few minutes later, the shuttle lifted off.

"We're going to Earth, Daddy!" said Cilnia.

"Yes, but first we're going to get on board the Lena," Zyzz said.

"And then we're going to Earth!" Cilnia said.

"Yep, I guess we are."

For a few minutes, it felt like a huge hand was pushing Zyzz forward against the seat straps. Then he felt his stomach going queasy when they went weightless, and he rose up against the straps. A few passengers got nauseated and used their plastic bags. Zyzz took an anti-barf pill with a sip of water through a straw from the bottle clipped into his armrest. Soon, he started feeling drowsy and fell asleep with his forearm linked to Zilla's.

On their way up to rendezvous with the interplanetary ship, he woke up when he heard the tech sergeant say, "The Lena is a state-of-the-art spacecraft. It's built of a ceramic-graphite-metal alloy complex that reflects radiation, reinforced by and bonded onto a spider-web silk frame. Now, just relax and enjoy your flight." He fell back asleep.

The shuttle ride and docking with the Lena went smoothly. Zyzz was feeling cramped; there wasn't much leg room. When they had all gotten aboard, Oxypilus helped them remove their gear and hang it up neatly on the racks that she rolled back onto the shuttle for the next set of passengers.

"Smallest on the left, largest on the right."

Chapter 30
Trip to Earth

She that traveleth far, knoweth much.

—Proverb from the *Book of Drell*

The Lena was headed toward Earth.

The Lena's engineer engaged the nuclear-powered hyper-drive to break loose from Venus orbit and get a good trajectory for the two-month trip to Earth orbit.

The ship's gravity simulation system created a Venus-like gravity, which gradually increased en route to get the passengers accustomed to Earth's gravity.

The initial excitement soon settled down into a boring routine. The crew followed Standard Operating Procedures right down the line, and there were no navigational surprises en route. Nothing like the movies. The library had a good selection of books and music on micro-disk, and the latest issues of some newspapers and magazines from all around Venus.

"You might like this," the librarian said as she gave Zilla a copy of a recent issue of *Reality Check*, a left alternative paper.

"I thought we weren't allowed to have these?" Zilla asked.

"Oh, we're well-supplied here," the librarian smiled. "We have just about anything you'd ever want on micro-fiche."

Zyzz preferred holding a book and turning the pages. After a few minutes of reading from a screen, his eyes felt like they were frying.

The lack of exercise soon got on their nerves. The ship's mini-gym was a poor substitute for hiking, climbing, and biking in the fresh air. Zyzz would wake up with excruciating leg cramps in the middle of the night, so persistent he had to stand up and dance around. Putting some weight on them helped, but Drell, they hurt!

One morning after a particularly bad night, he went into the clinic on "sick call". Doctor Frumm wrote him a prescription to pick up some potassium tablets. In the privacy of the doc's office, he told Zyzz that he was a member of Physicians for Reform and familiar with the ESP. As Zyzz was leaving, Frumm smiled, winked, and said, "We are everywhere."

The air on board the ship was chemically correct, but the lack of plants gave it a sterile, metallic taste. Tempers flared and arguments erupted over trivial things. The exiles slept a lot.

Personnel Management kept the passengers on a tight schedule. The wake-up alarm—a raucous rendition of an old Empire march—went off on the speakers installed in all quarters in the morning. Nobody could sleep through that, and there was no off-switch or volume control.

Per regulations, Zyzz made an appointment to meet with the ship's chief officer, Captain Bantia. He checked the "Support Request" box on the form before handing it to the receptionist.

At the assigned time on the appointed day, Zyzz knocked on the captain's office door.

"Yes, come in," barked Bantia.

Zyzz opened the door. The captain's office wasn't what he had expected. Paintings of idyllic, pristine landscapes hung on the walls. One covered the observation port. Bantia sat behind a desk, looking craggy and gaunt.

Zyzz walked up to the desk, stopped, raised both his fore-hands, palms open and, facing the captain in the traditional sign of peace, said "Zyzz reporting, sir."

Bantia's eyes had a sharp, mean look. He returned the salute and asked, "So, Mr. Zyzz. What was it you needed to talk about so badly?"

"Sir," he said. "I've been selected as our group's representative."

"Yes?"

"According to the Standard Operations Manual, I'm required to establish official contact with the commanding officer. Just thought I'd stop in to introduce myself, sir."

"So," Bantia said with a sigh. He stretched and leaned back in the chair, hands clasped behind his head. "How are your people doing on this trip so far? Everything to your liking?"

Zyzz caught a strong whiff of sarcasm from the captain. "The simulated gravity helps. We're pretty comfortable, all in all. A bit cramped; not much room in the cabins, but that's to be expected, I guess."

"Have you heard any complaints?"

"No, nothing about the ship, sir. People are missing their homes, their friends and families they left behind. And there's a generally shitty... uh... hostile attitude from the crew sometimes."

"Like what?"

"Just the general attitude." Zyzz couldn't think of any specific examples.

"Any disrespect toward you or your family?"

"No, sir, not really."

"Listen. This is a long trip. Small, insignificant things that you'd never notice back home can get downright irritating after a while on board in cramped spaces. The crew has been trained to remain cool and professional at all times, with zero fraternizing with internees. That's just the way it is. That's the way it should be. Now, if you have any specific complaints of departure from these norms, any personnel acting unprofessionally or playing favorites, bring that to our attention through the proper channels. Got that?"

"Yes, sir."

"All I can tell you is to make use of the library and other morale support activities on board. Warm enough for you guys?"

"Well, it is kinda cold on the Lena."

"Better get used to that, son. Earth is colder than Venus. Food okay?"

"Not bad. Kinda repetitious, but not bad. Better than some places we've been," Zyzz answered.

"Decent food does help with on-board morale on these runs. You've noticed that the lighting here on the Lena is adjusted to approximate Earth days and nights."

"Yes," Zyzz yawned. "Seems like as soon as I close my eyes, the damn alarm goes off and it's time to get up again."

"Better start getting used to it now. You'll have an easier time once you get Earthside."

Zyzz nodded.

"Will that be all then?"

"Sir," Zyzz said, "As you're well aware, many of us on board the Lena are trained professionals. We are chemists, foresters, engineers, physicians, all sorts of skills. I'm a botanist. We're specialists, trained in fields the Consortium needs on the extra-Venusian bases."

Bantia tapped his pencil on the desk calendar pad. "Well, whoopee-ding. So, why in the hell are you telling me all this, Zyzz?"

"We're not criminals, but sometimes that's how we're treated."

"I've been trying to tell you, Zyzz: don't take detached professionalism as an insult. Like I said, that's the way the crew is *supposed* to conduct themselves. You only have grounds to complain if they depart from those norms."

"And," Zyzz continued, "my group and I are concerned about what the Consortium has in mind for us when we get to Earth." This was the real reason that prompted his visit.

"Zyzz, I really don't give a flying fuck what happens to you and your bunch once you leave the Lena. My responsibility is to get your bunch to Earth orbit safely and intact. My duties to you end there. The contract is clear on that." He picked up a paper copy of the contract and held it up. "Listen, I'm in charge of this ship. That's all. What may or may not happen Earthside is really no concern of mine. I have no authority on that anyway."

"But..."

"Have you talked with Tenodara yet?"

"Uh, no."

"Do you even know who she is?"

"No, sir."

"She's the liaison between the Consortium's Earth Affairs Department and the decision-makers on Earth. They're the ones you need to work with, buddy. What happens or doesn't happen Earthside? That's all up to them, not me. I'll phone her secretary and put in a recommendation that she see you for a brief visit. I said brief: she's a very busy Drelb. And son, one more thing."

"Sir?"

"Ask her to have somebody brief you guys on the command structure on this vessel, will you?" he said, slowly shaking his head.

"Will do; thank you, sir," Zyzz said.

Bantia noticed that Zyzz was looking at the paintings on the walls. "Do you like them?" he asked.

"Who, the crew?"

"No. The paintings," Bantia answered. It was the first time in this conversation that he had laughed.

"Yes, beautiful. Scenes of… where?"

"Zimceria. That's my home area. I did them myself."

"You?" Zyzz was pleasantly surprised. "Zim… what?"

"Zimceria. Small town on the east coast of Lada, down by the Aino Sea."

"I've never been there. Looks nice."

"Very nice. Drell, I miss home sometimes," the captain said.

Zyzz looked at him.

"Yes," he went on, "It's one of my few hobbies. I find it a release. This job has its share of stress, believe me. It helps me remember places I love. Painting is good therapy. Helps bring back memories, the sounds and smells, and feel of a place."

Guess that would explain covering up his observation port. After a shift at the bridge, he doesn't need an observation port in his office, thought Zyzz. "Yes, I can see that. You really caught the feeling of those tree ferns." Zyzz pointed them out. "You can almost hear the crickets."

"Have you ever tried your hand at it?" Bantia asked. His expression had softened a bit.

"Painting? No sir, just sketching. Botanical taxonomy, that sort of thing. Nothing like this. This is good. This is art."

"Well, Earth should give you plenty to do in the botany department. The place is crazy with life; crawling with it, son. You know, you guys could have just as easily been sent to Mars or Mercury."

"What's it like there?"

"Mercury is a bitch," the captain said. "No atmosphere to shield ou from solar radiation; daytimes you'll be roasting at about 427°C, and nights get down to 200 below. No. I can't say it's my favorite place. And Mars? Not much better. It was once, way back. They've found evidence of old rivers, seas, liquid water, so it used to be livable. Then Mars cooled off; all the water evaporated, and pfffft! Nothing alive there anymore."

"Sounds like it could get old pretty fast," Zyzz said.

Bantia answered, "Yeah. It's cold there; cold as hell. And the air's bad. You can never go outside without oxygen tanks and suiting up, antennae to foot. Still, even so, it's a hell of a place. Beautiful in its own way."

"Sounds incredible. I'd like to go there someday, take a look around."

"You should consider yourself one of the lucky ones, son. Never forget: if you screw up on Earth, you could still end up there. Easily."

Zyzz just nodded. That possibility had crossed his mind.

"So, which of these do you like the most, Zyzz?" the captain asked.

Zyzz walked around, looking over the miniature art gallery. "They're all really nice, sir. Oh... this one, I guess. Reminds me of home. I can almost smell the swamp, feel the breeze. Beautiful. How long did it take you to paint this?"

"Four or five days. Earth days, that is. It's yours."

"Huh? No, I couldn't. Besides, where would I put it, sir? Things are pretty tight on board. No room."

"You're right about that, son. I'll have somebody deliver it to your quarters Earthside."

"Thank you, sir. This is beautiful."

"Well, I've got things to do, Zyzz. Thanks for stopping by for a chat. Oh, one more thing. While you're here, could I ask you to..."

Bantia walked over and took a book down from his shelf. "Could you sign this for me?" He handed it to Zyzz with his upper right hand, and offered him a pen with his lower right hand.

It was a well-worn copy of Zyzz's *Field Guide to Plants of Central Aphrodite.*

Zyzz said, "Looks like this one's been around some." On the title page, he wrote, "May your wanderings bring you joy. Zyzz."

"It's pretty good, Zyzz. Thanks," Bantia said. "Remember, my door is always open, but please, do follow procedures."

The interview over, Zyzz said, "Well, thank you, sir," stepped out into the hallway and walked back to his room. Captain Bantia: an odd mixture, for sure.

The chain of command on this jalopy was confusing. Zyzz shrugged. He had to stand his ground and play the game. There was plenty of time left before arrival at Earth orbit, and there wasn't much to do on board.

"What does Daddy do?" asked Cilnia.

"He's a botanisshzt," said Callibia. "Right, Mommy?"

"That's right, honey. Now both of you, say 'bot'," said Zilla.

"Bot," repeated the girls.

"Botta," said Zilla.

"Botta," repeated the girls.

"That's right. Now say Botta-nist."

"Botta-nizht," said the girls.

"What's a botta-nizht?" asked Cilnia.

"Hmmm. He's a kind of a plant doctor, honey."

"What's a plant, Mommy?"

"Remember back home? All those green things growing everywhere?"

"Like trees? Are those plants?" asked Cilnia.

"Yes, honey, those are big plants. But moss and ferns are too, and grasses. There are all kinds of plants."

"So when a plant gets sick, does Daddy go visit it?"

"Yes, sometimes he does."

"Does he have it open its mouth and say 'Ahh'?"

Mom said, "Oh, some of the time, not all of the time." They giggled.

"And what are you, Mommy?" Callibia asked.

"I'm a Mommy. That's a very important job."

They both nodded.

"And I'm going to be a teacher someday. Daddy's a teacher too."

On the way back to his room, Zyzz chanced upon Moorv in the hallway. "Hey, man, howzit going?" Moorv asked.

Zyzz told him in a lowered voice about the meeting he had just had with the captain.

"Find out anything important?"

"Not much. Just got sent on to somebody else. They got me doing the Bureaucratic Shuffle. How about you?"

"Nope," Moorv said. "I'm not even supposed to talk with anybody important directly. You're the rep; that's your job. You'd be getting any important information first, no?"

"Nothin' yet."

"No news is good news?"

"Yeah, guess so. See you later."

"Don't let 'em intimidate you, Zyzz. They'll have you dancing like a puppet on a string if you let them."

"We need to stay on good terms with them, as much as that's possible."

"Just watch it, Zyzz," Moorv warned. "These bastards are treacherous." He was emanating strong negative stress and anger.

"Something bugging you, Moorv?"

"Majanga. I miss her so much, man. I mean, how would you feel if they took Zilla away from you? What should I do?"

"Gotten any messages from her yet?"

"Oh yeah, every couple days. But anything important gets blocked out."

"Both ways?"

"Yeah. They delete any information that might be even remotely sensitive. This is 'communication'? Not!"

Zyzz shook his head, understanding. "It's gotta be tough. But don't blame the crew, man. Blame the courts, the judges; blame the Drell-damned system, but none of this is the crew's doing."

"Yeah, yeah, they're just following orders," Moorv said. He was giving off a pungent odor of cynical negativity that stung Zyzz's antennae. "Easy for you to say with Zilla here with you."

"The communications guys would get into a ton of trouble if they broke their orders."

"Yeah, yeah."

"When we get Earthside, go to Personnel as soon as you can. Find out what sort of paperwork you can submit to request that she be sent there. I mean, she's your wife, man. And tell her to do the same thing on her end. See if they censor that."

Moorv nodded.

"So, how's she doing?" Zyzz asked.

"Oh, she's okay, far as I can tell. Pretty bummed out."

Zyzz stepped up and hugged his friend, and Moorv broke down, trembling and crying. "Drell, I miss her so *damn* much, Zyzz!"

When Zyzz got back to the cabin, he asked his family, "And what have you guys been up to?"

"We talked about botanizzhts!" Cilnia said.

"Really?"

Next morning, Zyzz felt a growing hard lump of nervousness gnawing in his guts on the way in to see Tenodara. He needed to be persuasive and firm, yet respectful. Being in the dark, not knowing what to expect, was eating at him. He felt like he had to be polite without being too wimpy if he was going to get what they needed.

The printing on the door read "Liaison for Earth Affairs". He knocked, and a female voice told him to come in. Tenodara was by far the best-looking officer he had seen so far on this trip. She had a svelte build and gave him the feeling that she was in a hurry. They introduced themselves, then she asked how she could help him. She looked good, but no flirt-pheromones were coming from this gal.

Zyzz started to talk about his concerns. "We're wondering what the Consortium has in mind for us when we reach Earth. How are they going to use us? We're professional, specialists in our fields, not criminals."

"Well, technically, you *are* criminals. If you weren't guilty of some crime or other, you wouldn't be on this ship."

"But…"

Tenodara held up her hands, palms toward Zyzz, indicating "peace".

"Now, calm down. Of course," she continued. "We know that you have a cadre of highly trained and dedicated professionals in your group, Mr. Zyzz. The consortium is spending a lot of money to bring you people to Earth, and we are aware that we wouldn't be realizing much gain if we just dumped you off to fend for yourselves. That should be obvious. We'll be giving you all the assistance you need to get established."

Zyzz nodded in agreement and said, "Right" a few times as she explained.

She went on, "I'm working with the Chief Warden of the penal colony, Governor Chaeteesa on this. If I were you, I'd save my breath and talk with her at your first opportunity Earthside."

Toward the end of the interview, Zyzz started to have trouble suppressing a yawn. He told her about Moorv and Majanga's situation, and asked her what she'd recommend. She gave him a form. "He might as well start filling it out now," she said. "He'll have to wait until he knows his duty assignment though, so that he has a location to enter in this box." She pointed to the place on the form. "It'll save him some time when he gets Earthside."

On the way back to his quarters, Zyzz stopped at Moorv's room to see how he was doing and give him the form.

He felt worn out. Time to crawl into bed for a while.

One day a message came over the ship's intercom ordering all passengers to assemble in the cafeteria for a mandatory incoming message from home. Zyzz, Zilla, and the kids sat down just as it was starting. Everybody was sitting around looking up expectantly toward one of several video screens set around the facility.

The words "Emergency Management Central Committee" flashed on the screen, followed by the words "Director Bufo". This message was coming directly from the junta council that had seized power and was now running Venus.

Scattered hisses sounded around the room.

"Bufo? Bufo? That… that…" Zyzz cut himself off when Zilla elbowed him for talking too loudly.

"Slime-ball?" Zilla whispered back in his ear.

The words "Emergency Management Central Committee" appeared again, then the screen blacked out.

"Good day, my sister and fellow citizens. And it is a good day. I know you're busy, so I'll 'cut to the chase', as they say. As you're aware, there have been a few serious disturbances in the past several days at some Family Protection Centers throughout the Empire. This disorder has been instigated and led by a few criminal and disloyal elements who use discredited and false science to lead good law-abiding people astray. We could not allow these disruptions to continue.

"You will be relieved to know that we have taken stern measures to enhance and improve protection of all good citizens of the Empire. We will safeguard the public against this criminal conspiracy. You can be confident that the descent into senseless violence and chaos has been firmly halted. With your help and the guidance of the Goddess of wisdom and mercy, those guilty will be found and dealt with appropriately. Martial law will soon be lifted and orderly, normal life will soon return. I thank you for your cooperation. Together, we will put this behind us and return to normalcy soon."

Zilla and Zyzz suppressed their comments and hissing and watched in silence. They were getting good at that. When they returned to their cabin, Callibia and Cilnia asked them what it all meant.

"Emergency Management Committee," Zilla said. "What a pile of clorm-shit. Buncha syndicate toadies! Those morons are gonna set progress back for years."

"The jerks are gonna undo all we worked so hard for," Zyzz added, nodding.

"Mommy, what's a toadie?" Cilnia asked.

Zilla flushed. Little ears sometimes have big mouths. She'd have to be more careful what she said.

"A toad is an animal on Earth that sits around in a puddle waiting for a bug to fly by," said Zyzz. "And when it sees one, it flips its tongue waaay out, like this..." He flicked his tongue, then reached out, picked up, and hugged Cilnia. "...and gobbles her up!" She squealed and laughed.

The view of Earth grew to gradually fill up the entire observation dome. White cloud patterns swirled over cobalt blue seas. It was so bright that Zyzz wished he had a pair of sunglasses. The "jewel in the crown" of the colonial project. Zyzz watched in slack-mandibled awe from the observation deck as the Lena smoothly decelerated and slipped into Earth orbit.

On the way to the shuttle bay, they were all routed through a communal shower, then through a chamber where they were treated with a disinfectant mist to kill any remaining microbes and ecto-parasites. Then it was suits-on again.

There were five shuttles parked in the bay; three were already loaded with provisions and gear for the colonies, and two were for cargo plus passengers. Zilla, Zyzz, and their daughters were among those who boarded the shuttle for Beta Colony.

Moorv, assigned to a different Earth base to reduce collusion among leaders, was directed onto the shuttle destined for Alpha Colony, in the region that Earthlings referred to as the Congo.

CHAPTER 31
WELCOME TO EARTH COLONY

She that commandeth well shall be obeyed well.

—From the Book of Drell

The last leg of the journey was near.

Soon as the shuttle passengers were settled, the attendant gave the "all ready" signal to the cockpit. The pilot radioed the Lena's bridge, "Shuttle Beta requesting deployment."

"Bridge to Beta One. Deployment sequence initiated, over." The shuttle rolled into position. The air in the cargo bay whooshed into space as the door slid open and the craft dropped from the dock to ferry them down to a base in what they would come to call northeastern South America.

In those days, the Drelbi had two major bases and several outposts around planet Earth. The major bases were located where the climate was most comfortable for Venusians. Category 1 Offenders were added to the ranks of the other convicts sent to earth to work in mines and factories established by the Consortium.

Zilla and Zyzz's shuttle landed and taxied up toward the receiving area, while the flight attendant recited her standard welcome spiel. A few seconds after the shuttle rolled to a stop, they heard, "Airlock pressures equalized. Okay to exit."

When the seat-belt light went off, they unbuckled. "Well, this is it," Zyzz said quietly to Zilla. "Ready?"

"Hmmph. Ready or not, here we are."

It felt good getting up from their cramped seats. Stretching outside at last, taking his first breath of Earth air, Zyzz smelled the familiar odor of humid jungle, but it was different. Sweeter, but with a pungent slap. Suddenly, he felt woozy.

"Whew! I'm feeling weird! You okay?" he asked Zilla, who was also wobbling.

"Whooo!" she said. "I'm dizzy as hell, seeing stars and feeling faint." She grabbed Zyzz's forearm.

"I know what you mean, love."

"Take it easy," a flight attendant assured them. "You're okay. Just stand where you are a few seconds. Breathe deeply; try to hiss and stretch; it'll help clear your spiracles."

Several of the passengers were also feeling unsteady.

"It's normal to feel a bit odd during the change from weightlessness to full Earth gravity." After a couple minutes, the attendant led them toward an entryway that took them underground, told them where to report and how to get there.

"Drell, it feels good to get these damn things off," Zyzz said. It was a relief to get those pinching suits off and breathe freely again. "If Drelbi were meant to wear stuff like this, we would have been born that way!" They hung up the suits on the racks in size order, from small to large. They would be wheeled outside to air out for a while, then returned to the shuttle for re-use.

The passengers followed the arrows down into a corridor to room 200, and took seats. They were met by a burley Sergeant Bolbe. "On behalf of Governor General Chaeteesa and Chief Warden Mulf, I'd like to welcome you to Earth." The lights dimmed, and he went through a slide presentation about in-processing and an overview of the Consortium's projects on the planet.

"As you're probably all well-aware, the Drelbi colonies on Earth are in a tenuous situation. Earth bases are sited and our activities are adjusted to minimize contact with the human population. You'll notice that our buildings are primarily underground and at other well-concealed locations. We have one thing going for us. We can see much farther into the long-wave end of the spectrum than humans can. From tests we've conducted, apparently, their infra-red vision is so limited that they can't see bugger-all in the dark."

Zyzz and Zilla exchanged quizzical glances. Tests? How had these tests been conducted? Had they abducted some humans?

"Is all this subterfuge really necessary?" somebody asked.

"Indeed it is," answered Sergeant Bolbe. "As you will learn soon enough." He continued with his slide show.

Bolbe went through some slides showing the various buildings, burrows really, in the compound. The well-furnished interiors contrasted with their drab, camouflaged exteriors.

He ended with a slide showing the step-by-step in-processing checklist they'd all been handed on the way in, talked about that for a while, then asked if there were any questions.

Somebody asked about the weather. "How cold does it get here?"

"The major bases have been sited in seismically inactive locations where conditions are most like those back on Venus. Outposts tend to be located in less hospitable sites. Subterranean living quarters insulate residents from temperature extremes. You folks will feel right at home here. But there are places on Earth… hell, I'll be honest with you. Most of this planet can get so cold you'd freeze in minutes if you went out unprotected. Be glad you're here where you can breathe easily without having to wear protective suits."

"The Earth people…" somebody said. "How do they keep from freezing?"

"You're 'Earth people' now," answered Bolbe, to scattered, weak laughter. "As for the humans? Insulation," he continued. "They wear skins and furs they cut off from other mammals they've killed, or finely-woven fabric made from various plant fibers. What's odd about these humans is that many wear this fur or fabric even in the warm season, or in places where it's never needed at all."

Bolbe showed the group some slides of humans from around the planet wearing a variety of clothing. "Some of those living here in the tropics wear no clothing except for ceremonial occasions."

"How do they breathe? How do they get enough air with so many of their spiracles covered up?"

"Their respiratory systems are different than ours. They get most of their oxygen through their noses and mouths. Their spiracles are very reduced compared to ours. *Pores* would be a more accurate term."

"Strange creatures," said Zyzz.

"Indeed," Bolbe said. "Intelligent chordates! Evolution has sure taken an odd turn on this planet."

Zyzz nodded.

"Even with all these problems, Earth is the Consortium's best project, by far. You want cold? Go to Mars! At some time or other, many of you will probably be visiting some of our outposts. It can get cold at some of those too."

Several variations of "No thanks!" came from around the room.

"Instead of importing everything or growing food hydroponically, like they do on the Mars and Mercury bases—a complicated affair at best—hell, here we can just eat off the land once you know what's good and what's poison, that is. On the other hand, nothing on Mercury or Mars wants to eat *us*." Bolbe laughed. "On Earth, it seems like it's one damn thing after another." Some looked sideways at each other soberly, wondering what they were getting into.

Bolbe came to the end of his slide show. "Are there any more questions?" There were none. "Okay, that's about all for today. At this time you will all proceed to the barracks to your designated rooms and await further instructions." Then he asked, "Now, which one of you is Zyzz?"

"That'd be me."

"Okay, the rest of you can go."

As the rest were leaving the briefing room, Zyzz came up to talk with Bolbe.

"I understand that you were selected as this group's rep."

"Yes," Zyzz answered.

"You'll continue with that," Bolbe said. "Tomorrow at eight you have an appointment with Colonel Ameles. She's the warden's Chief Adjutant for Personnel. Somebody will be at your barracks to pick you up at 7:40 a.m. Think you can handle that?"

"Yes, sir."

Zilla, Zyzz, and the children were assigned a suite of adjoining rooms in the junior officer's quarters. The communal latrines were down the hall. This would be home for a while, maybe a long while. The higher-ranking officers were billeted down in the officer's burrows, a good distance across the base.

Zyzz set the alarm clock in their room to 6:40 a.m. At suppertime, the four of them went down to line up at the mess hall, where most on base took their meals. The food was the best they'd had since leaving home.

Next morning, a corporal knocked on their door at 7:42. After they got into the zoom, they made some customary small talk, and he asked Zyzz about the trip to Earth.

"Not bad," Zyzz replied. "Kinda boring, actually. Getting into and out of those damn space suits was the worst of it. Everything else was okay."

On their way to Personnel, Zyzz noticed that all the surface vehicles were olive drab, and asked about it.

"That's to make them less noticeable," the corporal answered. Humans were a recurrent topic in their briefings. Their population was growing; they were spreading around the planet, and there'd already been some unhappy encounters. Humans seemed to assume that they owned this planet. They were to be avoided.

They walked past some workshops that manufactured zappers, radios, and other equipment and spare parts to support the Earth bases. Most deportees were employed at these operations around the planet. Projects were underway to make the colonies more self-sufficient. They were still dependent upon costly shipments from the mother planet for many essentials.

"Build Self-Reliance!" was a common slogan, posted in large-character posters with smiling workers' faces above the doorways and on walls in many buildings. Colonists on each planet have different needs. There was little need for zappers on Mercury or Mars due to a lack of predatory animals, and there was no need for oxygen-producing technology on Earth.

Earth bases were already self-sufficient food-wise, but still imported some luxuries. Deportees and regular employees alike used Consortium Script to buy their supplies at the commissary. These company stores were the only Venusian retail outlets on the planet.

They went into the Personnel office and the corporal walked Zyzz to the Director's office.

Colonel Ameles was a short, rotund female. She wore scuffed-up boots and was all business, wasting no time on cordialities. After a curt introduction, she asked Zyzz, "So, who the hell made you the designated spokesperson for this bunch?"

"They elected me. I'm just lucky, I guess," he answered with a laugh.

"As this group's rep, you're getting the first interview, so pass this information along to your bunch. We've been through your files and intend to utilize your skills, experience, and training to the max. Each one of your group will be scheduled for an interview with me or an assistant. They'll be advised about their duty assignments. That's about all for that."

"Yes, Ma'am." Zyzz could almost smell the fragrance of clormshit on her boots.

"Dammit! Relax, professor. This should be good news for you."

"Izzat right, ma'am?"

"Yes. You're going to be lead botanist for this base. I have some of your books," she said, flicking her thumb up toward the bookshelf. "Not bad. I'm no botanist, but I can understand 'em."

"Thanks, ma'am. That's a sign of a good field guide." Zyzz' target audience for these guidebooks was the general public, not just other scientists.

"Yes, I suppose it is." She leaned back in her chair, clasped her hands behind her neck, and put her feet up on her desk.

"And I see that your spouse Zilla was an Education major, eh?"

"That's right, ma'am. General elementary education. She just recently graduated."

"Well, she'd better be ready for teaching; that's what she's going to be doing here."

Zyzz nodded.

"She'll get all the details when she comes in for her interview, but you can tell her that much."

"Okay," he said, adding a smile to his nodding.

"So, what do you think of our operation here so far?" she asked.

"From what I've been able to see so far, it's pretty impressive. You're doing a lot here."

Ameles nodded, then she stood up and started to pace. "Now, try to do all this standing on one foot with one hand tied behind your back."

"Ma'am?" Zyzz looked at her quizzically.

She walked over to a map on the wall. "All this subterfuge gets tiresome after a while. So damn tiresome. And, it's expensive. A royal pain in the ass, is what it is," she said. She tapped her palm with a riding crop she carried around.

"Izzat right?"

"Damn right it is. If we wanted to, we could just erase these worthless humans and have this place and all these resources to ourselves. Eliminate the lot of them. Just clean up this place. But, oh no. Instead, we have to hide like termites in hidey-holes." She shook her head in disgust.

"Whew," Zyzz felt his antennae stand up involuntarily. "Isn't that a little... uhh... extreme, ma'am?"

She pivoted, executed a smart left-face, and paced in that direction. "I don't think so. Some of them have already stumbled through our Area of Operations." She tapped her thigh with her crop.

Zyzz followed her with his eyes, wondering what she'd be hitting next. Something about this gal was making him nervous. "What happened then?"

"Nothing. Don't get me wrong: camouflage *does* help. They apparently didn't notice anything unusual, and went on their way, no problem. Dumb shits. And size matters."

"Huh?"

"Well, we can come and go pretty well as we please without being detected. If we and our shuttles were any bigger—say, human-sized—we'd have a lot more troubles."

"Yeah, that's good. Could we power the perimeter? An invisible fence to zap intruders?"

"Too expensive. And it's too damn wet around here. A perimeter force-field would malfunction in no time. Plus, it would probably just attract more attention. Nah. But one of these days..."

"Ma'am?"

"Well, one of these days we're going to be forced to take some corrective action, mark my words. These humans are spreading like a fungus. Too damn many of 'em. If they keep it up, they'll ruin this freakin' planet."

"Maybe," Zyzz nodded. He didn't like this kind of talk, and didn't know what to say. "How would we do it?" he asked tentatively.

There were a few seconds of silence. "Hell. It wouldn't be hard to launch a few lethal payloads to their population centers."

"Like what? I don't..."

"We could engineer strains of bacteria or viruses and start a few good epidemics. They need that to help bring their numbers down anyway. It would be easy to exterminate the whole mess of them."

"Which could easily backfire and wipe us out as well," Zyzz said.

"Nah. We'd only use human-specific lethal pathogens that wouldn't harm us in the least. "Or, we could do it the old-fashioned way."

"Like what?"

"Wage war on them." She turned her chair and angled her face up toward the skylight.

"Mega-zappers versus… what? Spears and arrows?" Zyzz asked.

"What we need is a good war. Take the gloves off. We could wipe their sorry asses off the face of this planet once and for all. Clean up this place for good. Show 'em who the hell's the boss around here, instead of hiding in these damn holes."

"Its… uhh… something to think about," Zyzz said. *Drell! This gal is nuts,* he thought.

There were a few silent seconds while Ameles shifted mental gears. "Okay, Zyzz," she said, remembering why he was there. "Everybody in your group that's been cleared for this duty station has passed their psycho-social profiles with flying colors. And you've all been assigned work that best aligns with your profiles."

"Yes, ma'am." *If anybody needs psychological profiling, it's this kook.*

"Yeah. To tell the truth, some of you did get some rather... uhh... shall we say unconventional... results in your social and political profiles."

"Yes?"

"Are you mocking me, or what? Is that all you can say?" Ameles barked.

Zyzz's face flashed a quick red. "Sorry. ma'am. I'm listening. Please go on." He couldn't find any comfortable way to sit. *How can I get out of here in one piece?*

"Well, as I was saying," she continued, "a botanist like you is probably going to be a tree-hugger. I can live with that."

"Thank you."

"Life here is pretty simple. We like it that way. You will live comfortably, but you *will* work. There's a helluva lot of work to do here. We need you, and you need us. We see ourselves as a family here. And we have rules that *will* be followed."

"Yes, ma'am."

"Your job? You're now on the Research and Development Team. You will be a squad leader for any botany-related field work."

Sensing this conversation had entered safer territory, Zyzz blew a silent sigh of relief, relaxed a bit, and asked, "How many on a squad?"

"Anywhere from three to a dozen, depending on the assignment," Ameles said. "You'll be given the acting rank of lieutenant. We'll start you out with just a few personnel, see how you manage, then maybe give you more. Your records indicate that you're an experienced fieldwork leader."

"And what's the mission of the R and D Team, ma'am?" Zyzz asked. All this military structure and formality was still new to him.

"The mission of R and D is whatever I say it is. Specifically, your mission is to follow orders. You know something about plants. The Consortium doesn't like to waste expertise. There's quite a variety of plant species on this planet. Many potential food and medical sources. We've tested many species and found many that are useful. You've had some in the mess hall. But so far, we've barely scratched the surface. That's where you fit in. You're to build on that. You will evaluate plants for their fitness for Drelbi consumption. Nutritional value, toxicity, potential industrial applications. Our labs have state-of-the-art analytical equipment. You'll be seeing that soon."

"Yes?" Zyzz said. *This is starting to sound interesting.*

"We want total analysis—stems, leaves, roots, the whole plant."

"This is huge. How many do you have working on this?"

"There's you and two more in your squad to start with, plus yours truly. That makes four. The lab supports you and several other projects. They're stretched pretty thin."

"Sounds like."

"Yes. The batch of recruits that you'll be leading has already started training. Several will be augmenting our lab staff."

"If you don't mind me saying so, you're talking about a pretty big project here, ma'am."

Ameles nodded.

"From what I've seen of this place so far, the sort of comprehensive inventory you're talking about will be way too big for just three field researchers."

"Hell," the colonel said. "There's enough work here for a hundred lifetimes."

"What are the chances of getting more people on the team?" He was thinking about Majanga.

"If the Consortium sees profits, yes. The more profits, the more chance of getting them to invest in this project. Not only food plants. Medicine, drugs. We need total analysis."

Zyzz nodded.

"I'll put it to you straight, Zyzz. We're a long way from the flagpole here. We like that. We don't need—and sure as hell don't want—any babysitters from Consortium HQ coming around here poking their noses into our business."

Zyzz gave her occasional nods and "rights" as he watched her pace around the room, tapping her riding crop against her leg.

"As long as we get good results, we can keep them off our backs. That's where you come in: get out there and find some good stuff."

Zyzz shook his head. "Damn, this is huge, ma'am."

"Yes it is. Start by studying these Standard Operating Procedures," she said, handing him a copy of the manual. The SOPs will help you and your squad get a handle on things. We've made some promising discoveries already."

"Yes? Like what?"

"Well, for starters, how about life extension?"

"Yeah, sure," Zyzz laughed. "What, some sort of fountain of youth?"

"From some preliminary tests on subjects, it looks that way. One botanical compound we've been working on shows some promise in reversing Mak's Syndrome."

Many suffered from that debilitating disease. Zyzz thought of his mother, growing more forgetful and absent-minded. Many elderly Drelbi ended up as vegetables, others as paralyzed blithering idiots. "Whoa! That would be fantastic," he said.

"And very profitable for the Consortium. And that's just the start. This place is a treasure trove of medical and commercial possibilities."

"Are there any carnivorous plants out there?" Zyzz asked.

"Sure, why?"

"Have you lost many personnel to them?"

"It's hard to tell. There've been some disappearances that have never been solved."

"Yeah?"

"Yeah. Actually, they're not much of a real danger here. There are just not that many of them. Very few species and small populations."

"Interesting," Zyzz said.

"Very," Ameles said. She sat down and put her feet up on her desk. "And that's another thing."

"What's that?" Zyzz asked.

"Why? Why are there so few carnivorous plants here?"

"Just an educated guess, ma'am?"

"Yes?"

"It probably has something to do with nitrogen availability."

She nodded. "You can work on that too?" She stroked her right antenna.

"Yes, ma'am. I was doing research on that back home. I was working on a field guide to carnivorous plants."

"Good, good. You'll be going out and sampling plant tissues, working with our biochemists and physiologists to run analyses of plant tissues in search of medicinally significant and other useful botanic compounds. You'll map ranges of plants that look promising. You'll cross-train with lab personnel to learn that side of the project. Oh, yes… and other duties as required," she added with a grin. "Now, about your dependants."

Zyzz's breath caught for a second and he felt something clutching his stomach.

"Relax, Zyzz! Your profile shows that you're very attached to your family. Knowing how close you are to them, it would have been a stupid waste of resources for us to separate you from them. You would have been less productive, if not totally worthless. We want to help you adapt to life here. That's in all our interests. You're here for a long time. I think you'll find that the Consortium is tough, but it isn't irrational."

Zyzz nodded, and listened. *This could be worse,* he thought. *If I was a geologist, I might have been getting this briefing on Mercury.*

"Of course, any breaches of discipline could trigger a re-evaluation,' she added."It's all in the Employee's Handbook."

"Breaches?" Zyzz asked. "Discipline?"

"There's one thing you need to keep in mind. It's a simple thing. You are now the property of the Space Consortium. Remember that. Everything else follows from that."

Zyzz cocked his antennae at an inquisitive angle.

"Number one rule: thou shalt not damage or be careless with Consortium property. Like I said, you are now Consortium property. One breach of discipline would be leaving the compound on your own. Why? There are birds, snakes, all kinds of wonderful things out there that would love to eat you for breakfast, given half a chance. Don't make it easy for them. We've lost too many people that way. You go out that gate, you're on the buddy system, or you don't go. That better become as automatic as breathing. Got that?"

Zyzz nodded.

"This is a dangerous environment. Never forget that. Days are shorter here. Much shorter. It's easy to get caught outside the gates when the sun goes down.

"The good news is that there are no megaraptors here. The bad news is that there are plenty of substitutes."

"No shortage of predators, eh?"

"All kinds. Bats, owls, tarantulas out for a snack—big guys—any of them can make short work of you. Going off base at night is prohibited without prior approval, and good luck with that. There's nowhere to go anyway."

Memories of some near misses he had experienced back home flashed through Zyzz's mind. *Seems reasonable enough, except for that 'property' stuff,* he thought.

"You have an opportunity to build a new and better life here, Zyzz. I suggest that you make the most of it. You're here to help us; we're here to help you."

She sat down at her desk, pushed a button on her speaker phone, and said "Mrzz, send in Zhaw."

Two minutes later, a young female in a loose, white lab coat came in and reported to the colonel, "Yes, ma'am?"

"Could you take Mr. Zyzz down to the lab and show him around?"

"Yes, ma'am."

Zyzz thanked Ameles, then went with Zhaw outside, and asked her, "Would it be okay if my wife and kids came along? I'd like them to see this."

"Sure," she smiled.

He started to jog down to the barracks. "Hey, it's okay. No rush!" she shouted after him, laughing.

He slowed a bit, but kept up a brisk pace. He ran down the hall, opened the door. They were all there.

"Come on, honey. You guys have gotta see this."

"What's going on?"

"Quick. They're giving us a tour of the lab where I'll be working. You too, maybe. Hurry up."

The four of them trotted back to the waiting lab technician and, catching his breath, Zyzz said, "Zhaw, this is my wife Zilla, and this is Callibia, and this is Cilnia."

"Glad to meet you," Zhaw said.

They walked to an entryway with a small sign that read "Laboratories", and went down some stairs to another long hallway flanked by doorways to the labs. Both in the equipment and in the conduct of those working here, this outfit looked pretty professional.

Zyzz was especially impressed with one stop on the tour. "Here," Zhaw began, gesturing broadly at some bench chemists and a Drelb sitting on a reclining dental chair apparently sleeping and getting tattooed by a technician. "We have a team of biochemists and physiologists that are developing a nutrition supplement program. This volunteer is receiving an implant containing chloroplasts. Now, who can tell me what a chloroplast is?" she asked, looking at the girls.

Zyzz looked Cilnia in the eye and nodded at her. She said, "Ma'am, a chloroplast is a cell that contains chlorophyll. It's where photosynthesis takes place."

Zyzz and Zilla smiled at her. He was surprised she remembered that.

"That's right," Zhaw said. "Looks like we have a budding scientist here!"

She continued, explaining, "When exposed to sunlight, the chlorophyll tattoo makes sugars that this volunteer's body will use to supplement his nutrition. This will enable recipients to stay alive through lean times when they can't get enough to eat. All they'll need is sunshine and air. In places like Mercury, where nearly everything, and all the food, has to be imported, this could have significant benefits. Even here on Earth where there's plenty to eat, this may prove useful. One of the problems with this approach is that too many chloroplasts can cause obesity. We're working out a chloroplast-to-body-weight calculus."

"Some people don't like tattoos," Callibia said, looking up at her mom.

"True," Zhaw said. "But for colonists on Mercury or Mars, this could be a life-saver."

Zyzz and Zilla nodded.

"This is a real team effort," Zhaw said. "Some physiologists are working on how to get around the tissue rejection problem. The body sees chloroplasts as pathogens—invaders—and the immune system kills them. The trick is to suppress that without screwing up the immune system. Can you tell me why?" she asked the girls.

Cilnia and Callibia shook their heads.

"So we don't catch some disease," their dad answered for them.

The next day, Zyzz was introduced to the two Drelbi that he would be leading in fieldwork, young guys named Klum and Schnorr. Before they'd be permitted to leave the compound, they had to go through a mandatory briefing given by Technical Sergeant Gorrf.

"Before you go out, make sure your canteens are filled. We have a good supply of potable water here at Beta colony, treated to reduce risks of waterborne diseases. Use this. Do *not* drink the water out there. Might look good, but it's nasty, full of pathogenic bacteria. Any questions about that?" Gorrf asked.

"Got it," they said.

"Each of you will be issued a beeper," the technician said. "That beeper will be set to go off an hour before sunset. Whatever you're doing, wrap it up and head in. Pack plenty of food with you. Always. If you get stuck out there and get hungry, you'll be glad to have it."

"Better to have it and not need it, than to need it and not have it," Zyzz said.

Gorrf nodded and walked over to a counter and picked up some berries, some red, others purple. "See these?"

"Yes," Klum said.

"Look good, don't they?"

"Yes."

"They're poison. Eat a few of these and you're an ex-Drelb. Within minutes. That's after severe cramps, pain, and barfing your guts out. Some birds can eat these with no apparent harm, but they'll kill you." Gorff waited for his advice to sink in.

"As far as your request for access to communications with Venus, yes, we can certainly schedule times when your people can come in individually and sign up to use the commo services. Those opportunities are limited and will be at our discretion. Be aware that there can be up to a fifteen-minute delay when communicating with home. Specialists will be assigned to help you, with orders to use the delays to ensure you don't stray into unpermitted topics. And there's regular mail service. Any questions?"

"How about when Venus is on the other side of the Sun?"

"When Venus and Earth are on opposite sides of the Sun, you can forget it. That blocks all communication between here and back home."

"Any other questions?"

There were none.

"Okay, that's about all for now. See you tomorrow."

Later, Zyzz told Zilla about his chat with Colonel Ameles. When he got to the part about what she had said about needing a good war, she shook her head slowly in disbelief. "Sheesh. Is anybody else talking like this?"

"Beats me. She never said, and I never asked. Hope not."

"Maybe she was just blowing off steam? Some of these people seem pretty stressed out around here."

"What blew me away was how quickly she switched subjects. I mean from horror show to normal, just like that," he said, snapping his fingers.

"Drell! Sounds like she only has one oar in the water. But what if she means it?" Zilla shook her head again.

Zyzz shrugged and shook his head too.

"Maybe she's been watching too many movies. Alien Invaders stuff."

Zyzz just shook his head again and sighed. "Keep your ears open; see if anybody else is talking like this."

Earth took some getting used to. Earth's gravity was stronger than they were prepared for.

"Drell; I feel so sluggish. Weak, you know? I mean everything feels heavier here," Zilla said. She bent over, picked up a pebble, and bounced it in her hand. "Even this feels heavier than it should."

"Feels like I'm wading in swamp water," Zyzz added. "The Lena's gravity simulator helped us some, but, yeah, I know what you mean."

Days and nights are much shorter on Earth than on Venus. The Drelbs' internal bio-rhythms that had evolved over the ages on Venus made it difficult to adapt.

The sun was smaller in the sky, dimmer, and didn't throw as much heat as it did back home. The cool daytime sky wasn't as dazzling as back home, and that alone was enough to plunge some Drelbi into a chronic funk of depression.

Overhead on a clear night the constellations looked odd from this perspective, twisted into different patterns.

The cold clarity of Earth's moon was the strangest of all, rising red and huge, seeming to shrink as it ascended the night sky. Looking directly at this orb didn't hurt their eyes like the sun did. Zyzz and Zilla loved to watch it as it waxed and waned through its phases.

"Lonely?" he asked her.

"I miss them. All our friends. Mom, dad, your mom; everybody," she said. "After all we've been through, this feels like such a let-down here, doesn't it?"

"Yeah, I know what you mean. We've gotta go through sort of a... a decompression, I guess."

Looking up in the evening sky, Venus glowed. Only the moon was brighter. Home: a terminally diseased gem shining brilliantly in the star fields.

Chapter 32
Tough Day in the Field

She who first breaks through the brush
gets the thorns.

– Ancient Thlargi proverb.

The Drelbi attempted communication with Earthlings.

When they left their dying home planet for Earth, the Drelbi tried to make contact with Earthling mantids. They looked like long-lost kin. Like their remote ancestors, they had the gift of flight, but their comparatively tiny brains suggested that little was happening behind their eyes. All Drelbi attempts at communication with their apparent brethren proved futile.

The exiles took most of their meals at the base cafeteria, also known as the mess hall; it simplified things. Otherwise, each family unit would need its own kitchen, which wasn't yet practical. The food was usually good; better than it had been on board the Lena, and much better than back at the Intake Station dining facilities. This mess hall was well supplied with fish, crab, and frog from the bays and rivers, and plenty of fruit. Honey, and the "honeydew" that aphids copiously exuded, tasted like sweet, concentrated splorff, and was a hit with the colonists.

One had to be careful about what was said in the mess hall, and all steered clear of political talk. Zilla and Zyzz tried to maintain some semblance of family life, but under these semi-military conditions, sometimes it felt like it was all slipping away. They were becoming part of one big extended family with all the other colonists.

At the first opportunity, Zyzz went to meet with his team-mates. Klum and Schnorr had been biology students and radical activists back on Venus. Here, they were lab technicians. Both wanted to continue their education and get advanced degrees, but with so many different research possibilities on Earth, and so little free time from their assigned duties, they were having trouble narrowing down their focus for their theses.

Zyzz, Klum, and Schnorr were issued hand-held communication devices. A technical sergeant named Ariusia met them with a welcoming smile and briefed them on how to use the radio units.

"Have any of you ever used these before?" None of them had. Ariusia held a radio unit and pointed at the button on the upper right side. "Okay. You press this button, right here, when you want to say something," They gathered around her as she demonstrated.

"You need to press this button," she said holding it up, "and hold it in like this. You say who you are, and who you're calling. Like this: 'Ariusia to base, Ariusia to base. Come in base. Over.' Then you release the button. When you want a response, you've gotta say 'Over', then release the button and wait for an answer. Somebody will be monitoring you at all times you're out. Remember: unless you say 'over', we assume that you're not finished speaking, so we won't respond. Keep your radios set at channel 12; that's where we'll be monitoring you. Make sure it's set on 12 before you try to use it. Any questions on that?"

There were none.

She put the unit aside, and picked up a geographic positioning device. "Now, have you guys ever used one of these trackers?"

Zyzz glanced at his men and said, "Not much. Go ahead."

"These will help us here at home base keep track of your location," she said. "Each time before you go off-base, make sure your batteries are fully charged, for both your radios and trackers. Got that?"

"Yes, ma'am."

"No 'ma'am' necessary, guys. Just call me Sarge. Okay, so when do you charge these?" Ariusia asked.

"Every time, before we go off-post," Klum said.

"Right," she nodded, then they followed her over to a cabinet, where she handed them their side-arms.

"Now, you've each been issued an electronic directional discharge device, also known as zappers." She held hers up. "Have any of you ever used these things?"

All three were familiar with zappers. Zyzz was more than familiar with them. He'd used his often enough back home, and they'd saved his life more often than he cared to count.

"Now, these are not your typical hardware-store models," Sarge stressed. "These units have been modified for local conditions to amplify the voltage. They can deliver a much stronger jolt than what you might be used to. Keep them ready. Always. Anything can happen out there. Standard operating procedure is to test them on medium and high settings prior to going out, to make sure they're functional. Use the test range by the gate. Then use them only if you need to.

"Keep this equipment on your utility belts," she continued. "Your tracker goes here." She snapped it into place. "Your radios go here, and your zappers here." She clipped them onto their belts to show them where they had to be secured. "And *only* in these positions. Get used to it, so it becomes automatic. You don't want to be fumbling. Sometimes just a few seconds can make the difference between life and death. Got that?"

"Yes, Sarge!"

Zyzz was itching to try out these things.

"Now, I want you to familiarize yourselves with these three tools. They'll help you stay alive. Spend the rest of the day with these things. We've created a familiarization module for you to work through and practice with. That should take you about two, maybe two-and-a-half hours, which we've slotted for you on the weapons range. Might as well head over there now; report to the range control shack. I'll test you on them tomorrow morning. Be at Range Control at 9:00 a.m."

They spent the rest of the day acquainting themselves with their new toys. They went into opposite corners of the compound, radioed each other and the home base radio shack, and checked coordinates. At the weapons range, they did some target practice.

Zilla, Zyzz, and the girls fell into the pattern of life in the Colony. It was relaxed here, and they felt a strong spirit of camaraderie with the other internees. Here, in Earth's humid tropical belt, it felt almost like home to a Venusian. Towards sunrise, the night fog dissipates, and mornings dawn clearly. Then, just before noon, the cumulo-nimbus rolls in, and it rains hard for a few hours. When it clears again, the steamy humidity swirls off the forest floor. After that burns off, it's a sunny afternoon. After sunset, the lightning bugs come out to dance.

"It rains a lot here," Zilla said one morning.

"No more than back home," Zyzz said.

"No way!"

"Don't you remember how it used to rain there... before things started drying out?"

"Yeah, yeah, now that you mention it. It was foggy too. I remember one night you were bringing me home. It was after that awful war movie."

"Yep. It was that bloody one about Drell in the Battle of Gunch."

Zilla nodded. "It was so foggy that night you were walking me home, you couldn't see a meter in front of you. We sat on the back porch swing for a while; didn't talk much, just sat in the mist."

"Yeah. That was nice."

"So nice," she said, putting her arm around him.

Callibia asked him, "Daddy?"

"Yeah, Snuggles?"

"Could we go with you tomorrow?"

"No, not this time, sweetheart. Not yet. Its daddy's first time out, and it's kinda dangerous."

"Oh, Daddy, please? Just me then? I won't get in the way. I promise!"

"What? Me too!" Cilnia squealed in protest.

"Maybe one of these days. Daddy loves you sooo much. You could get hurt. What would Mommy and Daddy do without you?"

"Oh, Daddy."

"Sorry, sweetheart. There are things out there in the woods that would just love to eat you up. Bad things. Besides, I need you two here to take care of Mommy. Now, enough of that, okay?"

"You just watch yourself out there, honey," Zilla said.

Their first few days out on field duty went without any trouble. A week later, Zyzz, Klum, and Schnorr were out in the rainforest collecting samples.

Sometimes, the forest was silent and still, not even a breeze stirring. At other times, the forest clamored with a lavish symphony of sounds; some familiar, others not. A medley of insects whirring, buzzing, and chittering; the croaking of tree frogs; and the chattering, barking, and howling of monkeys. The rich texture of sounds, of the wind rustling the trees, those amazing bird calls, the buzzes and burrs, the creaks and croaks and cackles of so many species—blended together to create a biophony that shared some elements with the forests of Venus, yet was so different.

To Zyzz's ears, the songs of the birds harbored a menacing undertone. Many were insectivores.

Some of the trees here were giants compared to those back home. The luxuriant plant life gave the air a rich, muddy, sweet taste. The unrolling giant fronds of tree ferns and the marshes emanated memory smells of Venus.

So much life here. They stood at the edge of a pond and watched. When the light hit them right, dragonflies, damselflies, and mayflies flashed rainbows of colors from their wings as they flitted here and there.

Mayflies were emerging from their old nymphal skins and skittering about. Unlike dragonflies, these were no threat. Once they broke the surface of the water to crawl up rushes to shed their old skins and fly away, they had a short lifespan. The business of an adult mayfly is to find a mate, lay eggs, and die. They didn't even eat as adults; but birds, dragonflies, and fish ate many of them. Defenseless, delicate, and graceful creatures; it seemed like a waste.

The forest bloomed with a thousand flowers that created a complex and heady bouquet. Zyzz felt like he was getting drunk on it.

"Drell! Will you just look at that," he said, pointing to a tree festooned with orchids in pink, blue, yellow, purple, and shades of infra-red. He went over for a closer look with the magnifier hanging from his neck by a shoelace, issued by base supply to replace the one they had confiscated back at the Intake Station.

The sunshine filtered down through the greenery. The moss seemed to glow from within, the sunlight backlighting the moss-covered branches. A spider sat on the center of its web, waiting. Flies and midges buzzed between the trees and got snagged on the web.

Another spider rappelled down on an invisible silken thread, landed on a twig, and then sat there, waiting. This one had a fat abdomen. Zyzz couldn't resist; he snatched it up and munched it. Tasted almost as good as they did back home, but then again, what doesn't taste better outdoors?

At the edge of a small pond, they watched frogs as they snapped up flies with their long tongues.

Using binoculars and keeping a safe distance, they observed mantids in their comings and goings. Some were typical green mantids; others were camouflaged and shaped like leaves, or pink like flowers. After days of observation, they found no evidence of social organization, nor any indication of any activity that appeared at all intelligent. Except for mating, these mantids led solitary lives. They appeared to operate on a sub-logical, instinctive level. There was no expansion on their heads that would indicate anything more than rudimentary brain development.

"We should take one in for examination. I would love to take a look inside that head," Schnorr said. His major work at the U had been in comparative anatomy and physiology.

"No way. We don't kill anything unless we can't avoid it. If we start something that would be perceived as hostile, there's no telling where the hell it might end up."

They neither heard nor smelled anything of concern. The three had no way of knowing that they had attracted a pair of eyes that was attentively, patiently, observing them from downwind. It drew closer slowly, very quietly. And still closer.

"Right. How about stunning one and examining it under anesthesia?"

"Yes, but not here. Let's bring it in, and let the guys in the lab help. Run a total scan while they're at it. Brain, organs. We need to do that anyway."

"We could do it now. Knock him out with a zapper and bring him in."

"How we going to get it to the lab? No, we need to organize this. We'll need a stretcher and enough volunteers to carry it. But we need to prep the scanner and lab equipment first. Schnorr, start putting together a checklist: what tests we should run, what equipment we need. Then, get with the lab and see what they think are the most important tests to run."

"Once we zap one of these guys and bring him in... or her... whatever, they'll only have a limited amount of time to run through tests and return the subject back outside the compound. Too much anesthetic could kill one of them."

"Right."

A sudden flapping of wings caught their attention, and they looked up. A big, bright yellow and blue toucan with a comically oversized bill landed on a branch of an avocado tree that was loaded with fruit and started eating.

"Good thing those things aren't carnivorous," said Klum. "Look at that mouth!"

A blue and red dragonfly whirred by. Then another monster—a long black one—glistened in the sunshine as it slithered across their path and slipped into the weeds. Zyzz caught his breath and felt his heart flutter.

"Damn! Did you see the size of that freakin' worm?" Schnorr said.

"Did you see that tongue flicking out?" Zyzz asked.

"Yeah."

"And did you see those eyes?"

"Uh-huh," said Klum.

"And scales? Do worms have scales?"

"Nope."

"Do worms have eyes? Tongues? Backbones?" asked Zyzz.

"Nope," said Klum. "Was that one of them snakes, professor?" He had read about snakes. Venus had plenty of worms, but no snakes. No vertebrates were native to Venus.

"Yep," said Zyzz. "They do look like worms though, don't they? But it's a vertebrate. They taste and smell with their tongues. We're lucky that thing wasn't hungry. Some of them get to be six feet long here."

"Drell! That's longer than a dozen freakin' Drelbi laid end to end!"

"Yeah, they molt like us. Shed their skins when they outgrow them. But they do it wide awake."

Then they heard a dry, rattling noise. Faster than lightning, a mantis jumped out from the undergrowth flew to Klum and grabbed him, piercing him in its pincer forearms. Klum's scream was cut short as the mantis bit his head off, and started eating him right on the spot.

"Fuck!" Zyzz said as he and Schnorr quickly pulled their zappers out of their holsters. In one movement they slammed the setting up to lethal range, and both of them fired at the mantis. It went down twitching, sizzling, and stinking of burnt bug.

"Filthy, stupid piece of shit!" Schnorr kicked the sizzling remains. Zyzz was bigger than the average Drelb male, but this thing was a lot bigger than him. He kicked the carcass too, for good measure.

Zyzz got out his radio and keyed the mike. "Zyzz to base, Zyzz to base. Come in, base, over," he said with a shaky voice.

"Base here. Over."

"Yes, we have trouble. A fatality. Bring a stretcher, over."

"What's wrong? What happened? Over."

"It's Klum. A mantis killed him. Bit his fuckin' head right off. Just bring the damn stretcher. Over."

"Okay. We've got your coordinates as [*deleted for security*] Please verify. Over," said range control.

Zyzz verified their location, then added. "Better make that two stretchers… and an armed guard. There are probably more mantises around. Over."

"Two? Drell! What the hell's going on now? Over."

"Tell the lab to prepare for a dissection of the biggest freakin' mantis you've ever seen. I want to cut this bastard up into little pieces. That's what the second stretcher is for. Over," Zyzz said.

Then he told Schnorr, "It's a damn good thing we had these zappers."

"Sure didn't do Klum much good." Both of them had a bad case of the jitters.

It had been a long day. Too damn long. When Zyzz finally got home, he broke down and wept, now that he finally could. Zilla came over and stood close. "I heard what happened, honey," she said quietly. "How ya doin'? Are you okay?" She wrapped her arms around him.

Zyzz held her tightly, his tears flowing. "Hell, not a scratch on me. But we lost a good Drelb today. So young."

"Its just awful."

"Drell. What have we gotten into? What in the *hell* have I gotten you into?"

"It's not your fault, honey."

They held each other a long time.

Some volunteers wrapped Klum's headless remains in a blanket. Next morning, out just beyond the perimeter, some co-workers dug a hole under a tall bush and gently laid Klum down into it. About fifty colonists came to stand around the grave and pay their respects. A few troops stood at attention holding their zapper-rifles at shoulder-arms. Standing next to Zilla was Klum's widow Vespa, stunned and quiet. She and Klum had no children, and she was feeling very alone. Zilla put an arm around her and asked, "Want to come stay with us awhile? It's okay."

Vespa turned to look into Zilla's eyes and nodded.

Zyzz began by saying, "We're gathered here to pay last respects to our friend and colleague, Klum. He was young; most of his life still lay ahead of him. Like the rest of us, he was not here by choice. He gave his life unselfishly for the advancement of science and understanding. He died not in vain. Amen."

He picked up a handful of soil, and saying, "From the body of the Goddess we came," threw some down onto Klum's body. "In the spirit of Drell, we live," he threw some more soil into the grave. Then, with the words, "To the calm pool of the Goddess and all her saints and prophets, we return to rest," he threw in the rest of the dirt and brushed off his hands.

Zyzz continued, "Until we are reborn again, in the infinite cycle of birth, death, and rebirth, I hear my mother calling, and I must be on my way. Amen." Several voices joined his to finish those old words. Vespa was crying hard now, and Zilla wrapped both her right arms around her.

Zyzz looked around at those gathered, and nodded to Colonel Ameles to say her piece of the ancient ceremony. Suddenly he couldn't breathe. He tried to breathe deeply, filled the bottom of his lungs, then the middle, but that just started him coughing and gasping. *What the hell is wrong with me*? he wondered. The others looked at him in pity.

Ameles said a few words about Klum giving his life for science and the Empire, that he had not died in vain and that he would join the honor roll of the brave souls who dared high-risk, but necessary, exploration.

Something was seriously wrong with Zyzz. He collapsed and Zilla caught him in her arms. "Sweetheart! What's wrong?" He held onto her, just shaking his head.

People assumed that Zyzz was simply overcome with grief. As Zilla walked him back to their apartment, gasping, a few more people made brief comments amid their weeping, then walked away from the grave, while a couple volunteers shoveled soil and leaves over the body.

Zyzz, Schnorr, and a few other technicians dissected the mantis. It revealed what they already strongly suspected: a tiny, rudimentary brain with very little gray matter, and well-developed wing musculature, compared to their vestigial Drelbi wings.

Zyzz probed around in the oral cavity. "Hmm," he said, pointing the probe at the base of the mantis' mouth. "Look at this."

"Whatcha got? I can't see anything," Schnorr replied.

Zyzz looked up at them and stuck his tongue out.

"Well, I'll be damned," Schnorr said. "No blinkin' tongue!?"

"It makes sense," Zyzz said. "Think about it."

"Okay."

"These guys never developed a tongue. And they lack any kind of thumb. Besides having a much smaller brain than we do, look: this guy isn't really much like us, is it?"

The techs shook their heads slowly. "Like our ancestors," Klum said.

"Very remote ancestors," Zyzz said, wheezing. "For some reason, the Goddess decided to give us two things: an opposable thumb and a tongue. Think about it. Our thumb gave us the ability to use tools. These Earth mantids never developed that. And our tongue gave us the ability to... what?"

"Well, to communicate, right?" another tech said.

"So we have two things coming together, guys. A tongue, which for whatever reasons developed in the first place, enabled us to develop better communication. Not just rubbing our legs together like crickets, but real, high-level communication. And a thumb, which allowed for tool usage. Can you see the implications?"

"Yeah." Schnorr said.

Guzz, one of the other technicians, added, "These two developments caused a huge punctuation in our evolution, and bumped us up to a new equilibrium, right? Over a comparatively short period, brain size increased over generations. The different groups competed, and our ancestors had a huge competitive advantage."

"Right," Zyzz said. "Our line was the winner. Tongues and opposable thumbs. Once we had these two things going for us, we could develop a higher level of communication. That led to social, coordinated labor, then to civilization and industry."

"For better or worse?" Schnorr asked.

"Good question, Schnorr. Damn good question," Zyzz said, then went into a coughing spell.

All the other organs were remarkably similar to those of the Drelbi. This mantis was a large one, about 11 cm. long.

Were the Drelbi the only intelligent invertebrates on this planet? Klum's death threw a blanket of fear over them. This planet was full of lethal killers that struck without warning.

Vespa was totally dazed and lost. She needed deep, strong comforting, and Zilla offered her the only solace she could. She held her as Vespa sobbed against her thorax.

The five went down into Zilla and Zyzz's burrow. "There's not much room here. Take our bed; we'll take the girls', and they can sleep on the floor," Zilla said.

"No," Zyzz said. He was still wheezing. "You two take the bed; I'll be fine on the floor."

Vespa shook her head. "You really need some rest, Zyzz. We'd all better share the bed."

That night, Vespa slept with Zilla and Zyzz. It helped pull Vespa out of the pit of despair. The bonding was welcome and felt right, like a painful place that needed to heal. The planet felt a bit less threatening and lonely, and she decided to stay with them awhile.

Other than Zyzz, Zilla had been friendless since leaving Venus. Vespa reminded her of Shirl, who she missed powerfully. Life without Shirl had left an empty place she would never fill. Vespa helped.

There is a noun in the Drelbian language: *Schluzz*. Of all nouns, it is the one that comes close to summarizing the most precious thing in the galaxy. It is intangible, and can't be measured. It defies calculation. It has no weight, but can be light or the heaviest thing. It has no size, no volume, no speed, but it can be huge and faster than lightning. It has no limits. It comes in all kinds, colors, shapes, and sizes. It has no monetary value, but nothing is more precious. Once you find it, you never want to let it go. It is incredibly complex and defies translation. The closest word in English is *Love*.

One morning, Vespa stayed behind while Zilla, Zyzz, and the girls went for breakfast at the mess hall.

On the walk home, Zilla told her daughters, "You're going to have two mommies for a while. Vespa will be living with us."

Callibia and Cilnia were wide-eyed and nodded.

"How do you feel about that?" Zyzz asked them.

"I like Vespa; she's nice," Callibia said.

"How about you, Cilnia?" Zyzz asked.

"Two mommies? Sure: that'll be neat!" she said.

When they got home, the girls gave Vespa a hug, and she looked at Zyzz and Zilla. They nodded and smiled back at her.

This planet had new experiences and species without number to discover and describe. A lifetime of exploration lay ahead of them. Enough for a hundred lifetimes, unless cut short by one of the countless predators in this place. It was heaven. It was hell. It was a huge, incredible challenge.

Not all killers on this planet were predators.

Zyzz was the first to come down with it. He first noticed something wasn't right the day after Klum was killed. A persistent shortness of breath and a bad cough, but no sneezing.

Zilla looked at him, worry all over her face.

"I'm okay; it's just a cold. Some kind of virus. Stop your damn fussing. I must've just caught a chill somewhere."

"Okay," she said. "You're sounding pretty bad, you know."

"I'll take some more of these anti-histamines," he said, taking some out of the pill bottle and tossing them down with a drink of water.

"You need some rest, honey. Why don't you take a nap?"

Zyzz stayed in bed until he couldn't sleep anymore, but still felt too tired and weak to get up. The pills didn't help much.

Then Zilla noticed she couldn't hiss. Normally, if she accidentally dropped something, she'd hiss involuntarily, without thinking. But now, even when she tried, she was so congested she could hardly breathe. In a couple days, any physical effort, even walking, would start her, Vespa, or the girls struggling for air.

"What the hell is this shit?" she coughed.

"Beats me. Just can't seem to catch my breath," he rasped.

"Honey, I'm going to take you to the doctor, if I have to carry you," she said.

"Yeah, I suppose I'd best go in. *All* of us."

"We gotta go see Doctor Gorp, Vespa," Zilla said. "Could you stay here with the kids?"

"Sure; no problem. Tell him I'll be in next."

"Something's seriously wrong, doc, whatever it is," said Zyzz when Zilla and he were talking with Dr. Gorp at the base clinic. "Our two kids and Vespa are starting to come down with it too."

Gorp nodded and took a sampling stick out of a drawer. "I'll need to take a sample. Now, this won't hurt," he said. He gently stuck the stick into one of

Zyzz's neck spiracles and scraped the sides. Then he walked over to a microscope and put in the sample. "Hmm. Take a look at this," he said.

Zyzz looked through the scope at a squirming mass of eight-legged creatures. "Holy jumping Drell! Spiders!"

"Yes," he said. "Spiracle mites, to be more exact. These spiders don't make webs and catch their food. These kill you more slowly. They're fairly common parasites here. They infect your spiracles, suck your blood, get fat, plug up your airways, and choke off your air supply."

Zyzz nodded. "Damn! I should've realized it was something like that."

"Sheesh: ugly things, aren't they?" said Zilla, looking through the scope. "So, how do we get rid of them?"

The doctor picked up a prescription form and started filling it out. "Let's see. Two adults and two kids."

"Make that three adults. Vespa's got 'em too," said Zilla.

"Doc, it seems that every time I sneeze, you hand me more pills to take," Zyzz said.

"Not this time, Zyzz. This is for soap," Doc answered. "Okay, three adults, two children." He handed Zilla the prescription slip. "This should be enough. Pick it up at the pharmacy. Each one of you, the kids too, take a sudsy shower with this stuff. Rub it into all your spiracles. Next day, do it again. They should be gone within a week. If it doesn't work, if this hasn't cleared up in a few days, call me. Okay?"

They walked home to get Vespa and the girls, then they all went to the barracks shower room. They soaped each other up into a lather, getting the giggles and making funny hats with the suds.

The miticide shampoo worked quickly; they all slept much better that night.

Chapter 33
Eco-cide

A small spark can start a forest fire.

—Ancient Thlargi proverb

A letter from home.

The only glaciers on Venus had been small alpine ones. When they melted, it caused a slight rise in sea levels. A few years after they disappeared, evaporation caused sea levels to drop back to former levels, then lower and lower. Shorelines the world over receded to record low levels, then kept falling.

Since the industrial revolution, massive amounts of sulfur and carbon dioxides had been dumped into the air, where it combined with water to form sulfuric and carbonic acids. It returned to Venus' surface as acid rain. As ocean waters grew more acidic, coral reefs and plankton—the base of life in the seas—started dying out. Crabs, oysters, clams, lobsters, ammonites—all species that people depended on for food—dwindled into scarcity.

All over Venus, the lakes, swamps, and bayous shrank. Even the oceans were disappearing at a quickening pace. As the seas evaporated, the fishing fleets were left high and dry. Little remained to catch anyway. With each drop of water that evaporated, the shorelines receded and hope also evaporated.

With the forests gone, there were no braking mechanisms left. The greenhouse effect spiraled out of control.

Water vanished into the sky, where it combined with carbon and sulfur dioxides. Rain evaporated back into the air before it could even reach the land's surface. The fertile fields of the New Agricultural Zones turned into deserts. Food prices and hunger surged in tight tandem.

"Yes, things are warming up a little, that's plain to see," the authorities said. "But this is all part of a natural cycle. There's nothing we can do."

Epidemics of deadly tropical diseases spread from the Hotlands into more urban areas.

Money lost all value. One female told a TV news reporter, "We worked all these years scrimping and doing without, to save for retirement so my husband and I could live out the rest of our lives in comfort and security. All this is worthless now!" she said as she tossed a handful of paper kecks into the air.

On a news special called "Crisis!" a Drelb said, "What we should have done is save the forests and save the air. We should have been banking real wealth. We should have switched over to solar power and left the damn oil and coal in the ground! But, oh no: instead, we burned all that crap and dumped tons of CO_2 into the air. Now the locusts are coming home to roost. May Drell save us from our stupidity!"

People packed their zooms with food and whatever other necessities they could grab and left their homes and shops behind. Crowds of enraged, frustrated Drelbi smashed windows and looted stores as they escaped to the cooler uplands. Many had no destination in mind as the hot lowland cities emptied out.

Those without zooms went on foot. Most zooms were already crowded as people swarmed toward higher country, so it was futile to try to hitch-hike. Mountain towns were soon overcrowded and overwhelmed. Many of the sick and elderly died. Many packed into churches and prayed to the Goddess, pleading for divine intervention.

"Listen: can you hear them? The sea, the land? This planet is crying and dying." Sister Boff led prayers at her packed church. "Oh Goddess, creator of all things seen and unseen, thank you for sending us your prophets to guide and teach us. Please forgive those who are fouling the beauty of your creation and bringing your garden to ruin. We pray that you save us now from the calamities and stupidity of the misguided ones."

Then the fires began.

At first, Zilla and Zyzz wrote letters to their parents and friends every couple weeks, but that tapered off. One morning after a mandatory formation, Zyzz stopped off at the mail room. The clerk handed Zyzz a letter. It was from Mom and, as usual, had been opened by the censors.

He read it, and the tears started. He folded it back up. He'd read this one to Zilla.

> Dear daughter, son, and dearest Callibia and Cilnia,
>
> I trust that things are going well for you and your friends on Earth. As you've probably heard, things haven't been going so well here.
>
> We've been having some crazy weather. Would you believe hurricanes? We never have hurricanes in Brzzt!
>
> I talked with your friend Guzz the other day. You two go way back. I remember you played together as children. He was a very good, dedicated fire-

Drelb. But they laid him off, along with many other firefighters. "Budgetary problems," they said. These were professionals. They knew the business!

Well, you've probably heard something about the horrible fires we've been having. One started on a hot afternoon when a rusty old power line snapped, sparking a blaze in the underlying brush.

There've been cutbacks in all the local Emergency Service and Public Safety Departments, and that's resulted in crippled response efforts. They tried, but volunteer firefighters were just no substitute for well-trained and equipped professional firefighters. Most of them had been laid off! [*Some words had been blocked out here.*]

Guzz did what he could to help the volunteers, but before they could even pull on their protective gear, the flames were already out of control. In a few hours, a huge dark thundercloud appeared, formed by the vaporized sap of thousands of trees. It towered over the mountains. Drell! You should've seen it!

Fireballs, windborne ash, and lightning strikes from the thundercloud started more fires twenty miles ahead of the fire front. Due to the shrinking water supply, there's not enough to mount more than a hopeless, pathetic firefighting effort.

Meadows, forests, and even swamps are on fire, burning out of control. Fire storms incinerate buildings. Fire tornadoes tear apart buildings, and scorch all that had been alive and green. Stately, majestic, ancient trees—ferns centuries old—are gone in minutes. So, so sad.

The governor came on the radio, warning people of the extreme hazard, and advising them not to panic. He didn't know, so he couldn't tell people that staying meant certain death in many places. Communities, built with only one way in and one way out, become traps, with no way out.

Sometimes, the smoke is so thick I can hardly breathe. People are suffocating from smoke and fumes more than are actually burning.

I fear that we haven't seen the last of these fires.

People are getting sick from drinking contaminated water. Supplies of safe water are drying up, and the big cities are hurting. Even the springs around Brzzt are drying up!

I miss you so much. I long to be with you, but am sure that's not very realistic. Even if they allowed it, the strain of interplanetary flight would probably be too much for me.

Where has time gone? Where did my youth go? Looking down the long road into the mists of yesterday, it has all flown by so, so fast, my son.

Do you remember that fellow that got kidnapped a few years ago? It was in all the papers and on TV. His name was Bufo. [*The censors had blacked out the next two lines*] He and his family all were killed in a terrible fire. His house, along with most of the other places in his hoity-toity high-security gated community? "Gone in minutes," it says. I have the newspaper right here.

Isn't it ironic how, if I would have been an active member of the ESP or some other radical group, we might have all been together now on Earth! [*One line blacked out.*]

I'd usually say that I wish you were here with me, but I can't say that now. Not anymore. It would break your heart to see all the forests and bayous that you love so much, go up in smoke. The situation here is grim, my beloved. If things continue as they are, it may well be the end of all of us, and all we have grown to love and take for granted. I have never seen it so incredibly hot.

I hope this letter gets to you.

With all my love,

Mom

The letter confirmed what they had been hearing.

Only a few left on Venus could be evacuated to safer places. A few insisted on staying, denying this was really happening, right up to the point of death, in hopes of things getting better, or praying and waiting for divine intervention.

Thousands traveled to the Space Consortium's offices in the cities and to the gates of the bases, in hopes of getting away, and offering their now-worthless money or begging. The spacecraft leaving Venus in those last days could hold only a tiny fraction of the desperate multitude.

The fires did get worse, and the greenhouse effect kicked into its final, runaway phase. The seas evaporated. The sulfur locked up in living and fossilized organisms and compounds was liberated by the fires and went up into the atmosphere, where it reacted with water vapor to form raging clouds of sulfuric acid. All the carbon in living and fossil biomass went up in smoke.

The swamps released their stores of methane, which made things worse. In place of lush, green forests and swamps, there were now parched, dead deserts. Nose-biting rains of sulfuric acid fell out of the hellish, churning cauldron of the angry sky. Rains of sweet water became a fond memory, replaced by death from above.

The clouds allowed the sun's heat to reach the surface, but didn't allow it to escape. The compounding heat raised temperatures on Venus to 7500K (477° C; 890° F.) year-round; hot enough to melt lead. Barometric pressures on the planet's surface increased by about ninety times. That's a pressure like that found one kilometer below the ocean's surface on Earth. There is no breathable, free oxygen left on Venus; it's all now locked up in sulfuric acid and carbon dioxide.

The space stations orbiting Venus held on for a while, but were unsustainable. Drelbi were taken to the colonies before supplies ran out. With no propulsion fuel, the stations soon lost orbital integrity; most crashed on the surface, and some were lost to space.

Things went quiet. No word from home for many Earth-years. Then one day, an all-hands announcement went out ordering everyone to assemble for a special meeting.

Colonists and refugees on three planets watched the coverage of the Venera 13 and 14 Soviet missions to Venus. The videos were intercepted and relayed via Drelbi communication satellite. Zilla, Zyzz, Vespa, and the kids watched the coverage from video-screens in the crowded mess hall, which by then had evolved into the base's Community Center. Zyzz felt a slow, sick feeling churning into nausea as he watched the broadcast. Things were far worse than he had feared. Little remained that was at all recognizable. There, on the hills where lush forests once hummed with life, lay bleak desolation.

Scattered voices of anger erupted from around the mess hall.

One Drelb stood up and kicked over the table where he had been sitting, scattering dishes and food on the floor. "Okay, what the fuck is this—some kind of sick joke?"

"Yeah, come on: what is this shit? Mercury? Mars?" asked another.

"Oh, it's real," Zilla said with a dazed expression. "This is Venus. This was home." She was standing, but now, feeling her knees giving out, she reached for Zyzz's fore-hand. He put a fore-arm around her and pulled her down to sit on the chair. He was feeling like he had been punched hard in the belly.

As usual for her, Colonel Ameles came into the mess hall late from her office. "What are you looking at?" she asked Zyzz.

"Looks almost like… no… Holy Mother of Drell, it's hard to tell, ma'am."

Most watched the horror show in numb disbelief. If you knew where to look, you could barely see traces of irrigation canals, streets, bridges, and roads, as even those were melting away. Fires and subsequent rains of sulfuric acid had eaten away all traces of the wooden structures and dissolved all the metalwork and concrete of the cities. It was like a gigantic eraser had come down and rubbed out everything.

It got so hot on Venus that carbonates in rocks sublimated directly into the atmosphere, where the carbon mixed with oxygen to form even more CO_2.

Oceans: gone. Boiled away, to combine with sulfur dioxide to form even more sulfuric acid. Trees, forests: gone. Nothing to be seen but ugly naked hills.

All this was crushing Zyzz. "This is fucking real," he said, his insides jostling with loss, anger, and a sickening sorrow. "Shit; that happened fast." His antennae drooped, framing his face. All the quantitative changes added up and brought Venus to a tipping point—a huge qualitative change.

Memories good and bad bounced around in his head. Those greedy, ignorant bastards had killed a planet. And they had escorted everybody left on Venus into the annihilation oven of an eco-apocalypse.

Brzzt? Bayview? Nothing left but memories. Mom? Shirl, Majanga; all their friends, all his students, past present, and future? Future? There *was* no future.

A world of music: gone. All art burned into cinders.

"You know what worries me?" Ameles asked Zyzz.

"Whuzzat?"

"The Mercury and Mars colonies. Ever think of them? All their supplies come from… came from Venus. How the fuck are they gonna survive now?"

As they talked, their eyes stared at the screen in a fascinated and horrified disbelief.

"Drell!" Zilla said. "What food we produce here on the Earth colonies is enough for us, but exporting it to other planets?"

"Mercury folks will have to leave; most will probably be coming here, some to Mars," Ameles said. "They're growing most of their food on Mars now."

"Soil's good on Mars," Zyzz said. "And their water generation projects are doin' well. Their food-production is in pretty good shape."

Ameles nodded. "Yeah; but Mercury? They're probably tightening down on food rationing already."

Zyzz shuddered at the thought of being trapped in a slow starvation scenario in some mining colony in that barren rock. "How much time would you give them, ma'am?"

"No more than a month."

"That's Earth months?" Zyzz asked.

"Yeah. Not much time; they'd better start evacuating. Get their butts out of that dump, now."

Zilla and Zyzz nodded.

"One thing for sure," Ameles added.

"Whuzzat?"

"None of us will be seeing any traffic coming from home anymore, food or anything. This is deep shit," Ameles said. "They must be having one helluva time at Consortium headquarters trying to figure all this out."

"What have you heard so far?" Zilla asked.

"Bugger-all," Ameles shrugged. "The Consortium holds their cards close to their thoraxes."

After the broadcast, people drifted away.

When he finally got alone with Zilla, Zyzz said, "I dunno. I just dunno, Zill. If we all would've just tried harder. If I hadn't been so into my work and tuned out of everything else for so long. If I would've gotten into politics sooner instead of holding back. If I had woken up sooner..."

"I know. Maybe if all of us had tried, each of us a little harder, it might have made a difference. But, shit, after you started coming out of denial, you *did* try, honey."

"Yeah, but if…"

"Fuck this 'if, if' clormshit. You did a helluva lot more than most did! Soon as you started to see what was happening, you were in there, love. Most of those syndicate clowns never came out of denial until their miserable asses were frying, "Zilla said. "Drell, how I loathe their stupid, greedy guts!"

Zyzz felt torn by conflicting emotions, like he was being stretched from different directions. "What the hell were we thinking? We couldn't change anything."

Zilla looked at him. "C'mon. You're kidding, right?"

"Kidding?" He looked up at her with teary eyes. "Hell, Zilla: you saw it. Nothing is left! Nothing! Nobody! Why bother with anything anymore? What the hell's the point? It's all gone, Zilla!"

Zilla kept quiet a while, listening. If he didn't vent, she knew he'd explode. Then, when he ran out of breath, she began quietly, "Stop feeling sorry for yourself. You did enough to get us deported, didn't you? You got our butts out of there. We could've been burned alive, for Drell's sake!" she said, holding him, looking into his eyes and shaking her head. "We are alive, dammit! You saved our lives. Now, stop dragging your ass around, you big, big… lunk!" She ran out of words and broke down and wept. They held each other, sobbing, and sank to the ground.

Zyzz drew in a deep breath and let it out slowly. "You woke me up, Zilla. If it wasn't for you, we'd all have been fried."

"This is home now," she snuffled. "And it's really not that bad a place."

"We'll probably be getting some new neighbors," Zyzz said.

"Yeah?"

"Sure: they'll be clearing out the Mercury bases."

"Yeah; I haven't given 'em much thought," Zilla said. "We've all been so occupied with our own problems."

"Most of them will be coming here, it makes more logistical sense than sending 'em to Mars. I wonder how many," Zyzz said.

"Try not to let it bother you. Ameles is right, honey. Let Consortium headquarters figure all that out."

"This is our home now," she added.

Chapter 34
Life on Earth

Don't undo your bootlaces
until you have seen the river.

—Old Thlargi saying

The colonists were adjusting slowly to change.

The Great Change back on the home planet led to changes in all her colonies.

When the colonists first arrived, they found that the base commissary was surprisingly well-stocked, with everything they needed to get by comfortably. But when regular flights between Venus and Earth were disrupted, there was a run on supplies. Anything imported quickly disappeared. If it couldn't be produced on Earth, it was no longer available. Just one of many examples: No more mandible/maxilla-paste; colonists would have to use locally produced sodium bicarbonate instead to clean their mouthparts. There would be no next shipment from home.

"Seems you guys might have been right after all," Colonel Ameles said to Zyzz one day. "All I can say is that I'm sorry, for what that's worth. I suppose that sounds pretty lame."

"Lame as hell, ma'am. So now what?"

"Hope you guys like it here. There's nobody left to go home to, even if we could. We couldn't live there anymore if we wanted to. Everything… everybody's gone. Dead. Drell, what the hell do we do now?" Zyzz had never seen the old gal so down.

"We live, Colonel. We live here. We make the most of it. Here. We learn from our mistakes and go on," Zyzz answered. "We're Earthlings now."

"Zyzz, as far as I'm concerned, you've proven your leadership potential. I'm authorized to give you a field commission. Will it be Major Zyzz?"

"Ma'am, with all due respect, no thanks. You can take your field commission and toss it in the freakin' river. This rank crap, all this top-down command system; I'm sick of it, aren't you? It's part of the problem, a big part. Drell, can't you see that?"

She just shook her head, nothing else to say.

After reading the last letter from his mother, Zyzz didn't feel like doing much of anything. He stayed home, mired in a deep funk.

"You should go to the lab," Zilla said. "It'd do you some good."

"Yeah, I suppose. Maybe tomorrow."

The next day, she took Zyzz by the arm and walked him over to the lab. After a few days, he started feeling antsy and ready to venture out again. He interviewed some candidates that Ameles sent over, and selected a new assistant to replace Klum.

Back home, Zyzz always sat where he could look out a window. It helped to relieve the hemmed-in feeling he got whenever he had to stay inside very long. He talked with a guy from the Facility Engineers shop about getting better light for his microscope work. They gave him a stronger lamp. Better, but what he really needed was a window in the lab that would let some sunshine in. Fat chance of that, stuck down here in a burrow like a mole.

Before the Change, Venus had been a hundred shades of green. The Drelbi weren't prepared for all the colors on Earth, and it took awhile for their eyes to become accustomed. They were awe-struck at the color and sounds of this place.

Zyzz was quick to notice that vertebrates—birds, mammals, reptiles, and fish—had filled many of the ecological niches that insects and spiders occupied back home.

There were plants on Earth that looked like the pitcher plants and fly-traps back home, but so far they saw nothing that sent out sticky tendrils to seek and subdue an animal and pull it in to the plant's mouth. Back home, plants gave off a variety of odors, ranging from sweet scents to smells like rotting flesh to attract a meal. On Earth, plants give off sweet odors to lure animals to pollinate flowers. Some species emitted nasty, rotten smells, but this was to attract pollinating flies, not to eat them.

Why were there so few species of carnivorous plants on Earth? Zyzz attacked the puzzle tenaciously and felt like he was closing in on some answers. In their field work around Beta Colony, Zyzz and Schnorr dug up plants and brought them in to the lab for analysis. He wanted to get a closer look at those odd lumps in the roots of many species. Another field discovery: fireflies taste good!

Zyzz was dissecting root nodules from a wild pea under the microscope. "Hmmm," he said.

"Whatcha got?" asked Schnorr.

Zyzz added some water, then purple stain to the mash and looked again. "Take a look at this," he said.

"Yes?"

"See those bacteria scriggling around down there?"

"Yeah?"

"I've got a strong hunch about those guys," Zyzz said. "I'm going to get together with some of our physiologists and see if we can measure net conversion of elemental atmospheric nitrogen into nitrates."

He got the results in a few days. In his report to Ameles he wrote, "Apparently the legumes of Earth add nitrates to the soil. That would account for the scarcity of carnivorous plants on this planet. Back on Venus, there's less nitrogen in the air, and nitrates, in the form that plants can use, is made available to plants by a different pathway. Carnivorous plants get their nitrogen from eating animals. When they drop leaves or die, they add their load of nitrates to the soil."

Then there were the animals of this planet. Some looked a lot like those at home. But there was a bewildering array of hundreds of new species of butterflies, flowers, and birds here, more colorful than anything he'd ever seen back on Venus. Zyzz was in a state of fresh rapture at every turn in the forest.

To Zyzz, it was a solace to see some familiar-looking animals like silverfish, dragonflies, and mayflies. The titanic dragonflies, their chief menace back home, were absent here. The bad news was that animals that were completely lacking on Venus, like birds, reptiles, bats, and amphibians, created a nightmare menagerie of predators on Earth. Many of them had a taste for mantids. Zappers bailed them out of many jams. Their use and safety soon became part of school curricula.

Adult Drelbi gradually grow brownish as they age. The compromised polluted atmosphere of Venus hastened premature aging. On Earth, brown-tinged Drelbi turned greenish by a few shades. Something in the climate was evidently beneficial, but they couldn't identify exactly what. Higher nitrogen and oxygen in the atmosphere? Less CO_2? Nutrients in the fruits and meat of this planet perhaps? The physiologists assigned these questions high priority.

From the beginning of their exploration of this island Earth, the Drelbi tried to communicate with native species.

There are no ants, bees, nor any other insects on Venus that had ever developed a four-stage metamorphosis. Drelbi had neither larvae nor pupae; they just hatched from eggs looking like white miniature adults, and grew.

Ants looked promising. Social animals that exhibit a high degree of organization, some species had even developed forms of agriculture. Drelbi observed columns of ants moving with military precision, cutting pieces of leaves to the same size and carrying them into their colonies, where they cultivated fungi to feed their larvae. Some tended aphids and milked them for their honeydew, similar to clorm-farming back on Venus.

Like Drelbi, ants secrete chemical odors and use antennae to smell, taste, and communicate. But when confronted, they didn't respond to any Drelbian attempts to communicate, even at the simplest sign-and-gesture level.

Ants lived in cities, but like no cities the Drelbi had ever seen before. Once, Zyzz watched as a moth landed on an anthill and within seconds was covered by swarming ants that tore it to pieces. They decided against walking up to that city. They tried to communicate with some isolated ants, well away from any of their cities. Again, they showed no interest in communicating with Drelbs. Programmed to operate on an instinctive level, ants showed no sign of any rational thought. Their swarm intelligence seemed robotic and bizarre.

Attempts to communicate with bees met with disaster. One Drelb was stung and died of respiratory arrest from venom poisoning. Bees make honey, but it was dangerous collecting it. When they found a productive nest under a rock overhang or tree hollow, they mapped it. Using zappers set at a mild voltage delivery, they soon found they could stun a whole nest long enough to collect a supply of the delicacy.

Some species of the odd, feathered vertebrates acted sociably, but not very intelligently. They had wings, but no opposable thumbs, so no tool usage. And, since evidence of tool usage was a primary indicator of intelligence, these were probably not intelligent enough to bother with.

Once, when Zyzz was out taking a close look at a flower, a bird flew right up to him. His reflexive, involuntary hiss bought him a millisecond of the bird's surprise, and he dropped to the ground, hunkering down until he thought it was gone. He barely missed becoming bird-food that day.

When talking with each other, humans sounded like an unintelligible recording being played absurdly slow. Although the Drelbi found them disgusting, ugly, and fearsome, the tall mammalian human bipeds displayed clear signs of intelligence. Their ways resembled Drelbi behavior. Unlike bees and ants, humans apparently responded to, and were driven by, much the same biological and social motivations as the Drelbi. Could the Drelbi ever communicate with these creatures?

One day while Zyzz and his two team-mates were out observing human agricultural practices near a village, one of a flock of the large, domesticated birds saw them and came over to investigate. Natives kept these birds, called *chickens*, for meat, eggs and keeping the village clean of insect pests.

When the chicken came too close and too quickly for comfort, Zyzz gave it a light jolt with his zapper. The loud squawking drew the attention of a furry four-legged animal that acted much like an overgrown snarf and a human, who came over to see what was causing the ruckus. Confronted by the dog and its boy, Zyzz tried to communicate. The dog tucked his tail between his legs, pointed his muzzle toward the sky, and howled and whined. The three beat a hasty retreat into the bushes, where they watched this human for a while. Pictures and movies hadn't prepared Zyzz for the real thing.

On another day out in the forest, Zyzz and Schnorr saw a large, four-legged furry predator crouching on the limb above a trail. An Indian was walking under it, totally oblivious to the danger waiting overhead.

They stopped. "Wait! Ssshhh! Watch this," Zyzz said.

The jaguar jumped off the limb and landed silently, close behind the man. Angry that it had so narrowly missed its prey, the big cat snarled, and the man stopped and turned, gripping his spear with both hands readying himself. It offered pathetic defense.

The cat crouched, tensing for the pounce. Zyzz felt a pang of pity for the man. He grabbed his zapper, cranked the setting up a few notches, and fired at the cat. Nothing.

"Crap! What the hell's wrong with this damn thing? Quick, gimme your zapper!"

"Got it, sir!" Schnorr reached down to his holster, grabbed his gun, and turned the power setting up a few clicks.

"Well, go for it! *Now, dammit!*" Zyzz called out.

Schnorr raised his arm, then lowered it to take aim, braced it with his other fore-arm, and fixed the sight of the weapon on the cat. He squeezed off a jolt that hit the cat in the left haunch. The cat froze in place. Trembling, it screamed in pain and jerked. Outraged and hissing at the stinging shock, she bit at the spot and hit at it with her paw. Schnorr fired again and popped the cat smack on the nose. It froze for a few seconds, then recoiled, shook, and yowled like a dog pissing on an electric fence-post. It quickly took off, running and snarling.

The Indian had never seen anything like this before. Relieved, but perplexed, he looked around and saw the two tiny Drelbi—the oddest mantises he had ever seen. Schnorr and Zyzz approached the man slowly enough to be seen by the man, and not just a blur. They made the sign of peaceful greeting with both right hands held up, palms facing him, saying, "Peace and friendship be unto you." They held still for what to them was a l-o-n-g time, but just a moment for the man. Because their sign looked similar to the sign of peace among his people, he returned the gesture.

The human was a bizarre, lumbering klutz, taller than twenty Drelbi, its head ridiculously small for its body and reeking with a strong odor. Long arms ended with stubby hands and short fingers. Slow moving, apparently slow-witted, this one was trying to say something, but all they could hear was a low, booming, bass croaking that made no sense. Zyzz felt sorry for this thing, apparently stuck in a grotesque state of slow motion.

All that the human heard was high-pitched buzzing and clicking. Then he saw a large centipede heading toward the mantises. He walked about a meter toward them. They thought he was going to step on them, but he stomped on the centipede instead. They made the peace sign once more, he returned it, laughed, and stood there for just a moment looking at them. Then he walked away, looking back over his shoulder. He shook his head. No way would anybody ever believe this!

"I know what I saw," said Kla-How-Ga, his name meaning *Cat-Killer* in the dialect of his tribe. "I can take you to see them for yourselves. They mean us no harm. If they did, they could've used their buzzing weapon on me, but no, they saved me, I tell you."

"I say we leave them alone. Sounds like bad medicine," Shtill-Kiutal (*Sick-on-Berries*) said. Up until now, Cat-Killer had been fairly dependable.

Cat-Killer talked three of his friends to go out with him and check out his story. He scanned the undergrowth where the incident had occurred just yesterday, but saw nothing unusual. No Drelbi were anywhere near this place now. The friends humored him by following him and searching for anything unusual.

Q'il-Sichna (*Dizzy-from-Mushrooms*) looked under a bush. "Nothing here," he said. He gave Sick-on-Berries a pitiful look, slowly shaking his head. Then he walked over to another bush and parted the leaves, making an exaggerated show of looking down and around. "Nope, nothing here either."

"Of course not. We scared them away!" Cat-Killer said. "But I'm telling you; they were *here*, man!"

After a few more minutes of this with no results, Dizzy finally said, "Nothing. This is nuts. You're crazy, Kla-How-Ga. There's nothing here but trees, grass, and weeds." He started to walk away, then turned around and gave Cat-Killer a brush-off gesture. "Crazy like your whole loco-weed story!"

Whenever they could get away to a place he had judged as being safe enough, Zyzz took Zilla, Vespa, the girls, and their new friends out hiking, talking about the strange creatures populating their new home and their ways. His daughters and their friends loved their ascetic, and increasingly mystic father.

Zilla missed home. One evening, Zyzz saw her standing out on the yard watching the sunset and came up and put his arm around her shoulder.

"Hi," he said. "How are ye?"

"Oh, Zyzz. After so much happening, all the political excitement and action, all the friends back home, this is so damn boring. This feels so, so… anti-climactic."

"Lonely?"

"Yes," she said. She felt her tear ducts start to tingle. "Very."

"Me too, honey. My Drell, I love you."

They stood holding each other and watched the big round orb of the red sun set in the west, under bands of purple and green and orange clouds.

CHAPTER 35
THE TEACHER

It is in teaching others that a teacher teaches herself.

—Thlargi proverb.

The colony was growing, and so were the children.

The family's suite in the barracks was getting too small as Cilnia and Callibia grew older. After applying for new quarters and waiting patiently while they worked their way up the availability list, they were finally moved into one of the detached family burrows. They would have five rooms: a big bedroom for Vespa, Zilla, and Zyzz, one each for Cilnia and Callibia, a kitchenette, and a compartment they used as humans would a "family" or "living" room.

Nothing fancy; even the officer's billets were plain and simple. But things were kept up nicely due to a priority on moral support and enabled by a good cadre of facilities engineers, such as carpenters and plumbers. And, Zilla and Vespa, who were fairly competent handy-Drelbs.

Zilla enjoyed teaching. She loved her job and her elementary school students loved her, usually.

One day, she brought in a clorm for the classroom terrarium. Compared to the clorms back home, this one was pretty dim-witted, and it made a lousy pet. Its single-minded mission was to eat leaves. After a week of gorging itself, it spun a cocoon. In a couple more weeks, a brilliant metallic blue butterfly emerged, bigger and brighter than any Venusian adult clorm. Zilla was even more astonished than her students. She led her small class outside to release the butterfly and pray to Drell that it would live long enough to mate and lay eggs, so that more of these beautiful things could hatch out.

"We live in an expanding universe," she said to the class another morning, putting her forehands together, then stretched, spreading them apart.

"What's a universe?" one of the younger students asked.

"Everything. All the stars, all the galaxies, all the planets and everything on them—trees, oceans, people, everything. The galaxies are all moving apart very fast."

"Fast? I can't feel anything," said another student.

"That's because each of us, along with Venus, Earth, the whole solar system, and our whole galaxy is moving together at the same speed. There's no way we can sense this. But scientists have figured it out."

"How?"

"Well, space scientists are pretty smart. They got us here, all the way from Venus safely, and they have very special equipment."

"That's what I'm going to be. A space-Drelb!" another boy said.

"Good!" Zilla said. "Now, someday..." she said, spreading her arms out as far as she could, "... we don't know exactly why or when, things will stop spreading out." She slowly brought her hands back together. "Gravity will take over and everything will start falling back in upon each other, until all the matter and energy and intelligence in the universe will be squeezed into one tiny little ball, incredibly dense, massive, and heavy."

"A big crunch!" said Zyria.

"That's right!" she said, laughing. Now, if you could take just one tiny spoonful of that stuff, it would weigh much, much more than the sun and all the planets put together."

Sensitive little Zarz asked, "When will that happen?"

Zilla saw the look of concern. "Oh, many, many years from now. Long, long after we're all gone. Now, all the wisdom in the whole universe will be in that ball. What would you call it?"

"The Goddess!"

"Very good, Zummy! You see, once upon a time, there was only this one tiny ball and nothing else, just darkness. One day the Goddess got bored. Have any of you ever been bored?"

A few raised their hands.

"Is it fun to be bored?"

Most of the children shook their heads, and said, "No way!", "Uh-uh!" and other negative responses.

"So one day the Goddess got so bored that she said, 'Enough of this!'"

Most of the children had heard variations of this old story before from moms, dads, and grandmas, but they still waited with wide-eyed expectation.

"So what did the Goddess say then?" she asked the class.

Everybody shouted, "Let there be Light!"

"That's right! And the light, the sun, and all the other suns and stars and planets were born and everything came out of that ball in a Big Bang, and things have been expanding ever since. You and I and everybody and everything else all comes from stardust. But someday it will reach a limit and things will start slowly falling back together again and start the whole thing all over again."

Zilla saw that she had their full attention as she continued. "Everything, including you and me, are all part of a big circle that goes around and around with no beginning or ending, but many beginnings and many endings. We're all in it, so we can only see a micro-teensy piece of it."

When they were about sixteen Earth-years old, Callibia and Cilnia went through their seventh molt. Drelbi children molt seven times before becoming adults, and that one is the most difficult and lengthy.

The day before her molt started, Callibia fell out of a tree and sprained her ankle. It hurt so bad she couldn't walk. Vespa and Zilla brought her to the clinic where Doctor Gorp called it a fracture of her lower leg.

"Can't do anything about it now, though," he said with the palms-up gesture. "You're about ready to molt, young lady. If we put a splint or brace on it, it would complicate things. Take a couple of these pills for the pain, and come see me after you wake up."

Drelbi emerging from their seventh molt share much in common with human teen-agers. Cilnia woke up from her week-long sleep about an hour before her sister, feeling weak and hurting in places she wasn't even aware of having. Zilla and Vespa were watching and waiting. When Cilnia crawled out of her old skin, her mother linked arms with her for support and walked her over to the table where she had a breakfast waiting.

"Well? How do you feel?" asked Zilla.

Cilnia stretched, the blood surging through her veins. "I'm hungry!" she said. "Gosh, I can hear my heart pounding in my ears. So loud! Can you hear it?" Cilnia sat down and put her left ear next to her mom's.

"That's normal, honey. And, no, I can't hear it."

"Here, eat something." Vespa slid a bowlful of sweet, juicy aphids and grub-worms to Cilnia.

Zilla looked over to where her other daughter was waking up and crawling out of her old, dried-up husk. While Cilnia sat at the table shoveling in her breakfast, Mom walked over to Callibia. Soon, Zilla had them both sitting at the table.

"How's your leg?" Zilla asked.

"Huh? Oh yeah. I messed it up before I fell asleep, didn't I?" Callibia lifted it, held it out, and rotated it, expecting pain. "Huh! Doesn't hurt at all now. It's like new."

"Good. Remember what they call that?"

"Uh, no."

"They call that *regeneration*, honey. It means you're normal and healthy."

Regeneration occurs during molting. Normally, most damages inflicted in the previous instar are corrected and healed during the process.

"But it kind of hurts down here," she added, rubbing her lower tummy.

"Does it hurt bad?"

"No, no, it doesn't really hurt at all, just sort of feels kinda… different. Funny. I dunno."

Vespa nodded. "That just means you're growing up. Did you dream?" she asked them, smiling.

"Yes!" said Cilnia. "Nice dreams. Funny dreams, I mean in an odd way, not ha-ha funny."

What did you dream about?"

"Gee, a lotta different things. Boys too," said Cilnia.

"That's good," Zilla said.

"I dreamed a lot too," Callibia said, nodding. "Strange how everything seemed so real! I dreamed about girls, though. Really nice dreams. It makes me feel funny down here in my crotch, kind of tingly thinking about it."

Vespa and Zilla glanced at each other and smiled. Zilla's antennae rose a bit as she said, "That's good too," and gave her daughter a reassuring pat on the back.

"Drell, I'm starved!" Cilnia said. "I could eat this plate!" As they ate, the girls soon started feeling stronger and less shaky… but different.

The girls' maturity presented some new parenting challenges to Zilla and Zyzz, with no grandparents to offer guidance.

It was time for some celebration. The daughters of Zilla were the first of the colonists to come out as adults on Earth.

To have a decent party, they'd need music. But, who had any instruments? Who could play? The girls helped

Zilla and Vespa make "Musicians Wanted" flyers and posted them on bulletin boards around base. They got enthusiastic responses—enough musicians to form a band of sorts. It was an assorted oddball collection of home-made whistles, banjo-like stringed instruments, and drums. They practiced until they didn't sound too bad at all.

The party was planned for the next month.

People started showing up at six. After a few familiar opening songs, the band started playing a Gorrf, a traditional dance. Singing in a lilting rhythm, the males called and the females replied in an older than ancient call-and-response custom that came from way back in mantid history. After a few minutes, a trance-like state tapped into deep wells of energy. A few shouted in words that had no logical meaning, but with emotions that were pretty obvious.

And that was how Callibia and Cilnia met their first lovers.

On their walk home after the party, the full moon was rising in such glory that Zyzz, Zilla, and Vespa had to stop and watch it a while. The strangest sight in this new night-time sky, its crater-scarred face had been slammed hard over millennia by bombardment of meteors. Yet, through it all, it still shone brilliantly.

When Zyzz woke up, Zilla and Vespa were still asleep. He swung out of bed, leaving their stereophonic snoring. *Gotta get some earplugs one of these days,* he thought. But he never remembered to.

He quietly closed the door behind him as he stepped outside and looked off into the forest, alive with sounds of early morning bird calls and cicadas whining electrically. It was the kind of morning that made him feel good to be alive. It had rained again yesterday. Now, the sun was rising over a clear morning. The air was strong with the smell of life and taste of death, growing and dying, birth and rot. A living cycle.

He let his thoughts drift. He was learning the ropes, but what would happen here, so much like the wilds back home, but so different. Would he handle the tasks and challenges ahead? Could they survive all the new dangers of this place? Yes, he had gained some competency in the swamps and jungles back home, across the seas of space and time, but that was there, and this was here. Here, on Earth, he was walking on shaky ground.

He started humming a country tune that was centuries old when he was a boy. Yes, there would be some rainy days ahead. No doubt. The morning sun felt good. This was home now. It was the beginning of a new day.

EPILOGUE

A Message to Human Earthlings from the Drelbi

The Drelbi pioneers on Earth had a rough time of it. They witnessed the demise of their home planet. Predators and mishaps claimed many lives. But they learned enough about their new home to survive.

For generations, they watched as the humans advanced and proliferated. The Drelbi observed the development of agricultural societies along river valleys in Africa and Asia. They observed as the Europeans re-discovered and colonized South America and Africa. The Drelbi developed ever-more effective and sophisticated means of subterfuge. They've had to shift their areas of operations several times; often, their very survival has been in question.

Humans presented an interesting set of questions and problems to the Drelbi. Humans communicated with each other and were apparently intelligent. Should the Drelbi communicate with them? How? They considered this, discussed and argued about it, and finally voted to attempt communication. This decision has had mixed results.

Your ancestors had a social life and rudimentary powers of reasoning, but our ancestors couldn't get through to them. When we tried to get their attention and communicate without adequate technology, all they saw were bugs. If they paid enough attention to hear us, all they heard was high-pitched clicking, chirping, and squeaking. From them, we heard only low mumbling and groaning, like a recording played too slowly. Mutually unintelligible.

Our linguists translated the major human languages into Venusian, and our technicians developed translating software so we could at least understand them.

Encounters with humans were kept to a minimum. Electro-magnetic emissions from Drelbi craft, which humans sometimes refer to as "flying saucers", unfortunately tend to disrupt the functioning of the engines of human vehicles and spazz out radios.

The human population was stable and lived in rough balance and harmony with nature until they started using fossil fuels on a major scale. This led to an industrial revolution in their Eighteenth Century—an artificial, unsustainable, and temporary increase in Earth's carrying capacity for the species, propped up by subsidies to fossil-fuel companies. We Drelbi have seen this movie before.

Our geneticists made perhaps the greatest contribution to Drelbi life on Earth. Gradually, over many generations, we were freed from our furtive, hidey-hole existence. Via anthromization—accomplished by chromosomal splicing and grafting—we attained human size and appearance and now easily pass for humans and walk among you.

Indeed, we have become Earthlings. As such, we take this opportunity to close this narrative with a word of warning to our sister and brother Earthlings of the Homo sapiens species.

The global climate of Venus was more precarious than that of Earth. Due to the greater amount of solar radiation Venus receives, it didn't take as much CO_2 and other greenhouse gases to reach the tipping point that sparked a runaway greenhouse effect that rendered the planet uninhabitable. Even sulfur-loving microbes that otherwise would have thrived the sulfuric acid rains, couldn't survive the increased heat and pressure. Some may still survive in the cooler upper reaches of Venus' atmosphere.

Earth is more forgiving, but not infinitely so. Please understand: you are now on a dangerous path. The parallels with your sister planet are ominous:

- Shrinking polar and alpine glaciers
- Rising CO_2 levels
- Increasing average temperatures
- Expanding ranges of tropical species and diseases
- Shrinking ranges of species adapted to cool climates

The warning bells are sounding. Ignore them at your peril.

Unlike Venusians, Earthlings have no livable, ready-made back-up planet to escape to. Earth is all there is. It's not too late to save it. It's within your power, but start now!

That means greatly reducing the burning of fossil fuels that adds greenhouse gases to your atmosphere. Stop scalping your forests and meadows and replacing living, carbon-sequestering ecosystems with your unsustainable buildings and barren expanses of asphalt and concrete.

We ruined our beautiful home planet. Don't ruin this one. Learn from our mistakes and avoid them!

We hear discussions about terraforming Mars. A commendable idea, but that will be a huge project, and you humans continue to pour your wealth and lives down the roach-hole of military squander. Welfare to the military industrial syndicates—or in your parlance, corporations—is taking far too much of your wealth, while space exploration is neglected and underfunded. That is a huge error you will regret.

You need to get serious about establishing sustainable colonies on Mars, and, yes, Venus. Can Venus be made habitable again? Can the damage be undone? Yes; but not easily, nor quickly, nor cheaply. But it will pay off far more than your military adventures. Venus is twice the size of Mars, roughly the same size as Earth.

Despite your war-plagued history and other evidence of colossal ignorance, your species shows a few flickers of promise. The United Nations, along with your peace, environmental, and socialist groups, offer signs of intelligence. Yes, your Green and Socialist parties are weak so far, but they are healthy, growing, and worthy of nurture. They have great potential. Join them, help them, and work for unity whenever possible. They need you, and you need them.

One of the plants in the Amazon watershed just south of the old Beta Colony site produces a substance that, in the right combination with other botanical extracts, has extended Drelbi life-spans and could extend yours as well, far beyond your meager eighty years. We're really not that much different, you know. Instead, you are threatening this plant species with extinction, along with its rainforest habitats.

So many questions remain unanswered.

For most of your species' time on this planet, you lived in a matriarchal society, but then things went wrong.

Are you degenerating? Can you recover? Can you bring your logarithmic population explosion under control?

Finally, why do you humans wear clothes all the time? Except for occasional, special ceremonies, indigenous humans throughout the tropics typically go nude, or did until contact with misguided missionaries and other outsiders—even at temperatures where clothing is apparently uncomfortable. This must be difficult for you. Wouldn't you be able to breathe, think, and function better if you didn't cover all your pores with textiles? Are you getting enough oxygen?

We do worry about you. We share your home. If you stay on this path, we *all* go down. Learn from our mistakes. There are too many dead planets already.

—Drelbi Central Committee

GLOSSARY

Ammonite

An octopus-like cephalopod that has a coiled shell, similar to a Chambered Nautilus. Some species remain in their shells; others can leave their shells to pursue food, then return to the shell where they usually stay. Shells can reach diameters of up to a meter.

Aphrodite Terra

The larger and more southerly of the two continents of Venus, it straddles the equator.

Borhgel

A birthing-aid scaffolding device to support the egg-containing froth produced by mantid mothers. Resembles a miniature tree in shape.

Brzzt

Zyzz's hometown. One of the isolated highland communities of eastern Aphrodite.

Calamites

A group of plants that were a major feature of the Venusian flora. This group flourished in Earth's Paleozoic era and survives in the genus Equisetum (horsetails or "scouring rushes") of present-day Earth.

Clorms

Large, 7-8 cm long, 3 cm tall caterpillarish grazing animal, domesticated for their meat and nutritious and sweet exudate (splorff), like cattle (milk) or aphids (honeydew) on Earth.

Drelbi

Literally, "the followers of Drell". The dominant life-form of Venus, a species of Venusian mantis with a reduced abdomen, vestigial wings, expanded brain, and, according to some racist mantidologists, comparatively higher cognitive abilities than the Thlargi race.

Drell
The only begotten daughter of the Goddess. The Jesus and Krishna of the more advanced of the two intelligent mantis races of Venus; their Jesus, Mohammed, Alexander the Great, and Napoleon rolled into one. Probably the single most significant figure in Drelbi history. Drell led her followers to victory over the Thlargi, enlightened them about the evils of cannibalism and sectarian warfare, and guided them in their shift from a purely carnivorous lifestyle to an omnivorous diet and agriculture.

Eco-Socialist Party
A political party of Venus, based on the premise that (1) the resources and means of production are, and should be treated and cooperatively and sustainably managed as, the common property of all—not the private property of a few, managed via syndicates, and (2) nature, ecosystems, and future generations have rights that must be considered in decision-making.

Epiphyte
A plant that grows on another plant, but is not a parasite and produces its own food via photosynthesis. Earth examples include certain orchids, mosses, ferns, and lichens.

Eurypterids
A group of large marine chelicerates (proto-spiders) that reached up to 200 millimeters in length.

Farra
Flat-topped volcanic features which look somewhat like pancakes and range in size from 20–50 km across.

Keck
A unit of currency used in the Venusian Empire.

Goddess
Referred to by humans by a variety of names, including Isis, Astarte, Jehovah, Diana, Hecate, Domita, Kali, Innana, Allah, Yahweh, or just plain "God". The celestial mother of Drell, the Savior, Teacher, and Communicator.

Gungkel
A fermented, but non-alcoholic, drink similar to the kefir of Earth.

Instar
One of several stages in the development and growth of an insect.

Ishtar Terra
The smaller and more northerly of the two continents of Venus.

Ishtar Forest Resources (IFR)
The major forest products planet-wide syndicate of Venus.

Mandibles
One of the pair of insect mouthparts that does most of the work of biting and crushing food. (Insects have no teeth.)

Mantids
The dominant life-form on Venus, strongly resembling Earthling mantises.

Maxilla
One of a pair of mouthparts in insects, lying behind the mandibles; assists in eating.

Muncho
Street food, sold from wagons. Typically, but not necessarily, inexpensive.

Odonaraptors
Large, dragonfly-like predators, similar to the genus Meganeura of Earth's Carboniferous era, often exceeding wingspans of 1 meter.

Riding
The basic political, legislative district on Venus.

Schlurpp
A shrimp-and-krill soup.

Snarf
An insect, often kept by Venusians as pets.

Spiracles
Small respiratory openings in an arthropod's thorax and abdomen that are used for breathing.

Splorff
A milk-like excretion from a variety of insects, especially clorms. A dietary staple and key ingredient in a variety of foods, including refreshments.

Syndicate
A combination of privately owned businesses. Having a central committee that owns the controlling shares of each constituent company enables it to control a market, absorb and/or eliminate competition, and dominate an entire commercial/resource sector, producing a de-facto monopoly.

Thlarg
One of the two advanced races of Venusian mantids, defeated in a genocidal war and restricted to ghetto-like reservations by the Drelbi.

Zoom
A vehicle that seats four or five passengers, resembling a jeep.

ABOUT THE AUTHOR

DAVID C. A. ZINK grew up in northern Minnesota on his family's fishing resort. Out in the serious boondocks, the family diet was mostly what they grew in their garden or caught. Dave fished for northern pike, rock bass, and walleye, and he hunted for venison, an occasional squirrel, rabbit, or snapping turtle. He spent a lot of time out on the lakes and in the forests.

Dave attended Lakehead University's School of Forestry, in Thunder Bay, Ontario, and earned Bachelor of Science degrees in Biology and Geography at the University of Winnipeg, with major work in Plant Taxonomy and Biogeography.

His long career of environmental activism includes 10 years as an Environmental Health Specialist in the U.S. Army's Medical Services Corps; 27 years service with the Washington State Department of Ecology, Washington State University Extension Service, as Master Gardener; and an active member the Native Plant Society and other ecological groups.

Dave currently resides near Puget Sound, where he teaches Botany, leads hikes at the Nisqually National Wildlife Refuge, and is active in the Tacoma Veterans for Peace organization.

Made in the USA
San Bernardino, CA
17 September 2016